UNDER AN ENGLISH MOON

BESS MCBRIDE

UNDER AN ENGLISH MOON

Copyright © 2013 Bess Mcbride

Contact information: bessmcbride@gmail.com

Cover Art by *Tamra Westberry*

Formatted by IRONHORSE Formatting

Published in the United States of America

ISBN: 1492314528
ISBN-13: 978-1492314523

BOOKS BY BESS MCBRIDE

Time Travel Romance
Forever Beside You in Time
Moonlight Wishes in Time
(Book One of the Moonlight Wishes in Time series)
A Smile in Time
(Book Three of the Train Through Time series)
Together Forever in Time
(Book Two of the Train Through Time series)
A Train Through Time
(Book One of the Train Through Time series)
Love of My Heart

Contemporary/Romantic Suspense
Will Travel for Romance Boxed Set Books 1-5
A Penny for Your Thoughts
A Shy Woman in Love
A Sigh of Love
A Trail of Love
A Penny for Your Thoughts
Jenny Cussler's Last Stand

Contemporary/Ghost Story
Caribbean Dreams of Love
On a Warm Sea of Love

Dear Reader,

Thank you for purchasing *Under an English Moon*. *Under an English Moon* is Book Two of the *Moonlight Wishes in Time* series, a series of Georgian-era time travel romances featuring time travel by moonlight.

In *Under an English Moon*, we find Lord Reggie Hamilton from *Moonlight Wishes in Time*, all grown up in 1827, and looking for love. Mattie Crockwell has married William Sinclair, and Reggie is all alone with no one of his own to love. But where to find his destiny? *Under an English Moon* continues the story of Mattie and William and introduces Phoebe Warner, a young woman living in New York City who loves Georgian-era romance novels and wishes she had a Georgian man of her own.

Although I am American, I am an anglophile in that I love all things British and Irish. I love the lyrical language of Georgette Heyer's and Jane Austen's dialogue, and I enjoyed trying to incorporate some of the dialogue into my own story while keeping the book a little more "readable" for modern-day romance enthusiasts. My advance apologies to my British reader friends who will note that the majority of the story is written and spelled in "American English" though many of the characters are English.

I know that I, like some of my fellow time travel romance readers, have wondered: How can I find one of Jane Austen's heroes for my own—a Georgian-era man complete with a firm moral code and impeccable manners with just a teeny bit of arrogance. If I did, could I really live with him?

Thank you for your support over the years, friends and readers. Because of your favorable comments, I continue to strive to write the best stories I can. More romances are on the way!

You know I always enjoy hearing from you, so please feel free to contact me at BessMcBride@gmail.com, through my website at www.BessMcBride.com, or my blog Will Travel for Romance.

Thanks for reading!

Bess

PROLOGUE

"Do not think to see me for some time," Lord Reginald Hamilton threw over his shoulder as he stormed out the front door. He jumped astride his horse, startling it into a whinny, and he grabbed the reins from the groom's hands.

"Have a care, Master Reggie. The moon is bright this night, but it is still dangerous to ride too hastily on these darkened roads." The small, wiry groom spoke with the familiarity of a long-time servant, and Reggie took no offense.

Reggie nodded. "Thank you, Gerry. I will," he ground out before turning his horse's head toward the gates and urging him on. He jammed his top hat securely down on his head and leaned into Sebastian's easy stride as they flew down the long drive of Hamilton Place. They reached the iron gates in ten minutes, and Reggie slowed his horse to a trot.

Gerry spoke true. It was too dangerous to rush the horse recklessly at night, especially onto the poorly maintained country roads. Even by the light of the moon, Reggie could see the deep ruts left by the spring rains several weeks before.

He looked up at the full moon—a luminescent white orb in the dark sky—and he felt the anger ebb from his body. It was as if the moon cast a soothing spell upon him. Reggie allowed Sebastian to slow even further, settling into a walk. His horse knew the road to the village well, having grown up on the estate and accompanying his master to the village on daily outings for exercise.

Reggie replayed the conversation in the library with his father.

"You cannot simply migrate to America, Reggie. It is unthinkable. I forbid it!"

"You *forbid* it? What right do you have to forbid me to do anything,

1

sir? I am of age and means. I do not need your permission." Reggie stood head to head with his tall father, irrelevantly surprised that he had at long last matched the large man in height.

His father blinked, seeming to realize the same thing.

"I forbid it because I am your father. If you leave, there will be no one to care for the estate."

"You do not need anyone to help with the estate, Father. You have many years ahead of you. And in the event something untoward should happen in my absence, though I hope it will not, Samuel will manage."

Lord Jonathan Hamilton shook his head and waved a dismissive hand.

"Bah! Your brother is interested only in books of late. He will not be equal to the task of caring for our holdings."

Reggie thought it more apt to say that Samuel might not *wish* to undertake the task of handling the estate. He *had* been buried in books for the past year, even to the point of declining to attend dinners and routs. Reggie and he had once been very close, almost inseparable, but of late they had seen little of each other.

"I am not going away forever, Father, but I *am* leaving."

"Reggie, my son, what has come over you? Only last year, I boasted to Lady Hamilton that you were an accommodating young man of a pleasant disposition. Now I find you willful, intractable, and dogged. Has this change come about because you fancied yourself in love with Miss Matilda Crockwell? Are you leaving England because your sensibilities were hurt by a woman?"

Reggie stiffened and his cheeks heated. His father exaggerated the matter but had not fallen very far short of the mark.

"As you well know, Father, her name is Mrs. William Sinclair now. And no, of course I am not leaving England because she married." Reggie narrowed his eyes and stared his father down. There was some truth to his father's words, but Reggie had no intention of acknowledging it. Even to his mind, the idea of migrating to another country for unrequited love of a now-married woman seemed excessive. But he felt restless, and he needed to explore. Miss Crockwell, a mysterious beauty from America, had incited in him a heretofore unknown curiosity about the world outside of England.

Before meeting Miss Crockwell, he had never thought of himself as other than Lord Reginald Hamilton, not yet five and twenty, the eldest son of an earl, Lord Jonathan Hamilton. He assumed he would marry a local girl from a good family at the appropriate time, settle onto his family's country estate with occasional visits to London, and take over management of the estate when his father passed away. He had wanted for nothing more, had expected nothing else.

And yet when copper-haired Matilda Crockwell, a distant cousin of the Sinclair's, had arrived unexpectedly from America, he had fallen under her spell and found himself wondering about America. What other delights did it hold? Miss Crockwell's mannerisms, speech, and habits had been somewhat different from that to which he was accustomed, albeit in a most engaging way, and he wanted to know if there were other women like her.

Reggie had not lied. His father promised to live a long life, and there was little for Reggie to do at the moment, certainly as far as the estate was concerned. Samuel was indeed immersed in his books, and his father had recently remarried a woman he had courted for years, Mrs. Lucinda Sinclair, now Lady Hamilton. With everyone in his family happily settled about their affairs, Reggie felt as if he had awakened from a long sleep to find himself without direction, without purpose.

Neighbors had recently migrated to America—Thomas Ringwood and his bride, Sylvie, and Louisa Covington, now Mrs. Stephen Carver. It seemed as if everyone had removed to America in the past year. He wanted to join the exodus—if only for a while—to discover for himself what lay across the sea.

"Impossible," his father roared. "You may have the money from your mother's inheritance, which I cannot withhold, but I will cut you off without an allowance if you leave."

"As you say, sir, I have my own money. Cut me off. It matters not to me." Reggie turned away and paused at the door of the library. He looked over his shoulder. "We do not have to part in anger, Father. I will return someday...perhaps in the near future."

"I am vehemently opposed to this, Reginald. I have nothing else to say to you." His father turned his back to him.

"As you wish," Reggie said. He crossed the foyer, ignoring his stepmother's murmurs of protest as she paused on descending the stairway. "Lady Hamilton," Reggie said as he reached the front door. "Do not think to see me for some time."

Now, Reggie rode on through the night aimlessly, uncertain of his immediate destination. He supposed he ought to take a room at the Village Inn for the night. It would not do to fly out of his father's house in righteous indignation, only to return as an abject child in search of his porridge and his bed.

Sebastian stumbled but quickly recovered his step. However, Reggie felt a dip in the horse's gait, as if he had injured his leg.

"Hold there, fellow," he said as he slid off the horse's back. He ran a hand down Sebastian's leg, and the horse shied away at his touch.

"Have a care there, old boy," Reggie soothed. "It seems you have sprained your leg, Sebastian. It is my fault. I should have taken more care." He patted the horse's neck and looked around. What Sebastian needed was a proper poultice on his leg, a task Reggie could entrust only to Gerry.

With a sigh, he turned the horse around. "Let us return home then, Sebastian. Gerry will tend to your leg, and I will attempt to tend to my father—though I may well be sleeping in the stable with you this night if Father has anything to say in the matter."

As Reggie led the horse back down the road toward home, he looked up at the moon once more.

"I am going to America, Lady Moon. Nothing will stop me. I feel my destiny awaits me there...whoever she may be."

As if in answer, the moon shimmered overhead, casting a radiant glow around him. Reggie, staring at the brilliant sight, misstepped and tripped in one of the ruts. He felt himself falling.

CHAPTER ONE

Phoebe Warner left the large office building on East 53rd Street which housed her employer, Sinclair Publishing, and strolled down the street toward her apartment only a few blocks away. She had worked late that night, and the moon was high in the sky, surprisingly visible between the tall skyscrapers of downtown Manhattan. She eyed it with appreciation—bright, white, the perfect sphere of a full moon. The apartment she rented at an outrageously low price from her wealthy, jet-setting cousin, Annie, didn't have a balcony, and she wasn't sure she would be able to see it from the apartment. It seemed too perfect to waste. She wondered if she should snag a cup of something warm at a local sidewalk cafe just so she could enjoy the rare sight of the moon.

Phoebe thought not. It was late. All she wanted at the end of a long hectic day at work was to take a warm bath, turn the television onto the twenty-four-hour Romantic Movies Channel, and savor a soothing glass of wine. If one of the movies was based on the novels of her favorite author, I.C. Moon, so much the better, she thought with a grin.

Sadly, Hollywood didn't use I.C. Moon's books for films anymore. The five books that had been turned into movies were done in the early sixties in black and white, and the Romantic Movies Channel showed them sporadically. She heartily wished someone would do a remake of any of the movies, just to see how they might look in color, or what current actors they might choose for the parts. Which up and coming British actors would they choose for the dashing heroes and heroines? She recalled that some of I.C. Moon's heroines were American though.

Phoebe had fallen in love with I.C. Moon's work a year ago when she'd landed a dream job at a publishing house in New York. Her job as copy editor at Sinclair Publishing was often exciting and demanding, occasionally tedious, but always rewarding, and she had worked on the re-release of several of I.C. Moon's books over the past year for the current market of readers of classic romances. At some point along the way, she'd fallen in love with the idea of England, of the Georgian and Regency eras, of old-fashioned courtship and romance. She hoped to visit England one day—to see I.C. Moon's English countryside. Someday...when she had enough money saved.

Phoebe reached the door of her building in fifteen minutes and greeted the doorman. Oh, to be rich like Cousin Annie! Nothing in her hometown of Lincoln, Nebraska, had ever prepared her for a doorman.

"How was your day, Tim?" she asked the short, stocky man dressed in a gray suit who faithfully manned the door five days of the week. In the year that she'd been living in her cousin's apartment, she'd only seen him take Christmas Day off and the weekends. The night doormen alternated, but Tim was always there.

"Good, Miss Warner. How about yours?" He held the door open for her.

"Long, but good." Phoebe smiled and moved toward the mailboxes.

"Have a nice evening, Miss Warner," Tim called out as he let the door close.

"Thanks, Tim," she said over her shoulder. She opened her mailbox to find it empty. Nothing new there. The mail consisted of either bills or nothing.

The elevator around the corner from the mailboxes took its sweet time arriving as usual, and Phoebe climbed aboard and pushed the button for the fifteenth floor. The image of the moon still lingered with her, and she wondered again if she would be able to see it from Annie's living room window. Maybe.

The elevator was no quicker going up than it had been coming down, and Phoebe rolled her eyes impatiently as the numbers above the door showed the elevator's slow progress. She finally reached her floor and headed down the ruby red-carpeted hallway to the end unit.

Inside, she dropped her oversize bag holding her gym clothes down onto the console table just inside the doorway, and she crossed the large living room to pull back the curtains and look out.

There it was! The moon—round, glowing, proudly preening high in the sky. Phoebe wasn't sure why, but she hadn't remembered having a view of a full moon from the window before now. Of course, the taller buildings across the street blocked much of the sky. Was the moon in a particularly unusual position that night?

What she wouldn't give for a telescope. Binoculars! Phoebe trotted across the dark living room to her bedroom, stubbing her foot on the coffee table along the way. Cursing and flipping on the lights, she limped to her closet and rummaged around on the top shelf for her small binoculars, used only two times for Broadway shows.

She returned to the living room, switching the lights off along the way so she could see the moon better. The binoculars, though not strong, magnified some of the moon's craters, and she perched on the windowsill and studied them for a while. Hardly an astronomer, she had no idea which shapes were the "seas" one heard of, but that didn't matter. She considered herself fortunate to be able to see anything on the moon beyond the naked eye. Surely I.C. Moon had never had the privilege of seeing the moon so close for all that she wrote so many books featuring moons...and charming Georgian men. Phoebe sighed. What she wouldn't give to find a Georgian-era man of her own.

Which reminded her—a warm bath, television, and hopefully a black and white I.C. Moon movie was what she wanted. Leaving the curtains open to allow moonlight to shine into the living room, she set the binoculars down on the sill and turned away from the window to head for her bedroom and bath.

"What the—!" Phoebe cursed as she stubbed her toe again, this time on something much softer but larger than the coffee table. She hopped around in pain and regained her balance before peering down to see a large shape lying on the white carpet. It muttered and attempted to rise. A man!

Phoebe screeched and jumped out of his way to run for the bedroom, slamming the door shut behind her. She locked it and waited, holding her breath. A quick scan of her room reminded her that she'd left her bag— with cell phone—by the front door. No help.

"What the deuce!" she heard the man say. "Where am I?"

Phoebe said nothing but pressed her ear to the door.

"Madam! Madam!" he called out. "Are you there? I cannot see. Where am I?"

His voice was unexpectedly appealing, deep and resonant, the accent British. British? A British intruder in her apartment? Didn't he have apartments in his own country to break into?

"Madam, please assist me. I mean you no harm. I saw only a glimpse of you as you ran past, but I know you are in there...behind that door."

His voice seemed to come closer, and Phoebe backed away from the door. She heard a thump, and he let out a curse.

"Oooff! What is this infernal piece of furniture? Madam, I have injured myself on this table of yours. If you do not wish to assist me, could you at least direct me to a candle so that I may see more clearly? Or perhaps the door? I promise you, Madam, I am as worried about my presence here as you are."

Phoebe almost laughed, but she suspected it would quickly turn into hysteria if she let it out. Was he serious with that accent? And the formal dialogue? He could be straight out of one of her favorite I.C. Moon books.

She gasped at the sound of his voice just on the other side of the door.

"Madam, my name is Reginald Hamilton. I am the eldest son of the Earl of Hamilton. I truly mean you no harm. Truly. Please at least tell me where I am."

"You're in my apartment, that's where you are, buddy," Phoebe barked. "I have a bat and, if you try to come through that door, I'll bash you with it." Phoebe promised herself that if she got out of this, she would get a bat.

"I assure you, Madam, I have no intention of bursting through your doorway."

He sounded insulted. Phoebe touched the doorknob. What was he doing here? What did he want?

"Are you a friend of my cousin, Annie Warner?" Phoebe asked. If he hadn't broken in, that could be the only explanation. In the first month of her stay in the apartment, a strange woman had let herself in with a key Annie had given her. They had scared each other half to death with their mutual surprise, and a quick call to Annie in Cannes had cleared the matter up. It did seem though as if her cousin might have handed out more than one key. Phoebe had promised herself at the time to have the place rekeyed, but she hadn't had any trouble since.

"Annie Warner? No, I am not acquainted with this person. Your accent, Madam, it sounds...American. Are you American?"

Phoebe heard a strange note in his voice that she couldn't interpret. Excitement?

"Well, of course, I'm American. You're not though."

"No, I am English."

Yes, he was, Phoebe thought, a twinge of excitement working its way up her spine. An Englishman with a delightful accent. She wondered if he looked as handsome as he sounded. Phoebe caught herself on the edge of opening the door to find out. She gave herself a stern shake and deepened her voice.

"So, what are you doing in my apartment?" she demanded.

"I have no earthly idea, Madam. I remember walking my horse, Sebastian, toward home in the dark, and stumbling on a rut in the road. I have no idea where Sebastian is at the moment."

"Well, I hope he's not here. I doubt he'd fit in the elevator." Phoebe stifled a hysterical giggle. "And exactly where were you when you lost

Sebastian?"

"El-e-vator?" he repeated. "I was only a mile from my father's estate, Hamilton Place, in Bedfordshire."

Phoebe swallowed hard. Did he mean England? Because she was pretty sure he wasn't talking about a town in nearby Massachusetts. Was he delusional? When, and if she finally opened the door, would she find a man in a red suit and cape, or a crown and an ermine-lined coat?

Phoebe couldn't resist. She had to know what he looked like. Her instincts told her she was in no danger. He *sounded* harmless. She opened the door a crack and peeked out.

Reginald jumped back as if he expected *her* to attack *him*. He rubbed a hand across his eyes and peered at her in the darkness.

"Miss...?"

"Phoebe Warner." She spoke through the partially closed door.

"Miss Warner! At last! Please be so good as to direct me to the door leading out of your apartments. I must find Sebastian."

Phoebe reached around the doorframe with a tentative hand and flicked the light switch on. Several lamps lit the room with a soft romantic glow. Cousin Annie delighted in ambience, if nothing else. No overhead garish lights for her.

Reginald blinked and stared at her.

Phoebe stared back.

"What on earth are you wearing?" she asked. She pushed the door open wider. No, not a red-caped outfit. He wore a historical costume in keeping with his formal speech and English accent.

Reginald blinked before his eyes traveled the length of her body.

"Good gad!" he said before turning his back to her. "I fear I have caught you *en dishabille*, Madam...Miss! Please forgive me."

Phoebe looked down at her suit skirt and low-slung pumps.

"Ummm...I'm fully dressed, Reginald." Now she *knew* he wasn't about to attack her. The back of his neck below thick dark hair was decidedly red. "You can turn around."

He glanced over his shoulder, dropped his eyes to her legs, and turned slowly. Phoebe noted he averted his gaze as if with effort and kept it on her face.

He bowed at the waist, his gesture catching her by surprise.

"Reginald Hamilton at your service, Miss Warner."

"So you said," Phoebe said in bemusement at the gallant, if old-fashioned gesture. She guessed his height at about six feet tall. Broad shoulders supported his greatcoat well. A high-necked silver waistcoat framed his firm jaw line, and a bright white cravat was knotted at his neck. His beige pantaloons suggested long, lean, muscled legs, and his highly polished Hessian boots showed dust around the soles as if he had indeed been riding.

That she knew the terms for his style of clothing was due in large part to the writings of I.C. Moon. The strange man in her living room wore clothes from the Regency or late Georgian era.

His clothing, although delightfully unusual, could not distract her from his handsome face. Thick wavy, almost black hair and long sideburns framed a lean clean-shaven face notable for dark eyebrows over slate blue eyes. He looked to be in his early twenties, close to her age.

"The door, Miss Warner?"

Phoebe blinked. "The door?"

"Yes, if you would be so kind as to show me to the exit? I do not know how I came to be in your apartments, and I apologize. Now, where did I drop my hat?" He turned to study the floor. "Ah! There it is."

Phoebe wasn't sure her eyes could get any rounder as she watched him pop a top hat onto his head.

"Where did you come from?" she breathed.

"Bedfordshire?"

"As in England?"

He inclined his head. "Yes, of course, England."

Phoebe took a deep breath to try to defog her brain, to bring herself back to reality. Or maybe it was Reginald who needed to be brought back to earth.

"I hate to tell you this, Reginald, but even if I show you the door, you're still not going to walk outside and find your horse...in England."

Reginald narrowed his eyes and scanned the room, stopping to focus on the window. He moved quickly toward the window and peered out into the night. Phoebe approached him cautiously, keeping a wary eye on him as she studied his movements. He swung his head from side to side as if to take in all the bright lights of the city, the neighboring buildings, the street below. He looked up at the moon, and she heard him exhale as if he had been holding his breath.

"I see one thing that is familiar," he said quietly.

"The moon?" Phoebe followed his eyes.

"Yes, that at least is a constant. Pray, what are all these lights?" Reginald nodded toward the buildings across the street. "Are those large edifices homes? What is it that twinkles on the street below? Surely not lanterns? That many carriages?" He looked down and then turned toward the room. "Where are your candles? How did you light the room with a button on the wall? What is the name of this place?"

Phoebe smiled despite her own confusion. She had no idea where

Reginald had come from before he entered her apartment, or whether he was delusional, but he certainly had a charming naïveté about him that seemed very real. Maybe he'd just never seen skyscrapers before, although she was pretty sure they had some tall buildings in England's larger cities.

"Obviously, each entire building isn't a single home—someone would have to be pretty rich and need a lot of square feet to call one of those buildings a home—but some of the lights come from apartments and some come from offices," Phoebe said as she nodded toward the surrounding buildings.

She looked down. "Ummm...twinkling lights? Cars? I wouldn't think there are any carriages on this street. Too far from the tourist areas." She turned back toward the living room. "There are candles on the fireplace mantle. I flipped the switch to turn on the lights, and the name of this place is my apartment in New York City." She thought she'd answered all his questions in the right order.

"Now seriously, where did you come from?" Phoebe asked, crossing her arms. "I totally believe you come from England, but I don't think you just left your horse on a road near your father's country home."

"But it is the truth, Miss Warner. I swear it upon my honor. I am as taken aback as you. I cannot possibly be in New York!"

Phoebe found his gesture of hand over heart irresistible, and she decided then and there she wanted to keep him. Not that he was a toy or anything, but he was the cutest confused man she'd ever met! He had a definite little-boy-lost thing going that entranced her.

"Look, why don't you take off your hat and have a seat, Reginald? I'll make us some coffee. Then we can figure out how to help you," Phoebe said in her best motherly tone. "I promise, you are not going to open that door and find yourself with your horse in England...not without a great deal of travel."

Reginald opened his mouth as if to protest, but closed it as Phoebe held out her hand for his hat. He removed it and handed it to her.

"Your coat?"

He shrugged out of his coat and gave that to her as well. Phoebe sighed inwardly. She *had* been right. He *did* have broad shoulders. His double-breasted cobalt blue dress coat showed a narrow waist. He looked like the quintessential Georgian-era Englishman, and she couldn't take her eyes off him.

"Shall I sit here, Miss Warner?" Reginald looked down at the chocolate brown chenille sofa.

"Yes, please," Phoebe said, releasing a quiet sigh. She laid his coat and hat across a matching easy chair and made her way over to the kitchen area of the open concept apartment.

"How do you take your coffee?" Phoebe called out as she threw a single serving of coffee into the instant coffee brewer.

"Cream and sugar," Reginald said.

"I hope milk and sugar are okay. I don't have any cream."

"Yes, that will suffice, thank you." Reginald rose and approached the breakfast bar of the kitchen. "Forgive me for shouting at you from across the room."

"Oh!" Phoebe murmured in some confusion. She hadn't thought they were shouting. The apartment was only about 700 square feet. "Okay. Have a seat." She nodded toward the high-backed, cushioned barstools. "Coffee will be ready in a second."

Reginald slid onto a stool and watched her with a look of avid curiosity. Phoebe's cheeks flamed under his gaze.

"Do you not have a cook, Miss Warner?" He looked over his shoulder. "For that matter, do you have a companion? Surely, you do not live alone."

Phoebe, in the act of popping another container of coffee for herself into the instant brewer, paused. She reminded herself that she really didn't know him and should use caution. No sense in revealing everything.

"A cook?" she laughed nervously. "No, not me. I think my cousin Annie has food delivered when she lives here. I mean, when she's here...which will be at any moment." A lie, but he would probably never know. It seemed likely that he really didn't know Annie. Had a previous owner left a key? Hadn't Annie rekeyed the place when she moved in?

"Ah!" he said. "Yes, of course, a cousin." He nodded toward the coffeemaker. "And what is that device?"

"An instant coffeemaker? It's my cousin's. I can't afford anything like this. It's pretty nice though, makes coffee in a jiff."

"And how is it heated?"

"Plug it in?" Phoebe wasn't about to start describing electricity. They had electricity in England.

Reginald shook his head in apparent confusion.

"Here." Phoebe handed him his coffee. "Let's go sit on the couch and figure out why you're asking me about coffee pots, Reginald."

He took the mug gingerly and followed her back to the living room, waiting to sit until she lowered herself to a chair across from the sofa. He set his mug on the coffee table and seated himself on the edge of the sofa.

"Reggie," he said.

"What?"

"If you intend to call me by my given name, please call me Reggie. I cannot abide the name Reginald."

"Okay, Reggie. What can I do to help?" Phoebe asked. She slipped out of her shoes and pulled her feet up under her. "Let's start at the beginning. How did you get into the apartment? I'm guessing you had a key somehow?"

Reggie watched her movements, his eyes straying to her legs and bare feet. Although she was covered, she realized she'd been rather informal with a total stranger. She straightened and thrust her feet back into her shoes.

"Yes?" she urged.

He dropped his eyes and cleared his throat.

"No, I did not have a key. I do not know how I came to be in your apartment. Frankly, I think I must be dreaming."

Phoebe could have taken that as a compliment, but the confused note in his voice didn't sound like he meant "dreaming" in the romantic sense. She sighed inwardly. No, she definitely hadn't conjured this guy up just by dreaming about him in the moonlight. Otherwise, she would at least have found a man who kneeled at her feet and swore that he'd fallen in love with her at first sight—perhaps placing warm kisses on the inside of her wrist as he whispered endearments.

She voiced her thoughts...some of them.

"Well, you couldn't just have dropped in by moonlight," she said. "Have you been drinking? You seem sober."

"Certainly not, Miss Warner. I am not inebriated," he said as he rose hastily. Phoebe watched him pace in front of the window.

"What was that you said about the moon?" he asked.

"I said you couldn't have dropped in here by moonlight."

She watched him stop and stare out the window before pacing again, seemingly trying to work something out.

He shook his head. "No, of course not. That is not possible." He stopped and stared at her. "Are you certain this is New York?"

Phoebe choked on her coffee and laughed. "Well, yes, I'm sure, Reggie." She jerked a thumb toward her chest. "*I'm* not the one who appears to be out of place. Where did you get that costume anyway? It's very attractive, looks quite authentic."

Reggie looked down at his clothing. "Thomas and Sons Tailors on Bond Street in London. Thank you. They do fine work."

Phoebe had expected to hear the name of a costume or theater shop, but somehow she wasn't surprised to hear him name a tailor in London. It would have been more ludicrous to hear him say "The Costume Shop on East 42nd."

Reggie stopped his pacing to peer down into the shade of a lamp. At the light bulb?

"What is the date, Miss Warner?"

"The date? April 23rd."

"The year?" He turned to survey the room, allowing his eyes to pause on her. Phoebe squirmed under his intent look. It was as if all her dreams had come true. A handsome historical gentleman gazed at her ardently. Well, more like shocked really, she thought.

"2013," she replied.

Reggie drew in a sharp breath and looked around the room wildly as if he would bolt. "2013?"

Phoebe swallowed hard and jumped up, feeling suddenly as out of control as Reggie looked. She turned one way then turned another, unsure of where to go or what to do. The shock in his voice was unmistakable. There was no doubt that the date surprised him. Which could only mean one thing.

She stopped and stared at him.

"Reggie, what year is it where you come from?"

"1827," he said a hoarse voice. "It is the 23rd day of April in the year 1827."

CHAPTER TWO

Reggie stared at the slender young woman standing before him, a stricken look upon her pale face. Had he been rendered unconscious when he fell and somehow awakened in the future? Or was this some fantastical dream—of twinkling lights, buildings which touched the sky, lamps which glowed without candles, and beautiful, if scantily clad, young women? Were it true, what a delightful dream he had engineered. If not, then some mystical force had transported him to the future—a future he could not possibly have imagined.

"1827," she gasped. Then inexplicably she began to laugh, a tinkling sound that soon devolved into something resembling a cackle. She clutched her sides and howled unbecomingly. Tears rolled down her face.

Reggie stiffened. "I beg your pardon, Madam. Your raucous laughter is unseemly at best. Please desist. What can you possibly find so amusing?"

Miss Warner stopped chortling, but the tears continued, accompanied by an occasional sob. Reggie was appalled. He had thought her tears to be from laughter but could see now that she wore an expression of alarm. Much as he felt.

"Come, Miss Warner. There now," he murmured, producing a kerchief for her. "Dry your tears. Forgive my harsh words. I suspected you to be mocking me. I cannot bear to see a woman cry, and have little enough experience with it. I have no sisters."

Miss Warner pressed the kerchief against her eyes and slumped ungracefully onto the settee. "No sisters," she murmured inconsequentially.

"No, alas, only a brother and a father, and lately a stepmother, but I

15

have never seen her shed tears, not even at the birth of her first grandchild."

"You're not married," she stated.

"No, Miss Warner, I am not, but I hope to remedy that some day."

"Oh! Are you engaged?" He almost imagined he saw her mouth droop.

"No, not as yet."

"Thinking about it?" A small twitch of her lips charmed him.

Reggie grinned. "One always thinks about one's future. However, I think our most pressing concern should be just that—the future. Either I hit my head when I fell and am now dreaming, or I have somehow been transported almost two hundred years into the future."

It seemed as if his own legs failed to hold him upright and he slumped into the chair opposite the settee.

Miss Warner straightened. "Did you fall? Hit your head?"

"Yes, I thought I mentioned that. While I was walking Sebastian back to my father's house, I tripped in a rut on the road and fell. I awakened here on your floor."

"Okay, but maybe you fell somewhere else, in the present time, and you've had a concussion, and you're kind of delusional." Her forehead creased as she contemplated her words.

"I think time travel would be preferable to the scenario you describe, Miss Warner. A delusional state of mind does not appeal to me."

"But maybe it's temporary. I could take you to a doctor."

Reggie shook his head. "And have them dispatch me to an asylum? I think not."

"They don't do that anymore, Reggie."

"I am pleased to hear it, Miss Warner, but no, no physician. He would as likely bleed me as anything, and I do not relish the thought."

Miss Warner stared at him intently, and Reggie squirmed under her gaze. Not so long ago, he had wished for the ardent look of another American woman. However, Miss Crockwell had but smiled at him kindly, having eyes only for William Sinclair.

"Miss Warner? Is there something amiss with my clothing? My hair?" He ran a hand through his thick unruly hair.

She blinked and shook her head. "Oh, no. No, nothing. You're all zipped up, if that's what you were asking. I'm just so confused."

"Zipped up?"

Miss Warner's cheeks reddened, and she smiled. "Don't worry about it. I'm beginning to think that you really don't know about zippers...or electricity."

Reggie shook his head. "I am afraid I fail to understand either word."

Miss Warner rose from her seat to approach the window. She seemed to stare at the moon.

"How do *you* think this happened?" She turned to face him, resting on the windowsill. "Because we don't have time travel in this century, and I don't think you all did either."

"Time travel," Reggie murmured. "No, I have not heard of it. Is it an American notion?"

"Not particularly. In fact, I think a British author wrote the first book having anything to do with traveling through time. Charles Dickens in *A Christmas Carol*. Somewhere in the mid-nineteenth century, I think."

"Charles Dickens," Reggie repeated. "I do not know that name."

"After your time," Miss Warner said. "And then British author H. G. Wells wrote *The Time Machine*, clearly about traveling through time with the use of a machine."

"I have not heard that name either."

"Also after your time," Miss Warner smiled. "Sooo...just supposing you did travel through time, how do you think you got here, and why would you end up here...in 2013, in my apartment?"

"I cannot imagine, Miss Warner."

"Phoebe, call me Phoebe."

"Miss Phoebe."

"No, just Phoebe."

Reggie raised a dark eyebrow. "It is unusual to address a lady so informally on such short acquaintance, but these are unusual circumstances, are they not, Miss Warner? And perhaps this is customary in your time. Phoebe then."

"Well, let's see if we can backtrack. So, you fell and hit your head."

"Yes."

"And what had you been doing when you fell? You said you had a horse? Did you fall off your horse? That would be quite a head injury. I got the impression you had been walking."

"Yes, Sebastian had injured his leg. My fault entirely. I should not have ridden him so carelessly in the dark, but I was angry." He pressed his lips together and waved a hand. "It is of no consequence. I had been looking at the full moon—as you have tonight in your time—and I misstepped."

"Oh, me too!" Phoebe exclaimed. "I was looking at the moon, too. Through the binoculars." She picked up an object which resembled two small telescopes attached at a base. "Want to see?"

He rose eagerly. "Binoculars. Yes, I have heard of binocular telescopes, but I have not seen them. May I?"

He peered through the binoculars and almost fell back as the building directly opposite seemed to leap at him. He lowered the binoculars and peered at the building. The monumental structure had not moved.

"These are quite strong," he grinned. "Now, where is the moon? Ah! There it is."

He raised the glasses again to study it more closely. Odd circular shapes and formations dotted the surface of what seemed like a luminous globe.

"Pon my word! What are those formations?" He turned to look at her.

"Craters from meteor impacts mostly, I think," Phoebe said with a bright smile. "It's beautiful, isn't it?"

Reggie handed the binoculars back to her, and she raised them to look at the moon.

"Yes," he said quietly. Indeed, she was beautiful. Shining dark brown hair grazed her shoulders, bouncing when she moved, so unlike the more restrained coiffures of the women of his time. He fought against an urge to run his fingers down the silky length. Her upturned nose delighted him as did her ready smile. Dark brown eyes, almost the color of her hair, dominated her face, and he longed to gaze into them yet again.

She dropped the glasses and looked at him, as he had hoped.

"We were both looking at the moon when you popped in," she said with a soft smile. "As hokey as it sounds, it's gotta be the moon."

"The moon, Miss Warner? How is that possible? I cannot deny that as a child I invested the moon with magical properties following the death of my mother, but I cannot truly believe it is responsible for such a momentous event."

"Your mother died when you were young?" she asked quietly.

Reggie looked away from the sympathy on her face. "Yes, when I was but a boy of eight. A long time ago." He cleared his throat. "I wished many a night on the moon for her return, but alas it did not come to pass." He smiled briefly.

"I'm so sorry," she said. "My mother passed away a few years ago as well."

Reggie bowed his head. "My condolences, Miss... Phoebe. And your father? Do you have siblings?"

"I never knew my father. He left when I was young." Phoebe's voice hardened, and Reggie thought he never wished to hear that note in her voice directed toward him. "No brothers or sisters." She shrugged and rose.

"Well, this is quite the dilemma, and I have no idea what to do. I think you'd better stay here though. It really isn't safe for you out there." She nodded toward the window.

"Not safe?" Reggie followed her eyes. "In what way?"

"Oh, gosh! In every way, I should think. It's fast paced, probably much more fast paced that you're used to. There are cars and people and streetlights and vendors. Just the hustle and bustle of the city."

"I have spent considerable time in London. London is a large city."

Phoebe shook her head. "It is now, I know, from the movies. I've never been there. But you have to trust me when I say the London you knew can't be half as chaotic and, well...as dangerous as New York is today."

"But how do you manage when faced with such peril? Or do you never leave your apartments?" Reggie approached the window again and looked out. "You reported your cousin was 'out' and would soon return. How does she fare?"

"I'm confusing you, I think. The city isn't *that* dangerous on a daily basis, not if you're careful. It's like any big city. There are good people and bad people. But I just think it would be very dangerous for *you*, Reggie, because you don't know your way around. So, I think you should stay here—while you're here—where I can help you." Phoebe paused. "And to be honest? I lied about my cousin returning. She lives in Switzerland right now with some young ski instructor."

"I see," Reggie said. London had its unsavory elements as well, and he thought he understood her concern for his safety. He noted she had a tendency to mother him, and he was not quite sure how he felt about it. Since he was as lost as a babe in the woods at the moment, her nurturing attentions were welcome, but he had fought too hard over the past few years to gain autonomy from his father's overbearing parenting to submit lightly to the dictatorial commands of a strange, if charming, young woman.

"I am uncertain how I arrived in your time, Phoebe, and even less certain how I shall return to my time. Just prior to leaving my father's home this evening...or then, I should say, I had argued with him as I told him I planned to leave England and move to America for an indefinite period of time. And now, here am I! In America, albeit in a different era than I had thought. My first instinct is to attempt to return to my time, yet that would be contrary to my expressed desire to come to America. Therefore, I shall not worry unduly about how I arrived here, and I welcome your assistance in settling in. As I...em...traveled without luggage and my pockets are empty, I must impose upon your generosity until I am able to secure funds for myself. Perhaps I could visit a bank tomorrow and arrange to draw upon my account. If I have not touched my money in two hundred years, it must have accrued a great deal."

Phoebe blinked. "Boggles the mind," she murmured.

"Boggles?" Reggie asked. "Do you think my admittedly impulsive plan without merit?"

Phoebe shook her head and smiled. "I have *no* idea. I can't imagine a bank holding onto an account for two hundred years though. My guess is they would close an inactive account after some years and absorb the money."

Reggie sighed. "Perhaps you are right. Then I must see what has become of my father's estate. I was due to inherit when my father—" The full scope of what had transpired seemed to hit him at once. His father dead? Samuel? No! Not possible. He knew a moment of horror and thought to launch himself from the window as if to fly home, but the instant passed. He would return home at some point...somehow.

"Oh, Reggie! Don't think about it!" Phoebe said with firmness. "Don't even think that way. This will all turn out okay, I'm sure of it. Come on. How about something to eat? Are you hungry? What do you eat?" She took him by the arm and urged him back to the kitchen where he reclaimed his seat on the barstool.

Having spent little time in kitchens, he watched her with interest as she bustled about preparing a meal.

"How about breakfast?" she said brightly. "At night. I don't know about you all, but we do it all the time here. It's one of the easiest meals to make."

"That sounds lovely, thank you," Reggie murmured. He noted she used no fire in her stove but seemed only to turn knobs and push buttons as she rattled pots, pans, and glassware. She withdrew cold items from a large silver container she termed a *re-frig-er-a-tor*. She spelled the word out for him.

"Do you have no servants at all then, Phoebe? No cook, no one to serve? Perhaps a maid?"

Phoebe looked over her shoulder and smiled. "No, not a one. Only the wealthy have a full staff, really, and I'm not wealthy."

"Oh, I see," he said. "The furnishings in your apartment, and the equipment in your kitchen, albeit smaller in scale than an English country home, are tasteful and appear to be of good quality. The kitchen of our townhome in London is not much larger, I think."

"So, you live with your father?"

"I do," he said. "I have often thought of purchasing my own apartments in London, but I spend more time in the country than in town. My mother's inheritance was entailed without land, so I reside with my father. Of course, I could purchase another property. I think I must if I marry. I would not wish to bring my wife to my father's house, especially now that it has a new mistress. My father's new wife would not welcome any interference in the household, I think."

A cacophony of ringing and other sounds resounded from the various machines in the kitchen as Phoebe cooked. Reggie listened to them with interest.

"And that noise stems from which machine?"

"The microwave," Phoebe replied.

"*Mi-cro-wave.* An expeditious means of cooking, I see."

"It is very fast," Phoebe replied. "So you were saying that if you marry, or when you marry, you think you'll buy another house for your wife? Like another country estate?"

"Yes, I think that would be best. I had not really given it much thought until now. Somehow, this...distance from England has given me some clarity."

"Tell me about your brother."

"Samuel." Reggie smiled. "Samuel has become an ardent book enthusiast. He reads often. He is not much interested in the running of the estate, which troubles my father not at all. My father is content to handle matters himself."

"So he doesn't work?"

"Samuel? No, not at any occupation. Our family do not 'work' in the trades. It is not necessary."

"But what do you do all day?"

"I ride, I visit neighbors. There are dinners and dances and balls and picnics. We are kept very busy in the country. I help my father in matters regarding the estate on rare occasions when he requires it."

"Wow! Nice life," Phoebe said as she settled food onto a plate and placed it unceremoniously in front of him. She sat down beside him with a bright smile.

"I hope you like it. Dig in!"

"You are so...American," he murmured with a smile. "I have known an American woman, and you remind me of her."

"Uh oh, I hear something in your voice. I take it you like this American? Where did you meet her? In England?"

"It is a long story. Perhaps another time."

Reggie eyed the pancakes on his plate before turning to see Phoebe pouring what looked like syrup from a container onto her pancakes.

He helped himself to the syrup, marveling at the light feel of the container. He cut his food meticulously and took a bite. Sweetness filled his mouth.

"Do you all eat pancakes?" Phoebe asked. "It seemed the easiest thing to make. I realized after I said I'd make breakfast that I didn't have a lot of groceries in the fridge. I hope they're okay."

Reggie struggled to understand all her words. He deduced "fridge" was a shorter version of refrigerator. "Groceries" sounded like something in which Cook might be interested.

"Yes, we do eat pancakes, although they look and taste differently. These are quite savory though. You are an excellent cook."

"Thank you!" Phoebe said, her cheeks taking on a rosy hue. "I never get a chance to cook for anyone."

Reggie quirked an eyebrow but said nothing. He was uncertain how to respond. Cooking was not something to which the women of his circles aspired. He thought he detected a forlorn note in her voice, and he wondered about her life, her acquaintances, her activities. Did she have a suitor? He rather hoped not.

He found his close proximity to her—seated as they were on the barstools and much closer than if they sat beside each other at a dinner table—played havoc with his senses, and he suspected he did not have enough presence of mind at the moment to truly comprehend the extraordinary situation in which he now found himself.

"And what daily activities occupy you, Phoebe?" The informal use of her name still sounded presumptuous and overly familiar.

"Me? Oh, gosh, let's see. I go to work, come home, watch TV—television—sleep, go back to work again. On the weekends, I run errands, shop for groceries, although not apparently enough," she said with a smile. "I go out to Broadway shows occasionally with a couple friends from work. Wow! My life sounds very dull, doesn't it? I don't think I realized. Work keeps me pretty busy. I love what I do."

"I did not realize you had an occupation. And what is it that you 'do'?"

"I work for a publisher, not too far from here. I'm a copy editor. I'm kind of low on the totem pole right now, but I have hopes of moving up one day to editor."

Phoebe's cheeks shone and her eyes sparkled when she spoke of her employment. He had never before met anyone who took such apparent joy in her occupation, and he found it most refreshing. He simply could not imagine the groomsmen or the maids in his father's home beaming thusly regarding their tasks.

"I wish that for you as well," Reggie murmured with a smile. "What may I ask is a 'totem pole?' Is this a structure at your place of employment?"

"What?" Phoebe looked startled, then she laughed. "Oh no, it's just an old figure of speech. A totem pole is... Let me think. It's a pole carved from a tree by the indigenous people of the northwestern part of North America. I think the symbols on the poles represent family lineages, stories, myths, events, almost anything they want to carve into them. And that's all I know about totem poles." She grinned and shrugged her shoulders, and Reggie was struck by the thought that he had not seen any of the young ladies of his time shrug in such a manner.

Phoebe continued. "But what I meant by the expression 'low on the totem pole' is that I am new to the publishing world, and I have to work my way up...wait for an opening, something like that."

"I see," Reggie said, though he really did not. He could not fathom a woman of Phoebe's obvious breeding and education working in any capacity other than as governess. His own education had been undertaken by a tutor, the most excellent Mr. Hartwood.

"And your cousin? You say she is away in Switzerland? With an instructor?" He had not understood all her words. A reference to a "ski"?

Phoebe wiped her mouth with a napkin of paper and discarded it on her plate. Reggie followed her lead.

"A ski instructor. Yup! Unlike me, Annie *is* wealthy thanks to her father's real estate investments, and she travels a lot. She recently met a ski instructor in Switzerland and decided to buy a place there and have him live with her. It's not the first time she's done something like that and may not be the last, but I wish her well. She's letting me live in the apartment while she's gone, otherwise I couldn't afford it. It's beautiful, isn't it?" Phoebe surveyed the kitchen and living room beyond.

"Yes, very lovely."

"Well, let me throw these dishes into the dishwasher and then decide on sleeping arrangements. This is only a one bedroom, so you'll have to sleep on the couch. Do you want to take a shower before you go to bed?"

Reggie jumped to his feet as Phoebe picked up his plate and stowed it in some sort of large silver-appearing cabinet. Her references to sleeping arrangements dumbfounded him, and he clasped his hands behind his back and watched her silently. She certainly could do with a maid or a housekeeper who could clean the kitchen as well as see to her guests' sleeping arrangements. The informality of life in America was eccentric at best, but he found it quite intriguing.

Phoebe looked over her shoulder toward him and favored him with her charming smile. He drew in a silent breath.

"It's called a dishwasher, and like it sounds, it's a machine that washes dishes. No need for a maid," she said almost as if she could read his mind. She shut the door of the machine and turned. "You know, I've often wondered who I would be if I hadn't been born in this time, Reggie. Have you done that? I suspect though that if I'd been born in your time, I would have been born poor, and probably married by now to a tenant farmer with four hungry children at my knees."

"I cannot imagine," Reggie said. "With your intellect, you could not have lived thus."

Phoebe's cheeks colored becomingly. "I doubt I would have had a choice, right? You're either born with money or not—in *your* time. You're either an aristocrat or not, right? Fortunately, in our time, that sort of thing doesn't matter—at least not in the United States or England. We can make as much money as we want if the circumstances are right. There are many fields of employment that pay tons of money if one is lucky enough to find work in them."

Reggie listened and tried to imagine the world she described, but it seemed fantastical.

"You are suggesting that the tenant farmer and the wife with four hungry children could have risen to become the masters? I do not think that is possible." He narrowed his eyes. Who then would work the farms?

"Absolutely," Phoebe said with a suspicious twist of her lips. Did she laugh at him? "If he took night classes, got a degree in business and a job on Wall Street, or if he moved the family to Hollywood and found a starring role in a television series. Or if *she* found a starring role in a movie. If he began an Internet startup company that made millions. Or maybe if they won the lottery. There are all sorts of ways the poor farmer could have found enough money to buy the farm."

"Then you would no longer be poor with four hungry children at your knees," Reggie grinned.

"Touché, Mr. Hamilton!" Phoebe laughed.

"I suspect this would be a most inopportune moment to advise you that my title would be more correctly addressed as Lord Hamilton?" He quirked an amused eyebrow in her direction.

Phoebe's mouth opened and shut in a most droll fashion. "Oh, sure, let's have the whole package! A handsome Georgian man drops into my lap complete with tight-fitting pantaloons and a cravat, an English accent *and* a title. Why not?" She curtsied.

CHAPTER THREE

At the sight of Reggie's bronzed cheekbones, Phoebe clapped a hand over her mouth. Had she really said "tight fitting?" She didn't want him to think she had been looking or anything.

Reggie dropped his eyes to his trousers, and Phoebe moved past him quickly.

"Well, let's see! Here's the couch. I'll get some sheets and a blanket. And if you'll follow me through the bedroom, here's the bathroom. There are fresh towels on the shelf there. I'm not sure you know how to work anything, so here...I'll show you." She spoke quickly, hoping he would forget what she had said earlier. After all, she was hardly the kind of girl who said, "Hey, Dude. Nice butt!" So telling a Georgian-era gentleman that she thought his pants were attractively snug was probably too much.

She showed him how to turn on the shower and adjust the temperature, how to work the taps in the sink, and how to flush the toilet. A quick glance at Reggie's face showed a kaleidoscope of emotions. Embarrassment, surprise, confusion, interest, and more embarrassment when she flushed the toilet. When Mattie pointed out the toilet paper, he coughed behind his ruffled sleeve.

"I have a few spare toothbrushes here from the dentist's office." She rummaged in the cabinet drawer. "You can use one while you're here. Here's a comb, and some disposable razors. Pink, but I'm sure they work just the same." She eyed his handsome face. "Don't cut yourself. They're very sharp."

Reggie picked up the small purple toothbrush enclosed in plastic, and he studied it.

"You don't use a toothbrush?" Phoebe wondered how that was

possible. His teeth appeared remarkably white and clean on his occasional smiles.

He shook his head silently, pressing his lips together.

"Well, here, I'll show you." She picked up her own toothbrush from a pink holder on her sink and loaded toothpaste onto it before brushing her teeth, albeit quickly. Reluctant to spit into the sink in front of him, she faced him and covered her mouth.

"So, you would rinse your mouth out with water. If you would just turn around..."

Reggie complied, and Phoebe rinsed out her mouth and turned to face him.

"So! I think that's about it. Do you have any questions?"

Reggie turned around. "A multitude, Madam, but I cannot even imagine what those questions might be at the moment. I am most anxious to use your paste though. Your smile is delightful, and if the paste is responsible, then I shall use it gladly."

"Well, that and a bazillion dollars in orthodontics, as my mom used to say."

"Orthodontics?"

"Teeth straightening. Big thing in our time. I'm not sure why."

He shook his head in apparent confusion and turned to survey the bathroom.

"I wonder, Phoebe, could you have a tailor attend me in the morning? I could pay him on account when I discover the whereabouts of my family's money. I could wear this clothing again tomorrow at the outside, but beyond that would be too egregious. I must have a change of clothes."

"We can go out in the morning and find some clothes for you. I don't think 'have a tailor attend' you means the same thing today as it might have in your day. Tailors don't usually make house calls, and I'm not sure if they make complete suits of clothing here in the United States. Usually just alterations."

"Oh, I see. I do not wish to trouble you. Could you then perhaps direct me to a men's establishment? I do not imagine you would be comfortable in such a place."

Phoebe grinned, and Reggie sighed.

He drew himself up. "Miss Warner. I see that some of the things I say amuse you, but is it possible for you to suspend your laughter for the moment?"

Phoebe pressed her lips together. "I'm sorry, Reggie. I really am. I'm not laughing *at* you, really."

"But I am not laughing, therefore, you are not laughing *with* me either, Miss Warner."

"Okay, please drop the Miss Warner thing. Not that I don't think it's kind of charming, but I know you did it because you're upset. I'll try to be more sensitive."

"I do not need you to be more sensitive. I am not a child to cry at miffed feelings, but if you could refrain from smirking when I do say things that seem unusual to you, I would be most grateful."

"Honestly, Reggie, I'm *not* smirking. I'm smiling. I think the things you say are cute." She sighed and moved past him to leave the bathroom but turned back. "Look, I'll take you shopping in the morning. Trust me. Women shop with men all the time, and men shop with women. It will be all right." She turned for the bedroom door but hesitated. "Umm...the only thing I have for you to wear to bed are T-shirts and sweatpants, all too small for you, I think."

"Do not concern yourself on my account. I shall do well enough in this clothing."

Phoebe nodded. "Well, I'll leave you to wash up if you want. I'll be out in the living room when you're done." She closed the door behind her and crossed the bedroom to enter the living room. With weak knees, she dropped herself onto the couch. Out of Reggie's presence, the enormity of the situation hit her, and she didn't know whether to laugh, cry, or call the police.

Her cell phone rang, and she scrambled up to find her bag by the front door.

"Hello? Mouse?" A familiar female voice spoke on the other end.

"Annie! You must be up late...or early." Annie didn't call often, and Phoebe wondered if she'd had a sixth sense about the arrival of Lord Reginald Hamilton.

"Not too early. I just arrived at the airport, at JFK. I thought I'd call ahead and tell you I'll be there within an hour. I didn't want to scare you when I open the door."

"What?" Phoebe almost shrieked.

"I know, I know! Sorry, I know this is a surprise. Johan and I broke up, and I didn't want to stay in that place for another minute. I thought I'd come home and lick my wounds for a while—you know—with my favorite cousin."

"Your *only* cousin," Phoebe said mechanically as she often did. She thought fast. What to do about Reggie? There was nothing she could do but tell Annie that he was her live-in boyfriend. She didn't think Annie would be able to keep her mouth shut about the truth, and the truth was not something New York City—or the world—was ready for. If indeed, Reggie was from the early nineteenth century. She wasn't sure how she felt about it herself.

"Yeah, thanks for telling me. Hey, I guess I should have mentioned that I have a guy...a boyfriend. And he's living with me. Maybe I should have asked. It *is* your place."

"No way!" Annie crowed. "Seriously? Just a minute." Some sort of commotion could be heard, and Annie came back on the phone. "Okay, I got my bag off the carousel. I'll be there in an hour. I guess I'll take the couch then. I could do a hotel, but that seems kind of weird. Besides, I wanted to see you. We'll figure it out."

"I'll see you then."

Phoebe disconnected the call and stared at the phone in horror. What was she going to do? How would Reggie react when she told him he had now become her boyfriend? Or suitor? And clearly, he wouldn't be sleeping on the couch.

She ran into the bedroom and hesitated at the sound of the shower. The situation seemed too difficult to explain through a closed bathroom door, so she would have to wait until he was finished. She almost hopped from one foot to the other impatiently while Reggie took what seemed like the longest shower in the world. Fifteen minutes later, the shower was turned off, and Phoebe knocked on the bathroom door.

"Yes?" Reggie called out.

"Reggie! I need to talk to you. Are you decent?"

"Decent? But of course. However, I am without clothing."

"Wrap the towel around you. I have to talk to you."

"A moment, please."

Phoebe gave it only a moment. "Okay, I'm opening the door, ready or not. We have an emergency."

She reached for the handle, but the door opened from within. Reggie stood in the doorway of the bathroom, one towel wrapped around his waist and another in his hand as he rubbed the moisture from his wet, wavy hair. Phoebe's heart thumped uncomfortably. Her Georgian boyfriend had all his body parts as far as she could see. Lean muscular arms and legs, a well-defined chest and toned stomach, and broad, broad shoulders as she had noted before.

She lowered herself to the bed on weak knees and faced him, trying not to gawk.

"Reggie, my cousin, Annie, just called. She's at the airport, and she's coming home. I think she's going to stay here for a bit. She'll be here in about forty minutes. I had to explain your presence here, so I told her you were my boyfriend and that you were living with me. I know this all probably sounds crazy to you, but..." Phoebe shrugged helplessly.

His eyes narrowed. "Phoebe, I cannot allow you to besmirch yourself on my behalf. I must insist on removing myself to other lodgings, perhaps to an inn."

Phoebe shook her head hastily. "No time, no money, no way," she said flatly. "I can't get you to a hotel in time and, even if I could, I really can't afford one. You actually don't have any money, pal, and Annie will be here before we can get out the front door. Besides, nothing has changed. I still don't want you wandering around New York City by yourself."

"But to suggest that we cohabitate? It is beyond the pale. I am not concerned for my own reputation, Phoebe, but for your good name." She caught her breath at the genuine concern in his voice.

"We do it all the time now, Reggie. It really isn't a scandal anymore. We'll be fine. I think Annie is a bit surprised because I've never actually lived with a man before, but it's not like I won't someday."

"You would consider such a thing?" he asked with narrowed eyes.

"Sure. Someday. Maybe." Phoebe ignored the feeling of being judged. Reggie couldn't help it.

She rose. "Well, hurry up and dry off so you can get dressed. We can't get you into any modern clothing before she gets here, so I'll figure out something to tell her." She moved quickly toward the bedroom door to listen for sounds of Annie's arrival. "Oh, I forgot! Annie won't know about you—about the time travel—and I don't think this is the right time to tell her. I'm not sure she could keep the secret. We don't want anyone to know about you yet. The implications of finding a time traveler are just..." Phoebe paused and shook her head. "I don't even want to think about it. So, let's just keep this between us." She smiled shakily and left the room.

Reggie emerged within fifteen minutes, fully dressed, his shining black hair combed and neatly parted on the side. He had apparently nicked himself shaving as he held a finger to the edge of his jaw.

"Let me see," Phoebe said. Reggie lifted his finger and she peered at the small cut. "It's not bleeding anymore. You're fine. You look refreshed," she said as she surveyed him. "She'll be here any minute. Just follow my lead, okay? I know this must be nerve-wracking for you, but everything will be okay."

"Not so 'nerve-wracking' for me as for you, I think, if I understand your meaning," Reggie said with a smile. "I feel quite calm, in fact."

"That's because you don't know Annie. She'll ask questions. Lots of them," Phoebe retorted. She heard the keys in the door. "She's here. Early."

She hurried toward the door and opened it for Annie who dropped her keys into her purple paisley carryon bag. Two matching suitcases rested by her feet.

"Mouse!" she exclaimed as she leaned in for a hug. "It's so good to see a familiar face." She grabbed one suitcase and stepped past Phoebe to move into the apartment as if in search of something. "Where is he?" she said. "Oh, can you grab that?"

Phoebe took hold of the other oversized suitcase and wheeled it into the apartment. By the time she cleared the short hallway, Annie had found Reggie.

"Annie, this is Reggie Hamilton. Reggie, my cousin, Annie Warner."

Annie thrust out a long, slender hand. "Hi there, Reggie." She kept her eyes on him. "You didn't tell me he was so handsome, Phoebe. Good for you, girl!"

Reggie bent slightly at the waist and inclined his head, his cheeks reddening.

"I am delighted to make your acquaintance, Miss Warner."

"Oh, and old-fashioned, too! You didn't tell me he was English either, Mouse. Where are you from in England, Reggie?"

"Bedfordshire, Madam."

Phoebe made a beeline for Reggie and tucked her hand in his arm in what she hoped looked like an intimate gesture. Reggie covered her hand with his own, perhaps thinking to reassure her. At the touch of his hand, a shiver ran up her spine, and Reggie dropped his eyes to her face as if sensing her tremor. Phoebe lost herself in his beautiful blue eyes for a moment.

"Hellooo," Annie waved a hand as if to distract them. "You are not alone," she intoned with a smile.

Phoebe dragged her eyes from Reggie's and returned her attention to Annie.

"Oh, sorry!" Phoebe muttered, her cheeks burning. "Yup, Reggie is from England."

Annie set her carryon bag down and turned for the kitchen. "So, what's with the getup? I was just in London three months ago, and I don't think anyone is wearing clothes like that. It's not Halloween, is it?" She popped a small canister into the coffee pot. "Coffee anyone?"

"Reggie is...a cover model," Phoebe surprised herself by saying. "He was just showing me the outfit for his latest cover." She dared not look up at Reggie again but kept her face on Annie's back as she poured coffee into a mug.

"Really?" Annie asked. She returned from the kitchen with her coffee. "Well, let's all sit down or something. You two are standing there like a couple of guilty teenagers."

Phoebe slid her hand down to Reggie's and led him toward the sofa while Annie slipped off her shoes and curled up in one of the easy chairs. Phoebe noted Reggie's eyes slide toward Annie's blue-jeaned legs.

"So, a cover model, huh? For your publishing house?" Annie asked.

"Yes," Phoebe agreed.

"Well, he's definitely handsome enough." Annie grinned.

Phoebe peeked at Reggie from under her lashes.

"Well, so anyway, that's why he's dressed this way. I'm sorry to hear about Johan."

Annie shrugged though Phoebe knew her well enough to suspect she masked her pain. Annie was always looking for "the one," but she seemed determined to pick men with whom she had nothing in common. Annie didn't even ski.

"Thanks. I'm sorry it didn't work out."

Phoebe glanced at Reggie then back at Annie. "We could talk about it later if you want."

"I'm talked out," Annie said. "No, I'd rather hear about your fella. How long have you been in the States, Reggie?"

Reggie opened his mouth to speak, but Phoebe jumped in.

"Not long, really. A couple of months?" She looked to Reggie as if confirming.

Reggie nodded and smiled politely.

"Do you always speak for him, Phoebe?"

"Oh!" Phoebe exclaimed. She turned to Reggie helplessly.

"No, not always, Miss...Annie," Reggie said. "Only when I am taken aback. I did not realize you would return to your home, and I was anxious to find my own lodgings lest you find my presence unsettling, but Phoebe has urged me to stay here. I fear you must uncomfortable with my presence here."

"Oh, no, I'm fine. I probably won't be staying long anyway. I've got a condo in Hawaii, and I think I might head off to that for a bit. You know, get some sun, melt the ice of Switzerland."

"And where is...?" Reggie began, but Phoebe intercepted the question.

"I love the Pacific islands. You are so lucky!" Phoebe took Reggie's hand and gave it a gentle squeeze.

"Ah, yes! The Pacific. Beautiful," he agreed.

"I know. I can't wait to get there. I'll look Kathy up when I get there. I think she's still living on Oahu."

Phoebe turned to Reggie. "Kathy is a college friend of Annie's."

"Indeed." Reggie nodded.

"Yes, indeed," Annie said. "So, what brought you over to the United States, Reggie? Just the modeling?"

Reggie looked toward Phoebe who bit her lip, hoping for the best. Annie was already wise to the fact that Phoebe had done most of the talking.

"Yes, modeling."

"How did you get into it? I've never met a male model."

Phoebe almost jumped when Reggie squeezed her hand, and she turned to look at him. One eyebrow was quirked in her direction, and she had a feeling he had just figured out what his occupation was.

"I began as a child, posing for a painter in my village."

"A woman who painted children playing," Phoebe edited. She was afraid Reggie's words would raise odd questions about the painter in this day and age.

"Yes, a woman."

"Oh, interesting! And then you just kept on with it as a photographic model?"

"Indeed," Reggie murmured. Phoebe pressed his hand gently.

"The painter? Is she famous? Would I have heard of her?" Annie asked.

"I do not think so," Reggie said.

Annie nodded. "And then you came here and met Phoebe."

"Yes, a fortunate event."

Phoebe's heart rolled over. Did he mean "fortunate" as in happy to meet her or lucky she was there to help him? She thought she'd take what she could get. The feel of his fingers laced through hers was both intoxicating and natural, as if she'd known him all her life. She never wanted to remove her hand from his. Never.

Annie finished her coffee. "Well, I'm exhausted. So, if I'm sleeping out here on the couch..." She fixed them with an expectant gaze.

Phoebe jumped up, pulling Reggie with her. "Oh! Sure. You must be exhausted. We'll go to bed. Are you absolutely sure you don't want us to sleep out here?"

Phoebe felt Reggie's hand jerk. She hadn't quite warned him about the sleeping-together-in-the-bedroom scenario. She kept her eyes on Annie.

"No, no, two of you, one of me. I'm not kicking you of out of your bed just because I can't get my love life straight. You go on." She shooed them away. "Just bring me a sheet, blanket, and a pillow, will you?"

Phoebe nodded and pulled a very stiff and resistant Reggie toward the bedroom. She shut the door behind them.

"Miss Warner! Phoebe! I feel as if I have entered a brothel! I cannot spend the night with you in your bedchamber! This is outrageous!" His ramrod straight posture mirrored the emotion of his words.

Phoebe stopped and stared at him. "A brothel? Reggie, I can't believe you said that!" She turned a shoulder on him and headed for the walk-in closet. "I should have explained what would happen when Annie got here earlier, but there wasn't much time...or maybe I was afraid you'd have this kind of reaction. Don't worry, Reggie. I'm not going to 'violate' you!" She pulled some extra bedding from the top shelf in the closet and eyed what was left. Someone wasn't sleeping on the bed, and she suspected it would probably be Reggie. He would need some bedding of his own.

"Violate me? Miss Warner, are you deliberately trying to provoke me? What nonsense! I really must insist on finding other accommodations."

Phoebe understood Reggie's concerns—if indeed he did come from the late Georgian era. She had been prepared for some resistance from him, but every now and then he showed an innate arrogance that grated on her, and he was in the throes of an arrogant fit at the moment. She suspected that ordering him to stay might not work.

"Okay, Reggie, just please wait until I take these out to Annie. Then we'll talk about what you want to do."

She opened the door and passed through with her load, and the awful feeling that Reggie, had he been a modern guy, would have rejected sleeping in her bedroom just as vociferously as he did now. Was she that undesirable? Her face flamed as if she had just propositioned him and he had turned her down.

She dropped the bedding on the couch. Annie emerged from the half bath in the hall, her toothbrush in hand.

"Oh, thanks. I'm going to need a shower in the morning, but I'm too tired to worry about it tonight."

"I hate to see you sleeping on the couch in your own place. I'm really very sorry about the inconvenience. Reggie...um...gave up his own apartment when he moved into here, otherwise, we'd stay at his place and let you have this one."

Annie waved a careless hand. "No problem. I'm the one who dropped in. This is your home too, Mouse."

"Okay, well, good night," Phoebe said. She hugged Annie.

"Phoebe?"

"Yes?"

"A male model?" Annie asked. "I can't see you with a male model. I would never have thought that would be your sort of guy. I thought you liked computer geeks and nerds. At least, that's what you've dated in the past."

Phoebe shrugged. "Well, just because he does some modeling doesn't mean he isn't intelligent."

"Oh, I'm not saying that. He sounds very smart, but..." She paused. "Does he do anything else for a living? He can't just make a living as a cover model, can he?" Annie's eyes narrowed. "He isn't an exotic dancer or something, is he?"

Phoebe laughed. "No! And he's not an actor wannabe either. No, just a model. I think he makes a pretty decent living at it."

"I know it's none of my business, hon, but does he contribute financially? I'm just kind of worried. You never mentioned him, but you say you've been together for..." She narrowed her eyes, and shook her head. "I don't think you said. Anyway, you'd said he'd only been here a couple of months and now he's given up his apartment? Cover models really can't make that much, can they?"

Phoebe gritted her teeth and held back retorts regarding Annie's flawed personal life. She had little enough room to be concerned about Phoebe's life.

"Well, cousin, Reggie does fine. He contributes. Actually, he comes from a wealthy family in England, some sort of aristocracy. I'm not too worried about it. So, not to worry." Phoebe turned for the bedroom. "Sleep well."

"I will," Annie yawned. "What are y'all's plans tomorrow?"

Phoebe paused at the bedroom door. "Oh, shopping," she said on a forced careless note.

"Can I join you?" Annie asked. "I need to do some shopping, too."

"Ummm...sure! I think we're mostly shopping for him though. He wants to buy some new clothes." How was she going to explain his clothing to Annie in the morning? She'd have to think of something. Phoebe didn't want to imagine how a shopping expedition for Reggie was going to go with Annie along.

"Night!" Phoebe said and entered the bedroom.

Chapter Four

Reggie, in Phoebe's absence, paced the room, stopping occasionally to peer at the various pieces of furniture, photographs and a square black box with a glass face. He fingered the bedclothes and the curtains, noting a feminine flower pattern on both. The carpet, tan in color, covered the floor in its entirety, and he searched for the edge to lift in order to peer under it, but he could find no edge. The carpet appeared to be attached to the walls.

To say he was discomfited failed to adequately describe his state of mind. He fully understood that he had arrived not only in America—as he had desired, but almost two hundred years into the future. Had customs changed so much that it was now permissible for an unmarried man to sleep in the bedchamber of an unmarried young lady? Of course, were the need to share a room with her to become a necessity, there was absolutely no question that he would behave toward Phoebe in any manner other than as a gentleman. Nevertheless, he was adamant that he find other sleeping arrangements.

Phoebe returned, and he stopped his pacing and turned to face her, his hands clasped behind his back.

She gave him an uncertain look and took a chair next to a bureau.

"Could you sit down for a minute, Reggie? We need to talk," she said softly as she nodded toward an upholstered tufted bench at the end of the bed.

"If it pleases you, Phoebe, but I warn you, I will not be dissuaded. I will not sleep in your bedchamber." He took a seat reluctantly and waited.

Phoebe's cheeks flamed, and he knew a moment of remorse.

"Look, Reggie, we're in a bit of a bind here. I would never suggest that you sleep in my bedroom under any other circumstances, especially since I can see that the idea repels you."

Reggie sought to protest but Phoebe continued.

"Things are different now as I've probably already told you a dozen times. No one is going to say anything about you or me if you happen to sleep in my bedroom. No one is going to know. I understand that this isn't done in your time, but it actually *is* in my time. I really, really, really think it would be a bad idea for you to go to a hotel, and frankly, you don't have any money."

Phoebe folded her arms across her bosom in a mutinous fashion much as he had done as a small boy when at odds with his father. He could hear the discomfiture in her voice when she used the word "repel," and he cursed himself for being an ungrateful cad. Further, Phoebe was correct. He had no money, nor was he certain he could take lodgings on account since he was unknown.

"Forgive me, Phoebe, I fear I have insulted you. I never meant to suggest that you 'repel' me or that the notion of sharing a bedchamber with you," his voice took on a husky note, "did not hold appeal for me. I have heard your assurances that this sort of *arrangement* would not be accompanied by the inevitable scandal as it would in my time, and I believe you are the best judge of that. You are correct in your statement that I lack funds at present. It is a humiliating situation for me, and one I hope to remedy soon. With your permission then, I shall find a corner of the room and prepare a makeshift bed." He rose and bowed. "Please accept my assurances that nothing untoward will occur, and that your virtue will be safe with me."

Phoebe clasped and unclasped her hands. "I'm definitely not worried about that, Reggie." She smiled faintly. "I'll get some stuff. Too bad I don't have an airbed. Maybe we can pick one up tomorrow while we're out." She stepped into the closet and spoke from within its confines. "At any rate, if Annie leaves for Hawaii like she said, and you're still here, you can always take the couch like we originally planned."

Reggie said nothing. He could not forget the wounded expression on Phoebe's face. Did the girl actually want him to sleep in her bedchamber? He cleared his throat and put the thought from his mind.

"Phoebe," he began. "Why does your cousin call you Mouse?"

Phoebe emerged from the closet, her arms laden with bedding. He stepped forward to take the linens from her arms.

"My middle name is Minerva, and she calls me Minnie Mouse on occasion."

"Minnie Mouse?"

"It's a character in a cartoon."

"I do not know what a *kar-toon* is, but Minerva is the goddess of wisdom and often depicted with an owl, not a mouse."

Phoebe put her hands on her elbows and surveyed the room.

"Yes, she was, and that is why you should trust *me*. I'm sure my parents knew what they were doing when they named me." The corner of her lips twitched, and Reggie's heart lightened. Although he did not understand the nature of his indiscretion and had sought only to protect her reputation by insisting upon other sleeping accommodations, he vowed to let the matter rest—if only to see Phoebe smile again.

He bowed his head. "I put myself in your care."

Phoebe looked up sharply. "Good! Well, where shall we put your makeshift bed? Have you ever slept on the ground before?"

Reggie allowed that he had not.

"How about over here against the wall, near the bed? That's the only spot I can think of with enough room." She surveyed him from head to foot, and he stiffened for a moment, unused to such frank assessment from a woman. "You're pretty tall."

She took the linen and bent on her knees to smooth out a sleeping area for him. Reggie wondered how he would sleep, but he did not care to alienate Phoebe further. He knelt down to assist her, enjoying the close proximity to her. She seemed remarkably agile for a young woman, especially one in a skirt which reached only to her knees.

"There," she said as she straightened. "It doesn't look very comfortable, but we'll figure something out tomorrow, okay? There is no way I can share the bed with you, and I seriously think you'd have a heart attack if I suggested it."

Reggie thought he might have an apoplectic fit were he forced to lie next to her in a bed all the night, but he now knew to remain silent on the subject. "The bedding looks to be very comfortable. Thank you."

"You're welcome." She rose to her feet. "Well, I need to take a shower. I'll just change in the bathroom and then hop into bed when I come out. Don't wait up!"

Reggie rose hastily and bowed again. "As you wish." He waited until she gathered her things and closed the door behind her before sinking down onto the bench at the end of the bed. Unable to resist the softness of the mattress behind him, he leaned back, resting his head on the bed and staring at the ceiling.

If nothing else, life in the twenty-first century felt very comfortable, even luxurious—from the smooth texture of the living room furnishings and carpet to the equipment involved in the preparation of meals, and from the instant hot water in the gleaming bathroom to the softness of the mattress upon the bed. Although he had only experienced the interior of

Phoebe's apartment, he had no doubt the world outside would prove equally comfortable.

He looked forward to their excursion to a clothing shop in the morning as he was in desperate need of a change of clothes. He would most certainly need a nightshirt given that he was required to sleep fully clothed this night with the exception of his coat and boots which he thought he could safely remove with impunity.

Reggie closed his eyes for a moment and listened to the sound of the "shower" in the bathroom. A marvelous invention. He would insist on installing such a system immediately upon his return to England...and his own time. For he had no doubt that he would return. One did not simply travel in time to a distant place, never to be heard from again, did they? No one in his acquaintance had ever done so. Even Sylvie and Thomas Ringwood, and Louisa and Stephen Carver sent letters to Bedfordshire with news of their new life in America.

He opened his eyes. Were they here? In New York City? No, no, of course not. It was not possible. Though they had indeed emigrated to America, they had done so almost two hundred years prior. Still, he thought, would their descendents still live? He would ask Phoebe in the morning.

Reggie closed his eyes again, vowing to rise in only a moment's time to make use of the bed Phoebe had so carefully prepared for him. In just a moment.

****

Reggie opened his eyes to the sound of tapping on the bedroom door. He bolted upright and rubbed his eyes. The room was dark though it had been lit by lamps only moments before.

The door opened.

"Mouse?" Annie whispered as she thrust her head just inside the door. "Are you awake yet? I really need a shower this morning."

A gasp from the direction of the bed behind Reggie caught his attention, and he turned. Phoebe sat up in bed staring at him. She touched a lamp next to the bed, and a soft glow filled the room.

Annie opened the door wider, and stepped in, surveying the room with a quick glance.

"Did you sleep there, Reggie?" she asked.

Reggie jumped up. Had he fallen asleep and slept the night through?

"I am not certain," he began. "I only sat for a moment."

"What is that on the floor? Is that a bed?"

Phoebe scrambled from the bed and came to stand beside him. She took his hand in hers. Reggie dropped his eyes to her sleeping garment—a scanty blouse with straps and pink trousers of some sort. He looked away hastily.

"Yes, he did. When I came out of the shower, he was asleep on the ottoman, and I didn't want to wake him up to go to bed."

Annie tilted her head to one side as if she did not believe Phoebe's story, which was indeed probably the nearest thing to the truth either of them had told her cousin.

"But what's that on the floor?"

"Ah! My back pained me last night, and I did not think I would be able to sleep upon the luxurious mattress," Reggie offered. Phoebe squeezed his hand, and he thought he had done well.

"Well, I'm sorry to bust in on you guys like this, but I'm filthy. I really needed a shower. My clock's off, and my body is on Switzerland time." She scrutinized a bracelet on her arm. "It's almost seven o'clock. I hoped I wasn't too early."

"No, no," Phoebe said. She kept hold of Reggie's hand, and he minded not one bit.

"Okay, well. I'm going to go shower." Annie moved into the bathroom and shut the door behind her.

Phoebe dropped Reggie's hand as if he were a leper. Had he said something amiss? Again?

"Sorry about that. I just thought I should grab your hand since we're supposed to be a couple."

Had she thought he was displeased? That he did not care for her touch? Nothing could be further from the truth.

"Phoebe..." Reggie began with a thought to speak his mind.

"No problem," she said. "I'll probably have to grab you a few more times while Annie is here, but it's for a good reason." She rubbed her eyes and yawned. "When I came out of the shower last night, you were passed out on the ottoman there, and I didn't have the heart to wake you. So, basically you slept there all night. Does your back really hurt?"

"Not at all. I thought that a plausible excuse for the bedding on the floor."

"That was good!" Phoebe smiled. "Well, why don't you use the bathroom in the living room while I get dressed? I'll be out in a minute."

Reggie inclined his head. "As you wish." He did not know if he could get used to being directed about like a child—especially regarding matters of hygiene. As he had said, he was a babe in the woods, but that did not mean he relished being mothered at his age.

He put it from his mind at the moment and refreshed himself in the small washroom as Phoebe had suggested, an interesting room to be sure, much like a closet and containing many of the fixtures of the larger bathroom but without the "shower," which he absolutely delighted in. He regarded his hair, mourning the absence of a comb, and he attempted to bring it under control with his fingers and a bit of water. The wilted state of his cravat was mortifying, and he knew an urgent desire to find a men's establishment and acquire fresh clothing. This morning, Phoebe had said. There was nothing he could do meanwhile but hold his head high and appear not to notice the certain stares of passersby on the street as they beheld his wretched appearance.

A quick glance at his boots reminded him they were dusty from the road, and he reached for the paper which Phoebe had called "toilet paper" to dust them off. He must acquire boot black. Reggie searched for a waste bin in which to discard the paper but could find none. He eyed the toilet with interest. Phoebe had indicated the paper should be used for that purpose. Tossing the paper into the bowl, he pushed the handle, let loose the water, and watched the paper seemingly dissolve and disappear. Curiously, he pushed the handle again to see if it would reappear, but it did not. Fascinating!

A tap on the door startled him, and he jerked upright as if he had been caught doing something he should not.

"Are you okay in there, Reggie?" Phoebe called through the door.

"Yes," Reggie called. He tugged at his waistcoat, gave himself one last glance in the mirror and opened the door. Phoebe awaited him with a cup of coffee in her hand. He noted she wore a colorful blouse with short sleeves ending above her elbows. Her lower limbs were encased in what appeared to be a pair of dark blue men's trousers, as form-fitting as his own. She wore Roman-style sandals upon her feet. He took a deep breath and kept his eyes upon her face and way from her limbs.

"I used the paper to remove the dust from my boots. I hope that was acceptable," he said solemnly.

Phoebe laughed then covered her mouth as he frowned. "Ummm...yup...that's fine. You would probably like a shoeshine today, wouldn't you? I don't know where they do that anymore except at the train station." She assessed his Hessians frankly. "We'll probably have to get you some different shoes today. Those are very attractive, but they're just different."

He looked down at his boots. "Different?"

Phoebe shook her head and offered him the coffee. "I can't explain it. Just different. The tassels. Probably not."

Reggie lifted his chin and clasped his hands behind his back. "These are very expensive boots, Miss Warner, from the finest bootmaker in London."

"Uh oh, you're calling me Miss Warner again. That's not good." Phoebe sighed, and Reggie relented and took the coffee from her. "They are great-looking boots, Reggie, but you're not going to be able to wear them with our modern clothing. I'm sorry."

Reggie dipped his head. "It is I who must apologize, Phoebe. I am being missish. You must think me quite the dandy. The truth is that appearance is very important where I come from, and any deviation from the accepted standards subjects one to public ridicule."

"I know, Reggie." She moved toward the kitchen, and Reggie followed.

"But how *can* you know?"

"Books, Reggie, lots and lots of books, some of them written by authors of your time discussing the customs and traditions of the early nineteenth century." She poured a cup of coffee and set another to brew, presumably for her cousin.

"I would be most interested in reading some of these books. To hear my time referred to as the 'early nineteenth century' or the 'late Georgian era' sounds so strange."

"Good morning, everyone," Annie said as she emerged from the bedroom. "Any coffee for me?" She approached the kitchen dressed in clothing similar to Phoebe's, and Reggie supposed they wore the equivalent of morning gowns, such as those his stepmother wore at home.

Phoebe handed her cousin a cup of coffee.

"Morning," she murmured.

Reggie bowed. "Good morning."

"I love that bowing, Reggie. Did you spend time in Europe? It seems to be more of an old-fashioned Continental trait than British."

"I have traveled the Continent," he replied with a quick look in Phoebe's direction.

"Well!" Phoebe intervened. "Shall go out to eat for breakfast before shopping? I really don't have anything here." She addressed herself to Annie with a shrug.

Annie cocked her head.

"Are you going out in that getup, Reggie?"

Reggie stiffened. What in the infernal blazes was amiss with his clothing other than it was no doubt somewhat dated?

"And are you going out in that 'getup,' might I also ask?"

CHAPTER FIVE

"Reggie!" Phoebe sputtered. She couldn't help laughing, although acutely aware that she needed to calm the tension between Reggie and Annie, who looked very irate.

"Forgive me," Reggie bowed almost immediately. "I cannot believe I spoke in such a manner. Forgive me, Miss Warner."

"Which one?" Annie said with narrowed eyes.

"Both of you as you are so similarly dressed."

"Okay, Reggie, enough teasing now," Phoebe urged. "You know very well that these *jeans* are my favorite pair, and I wear jeans everywhere." She turned to Annie. "He's just teasing, Annie, really."

"Yes, of course, I jest." Reggie's serious expression didn't look like he had been jesting, but short of tickling him, Phoebe didn't know what else she could do to put a smile on his face to soften the moment.

Poor Annie, she thought. The sooner she headed off to Hawaii, the better off they would all be. Phoebe regretted that Annie had invited herself along on the shopping expedition, but there was nothing she could do. Had Reggie not appeared, Phoebe would have set herself to pampering and soothing Annie's broken heart, but she simply had her hands full with Reggie.

"Well, I'm sorry if I sounded like I was insulting your clothing. Why are you wearing it, by the way?"

Annie never could leave well enough alone, Phoebe sighed inwardly. She improvised.

"That's what he's going to wear on his photo shoot today, which he has to do before we go shopping. I forgot about that." She checked her watch for no reason at all other than it helped her focus on her lame story. "So, I've got to run him over to my office this morning fairly early. In fact, I wonder if we shouldn't head over there now so we're not late. We could meet you for breakfast after the shoot? Say in about an hour?"

Annie wasn't buying the story, and Phoebe didn't blame her. Reggie watched them but said nothing.

"A photo shoot at the publishing house? Do they do that? I thought that would be done in a studio? Uploaded online?"

"Special deal with this cover. The author wants to approve it, has that written into her contract, so the photographer is coming over to our place. Really complicated, too complicated to explain." Phoebe put a hand behind Reggie's back as if to urge him to the door. "Where do you want to meet? Charlie's Place down the street?"

She took Reggie's hand to pull him toward the door, grabbing her bag along the way. Reggie picked up his top hat from the hall table and settled it on his head. Phoebe rolled her eyes. He would definitely stand out in the top hat. Well, maybe someone would think he was a doorman or something.

"Okay, see you in about an hour then!" Phoebe called out without turning around. She opened the door and pulled Reggie through, not an easy task given his much larger size.

She pulled the door shut and turned with a finger to her lips when Reggie opened his mouth to speak.

"Wait till we get downstairs," she whispered. She dragged him down the hall toward the elevator, with Reggie lagging somewhat as he turned this way and that to study the hall. Right! He'd never even been outside of the apartment.

Phoebe stopped in front of the elevator. "Okay, Reggie," she said, keeping her voice low. "I'm sorry about all that. I don't think Annie believed me one bit, but I couldn't come up with anything else at the moment. Hello?" She looked up at him. Reggie seemed not to hear her as he ran his fingers along the shining steel of the elevator doors and over the lighted button she had pushed.

"This is the elevator I mentioned last night. We're in a tall building, and this carries us up and down the floors. By a cable," Phoebe added.

"There are no stairs?" Reggie asked.

"Well, yes, but we're on the fifteenth floor. That's a lot of climbing everyday."

"Fifteen floors?" he murmured with a shake of his head.

"The elevator is slow," Phoebe added with a sigh as she looked beyond him to assure herself that Annie wasn't following or setting out from the apartment herself at the same time.

A ding announced the arrival of the elevator, and the doors slid open.

Reggie jumped back, startled.

Phoebe grabbed his hand again. "Come on. You'll get used to all of this, you really will, Reggie."

Reggie allowed himself to be led inside the elevator, keeping one eye on Phoebe and a wary eye on the door as it shut behind them. He grabbed the rail as the elevator began to move, and Phoebe was grateful he couldn't see the actual motion of the elevator.

The realization of the complications inherent in taking care of this tall, handsome and very lost young man started to weigh on her. How could she possibly keep him safe, educate him in modern ways, even clothe and feed him? She had no experience with children, had never been called upon to babysit. Not that he was a child, of course, but she couldn't help worrying about him as a mother might a child—as her mother did about her. The quintessential worrying mother of an only child, Minerva Warner never left her daughter any doubt that she loved her more than anyone else in the world, and Phoebe missed her terribly. The prospect of being a single mother of a one-year-old infant in those days must have been daunting, but her mother had risen to the challenge and been both father and mother to her, albeit with a more watchful eye than some of the other parents in their Midwestern neighborhood.

Phoebe suspected she was channeling some of her mother's anxieties at the moment, but knowing that didn't help her wonder how she was going to take care of Reggie.

The elevator arrived at the ground floor, and Phoebe took a deep breath as she waited for the slow doors to open. Past the doorman they would go, and out into the street. Her immediate plan was to take Reggie to a store right away and get him some clothes before they met Annie for breakfast...so they could go shopping again. She looked up at Reggie, hoping he was an easygoing man who wouldn't fault her for coming up with such a harebrained scheme just to deceive Annie.

Reggie caught her eye and gave her a smile as if somehow reading her anxiety.

"Ready?" she asked as she took his hand again. She quite enjoyed this part of taking care of him—the touching.

Reggie surprised her by tucking her hand between the crook of his elbow and his side.

"It is only proper that I offer my arm to you, Miss Warner, and I am pleased to do so."

Phoebe blushed, feeling a bit like a gal in one of her romance novels, but she said nothing. The doors finally opened, and they entered the lobby. Tim was off as it was Saturday, but a middle-aged tall and thin man in a gray uniform greeted them.

"Good morning, Miss Warner, how are you today?" He held open the door for them, but Phoebe paused for a moment. No time like the present to introduce Reggie to the doorman.

"Hi George, good morning. Ummm... George, this is Reggie Hamilton. Reggie is going to be staying with me for a while...maybe a long while." Phoebe avoided Reggie's eyes. She didn't think she could bear to see him protest "Oh, no, not a *long* while. No, no."

"Welcome, Mr. Hamilton." George nodded and smiled.

"Thank you, George," Reggie said with a regal air as he inclined his head.

If George had any thoughts about Reggie's clothes, he never let on.

"Thank you, George," Phoebe said. She sashayed out the door on Reggie's arm but was brought up short by Reggie, who stopped and stared.

"Pon my word, Phoebe. Where on earth are we? Is that a horseless conveyance?"

Phoebe surveyed the street in front of her apartment building, trying to see it through his eyes. It was relatively quiet for a Saturday morning, with cars parked along the curbs on both sides of the street. Small city-size trees dotted the otherwise neutral gray concrete landscape. A passenger car meandered down the street.

"New York City, Reggie. And yes, that is most definitely horseless. We call it a car. You'll probably get a chance to ride in one, a taxi...if you're here long enough." Phoebe heard her voice drop on the last words.

She looked up at Reggie to see him busily scanning the street, probably trying to comprehend everything. She wasn't sure what she would do or how she would feel had she been the one who traveled to the twenty-first century. Luckily, he hadn't heard the wistful note in her voice. She plastered a smile on her face, promising herself to make his visit a pleasant one.

"I think we should get moving just in case Annie comes out. So, the immediate plan is to get you to a store, find some clothes, and get you dressed before we meet Annie for breakfast. I'll have to give you some sort of scenario for this supposed photo shoot that I lied about." Phoebe tugged at Reggie's arm. "Reggie? Are you listening? Come on, you can stare while we walk down the street."

Reggie dropped his bemused eyes to her face and nodded.

"Is life always so complicated for you, Phoebe?"

Phoebe laughed. "No, no. I lead a very dull life. That's why I'm not very good at this subterfuge thing."

"Let us proceed then. I put myself in your hands for the time being."

While they walked in the direction of Sinclair Publishing—and some stores—they discussed how best to convince Annie that Reggie had gone to her office for a photo shoot. Or at least Phoebe discussed and Reggie listened with half an ear while studying his surroundings with wide eyes.

"Reggie, are you listening?" she asked, feeling much like a long-time couple with her hand in his arm and asking the age-old question that women always would.

"Yes, yes, I am. Well, I am attempting to listen," he muttered. "What in blazes is that noise?" He nodded toward a multitude of taxis as they jostled each other on the now busy streets, the drivers fighting for position via blaring horns. Phoebe hardly heard the noise anymore, but she remembered being shocked when she first arrived at the amount of noise in the city.

"Taxis. Horns. They're only supposed to use them in emergencies, but the drivers use them to communicate, to say, 'Watch out! I'm mad as heck! Take that! Get off my rear!'" She looked up at him. "You all have hansom cabs in London, right? I'll bet they're noisy. Same drivers—different century?"

Reggie grinned and nodded. "You may be right about that, Phoebe. Certainly, there is a great deal of shouting amongst the cabs."

"Here we are!" Phoebe said with a flourish. She dragged him into the chain department store, doing her best to ignore the curious glances of passersby toward Reggie. Her lips twitched as several women in the cosmetics department eyed him with appreciation. *Yes, indeed, ladies, feast your eyes. Isn't he handsome?*

"Let's see." Phoebe stopped to read the store directory. "The men's clothes are upstairs."

"Shall we take the elevator?" Reggie asked.

"Nope, escalator this time." She paused in front of the escalator, dropping her hand from his arm. "No, let's not," she said with misgiving. "Let's take the elevator. I don't think they have any real stairs in this place. I don't want you to fall."

"Nonsense," Reggie said, eyeing the escalator with appreciation. He watched people ascend and descend. "I believe I can negotiate these moving steps with ease. If you please?" He bowed elegantly and gestured for her to precede him. Several ladies behind them waiting to step onto the escalator giggled. Phoebe hung back to let them go ahead of her.

"Oh my," one of the little silver-haired women said. "Well, if you aren't just the cutest thing. Isn't he a doll, Mary?"

"Yes, indeedy. Do you work here, young man?"

"Not at all, madam," Reggie said with a grin. "I am here to purchase men's clothing."

Phoebe covered her mouth with her hand. She agreed with the ladies. He was the cutest thing, but he wasn't going to be too happy to see her laughing.

"Allow me," he said as he took the hand of each lady and helped them onto the escalator to the sound of their continued twitters. He turned to Phoebe.

"Shall we?"

Phoebe smiled and stepped onto the escalator, turning immediately and holding her breath to see Reggie hop lightly onto the first step without incident.

"That went well," Phoebe breathed.

"But of course, Phoebe. I am not a child. I can race a stallion over miles of rough terrain. I can certainly negotiate moving iron stairs."

"I know, I know. I just worry."

"Do not." Reggie, on the step below Phoebe, took her hand and pressed it to his lips. Phoebe drew in a sharp breath. She could hear the "ooooh's" of the ladies just above them as they watched.

"Oh my," she echoed their early words. Mesmerized by his gesture, she failed to see that they had reached the top of the escalator. The front of her sandals jammed against the immobile lip at the top of the stairs, and she pitched forward with a cry.

Strong arms caught her from behind, wrapping themselves around her waist. She looked up from an awkward position precariously near the floor to see Reggie holding her. He pulled her up and set her on her feet. Out of the corner of her eye, she saw the two little old ladies watching with concern.

"Are you injured?" Reggie asked in a rough voice. He bent his head to peer into her face, his breath fanning her cheek in an intimate way.

A faint sound like mice clapping caught her attention, and she turned toward Mary and her companion who patted their hands together in admiration of Reggie's gallant catch before moving on.

"I'm fine, I'm fine," Phoebe murmured with a shaky laugh. "I can't believe that, after worrying about you, *I* was the one to fall on that thing."

"I can see that it does have the potential for danger," he said with a look over his shoulder toward the escalator. "You were right to be concerned." Reggie straightened and removed his hands from her waist. Phoebe wondered idiotically if she could repeat the event on the way down, if that would guarantee him placing his hands around her waist again.

"Well, let's head for the men's clothes," she said. She avoided grabbing his hand as she had that morning, shyly keeping her hands to herself. He did not offer his arm, and she thought it best given the crowded store. People continued to stare at him, especially his top hat, but she was rapidly growing used to it. She would have stared too...happily.

"Well, here we are," she said on arrival in the men's department. She checked her watch. "We've got about thirty-five minutes. I don't know a thing about men's sizes. I'd better get a salesperson." She flagged down a saleswoman who came over to assist. The bored-appearing, middle-aged woman eyed Reggie with a raised brow, her eyes blinking when she looked at his top hat, but she said nothing as she fished a tape measure out of her pocket and ran it around his neck and then his waist. He threw Phoebe a harried look when the saleswoman wrapped the tape around his waist but said nothing, and raised his arms accommodatingly.

"Sixteen," she saleswoman said. "Thirty-two."

The saleswoman reached down to measure Reggie's inseam, and he jumped back.

"Madam! Enough! Is there no proper tailor who could attend me in private?"

The saleswoman straightened, her cheeks red. "Well, we could go into the dressing room, of course, but there are no men working the floor if that's what you mean by a 'proper tailor.' This is a ready-to-wear store, you know."

"Reggie, it's all right. She's just trying to help. We really don't have time for a tailor this morning, and I don't know if they make complete suits anymore. How about if I measure your inseam? Unless you know your size already?"

Reggie eyed her, a little wildly in Phoebe's opinion, and he shook his head. "I do not. My tailor has my measurements." He raised his eyes to the ceiling. "If you must, then I prefer you take the measurements, Phoebe."

The saleswoman thrust her arm out with the tape measure, and Phoebe gave her an apologetic smile and a shrug disowning Reggie's tone of martyrdom. She bent, quickly placed the tape measure against the front of his leg at approximately the same position as if she had actually measured his inseam, and read the measurement as fast as possible.

"There! Done. Simple." She handed the saleswoman the tape and thanked her. "Now, we know what size to get you." The woman walked away, tossing a narrow-eyed gaze over her shoulder.

"Ah! My tailor usually places his tape to the inside of my lower limb, and that is what I imagined the woman thought to do. I see that has changed. I apologize if my response seemed melodramatic."

Phoebe grinned. "Oh, no, we still measure the same way, but I thought you'd flip out if I did that, so I guessed at your measurements. It will be all right. We're just getting you a pair of jeans this morning."

"Flip out?" Reggie lifted his chin, one eyebrow raised.

"You know what I mean, Reggie. Don't act like you don't. Come on, we're running out of time." She grabbed a pair of jeans from a nearby table, a shirt from a rack and sent him into the dressing room. "Just change into the clothes. I'll pay for them while you're changing. Wait! I think I'd better get you some underwear while we're at it. Oh, man, we need shoes, too!"

Phoebe rushed over to the men's underwear department carrying the clothing, and Reggie followed. She was definitely out of her league now, having never bought underwear for a man before. Which? Briefs? Shorts? Boxers?

"See anything you like?" she asked. Reggie picked up a packet and eyed it with a raised eyebrow.

"Is this what I am meant to do? Is this then a male model?"

Phoebe couldn't hold back her laugh. "No, no." She shook her head but then nodded. "Well, yes, that is a male model, but not a 'cover model.' I suppose he's called an underwear model. No, Reggie, that's not what I meant." She bent over in a peal of laughter.

"Phoebe..." Reggie warned. "You laugh at my expense again."

Phoebe tried to stop. "I'm sorry, Reggie. I really am. But this is really awkward. I don't think you'll be buying those underwear anyway." Reggie held a package of thongs in his hand.

"Here, let's buy two kinds, and you can try them both on and decide for yourself. We'll just keep the other pair." She grabbed a package of conventional white briefs and a package of boxers. "Come on. Shoes!"

She raced over to the shoe department, luckily nearby. "Sneakers, trainers, athletic shoes, whatever they call them these days. That's what we're getting." She found a shoe-measuring device. "Take your boots off and stick your feet in there. I'll measure your feet."

"What the deuce is that? It resembles a trap. Is it painful?"

Phoebe pressed her lips together and shook her head in answer to his question. A million thoughts ran through her mind at the moment—how adorable Reggie was, how confusing the present must be for a time traveler, and how the shoe-measuring device really did look like it might be painful to someone who had never used one. She wondered if she was expected to kneel down and help him remove his boots. Not that she minded.

Reggie settled the question for her by taking a seat on a nearby bench and deftly removing his boots on his own. Of course! He had taken them off the night before to bathe and sleep. She noted he wore thick white stockings.

He gingerly settled his right foot into the device, and Phoebe bent down to measure his foot. Size eleven. She measured the other foot, and then rose to look for shoes.

"Okay, try these on." She opened a box with a pair of white athletic shoes and held out the right shoe. Reggie reached for it and studied it with interest.

"You call these sneakers?"

"Or athletic shoes. I think the British call them trainers."

"This term 'sneakers' is intriguing. Why are they called such?"

Phoebe glanced at her watch. Why hadn't she given them more time, told Annie they would meet her later? Reggie had so many questions, all natural, and she couldn't bear to blow them off or rush him like she was—not on his first day in the twenty-first century.

"I imagine because they can be quiet and people could sneak around in them?" She fished for her cell phone in her bag. "I'm going to call Annie and tell her we'll meet her an hour later."

He eyed the phone with interest.

"And what is that device?"

Phoebe opened her mouth to speak, but Annie came on the line.

"Hello?"

"Hey, it's me," Phoebe said. "We're running late. Can we delay breakfast by an hour?"

"Sure," Annie said. "I'm still just hanging around, doing a lot of nothing. How's the shoot going?"

Phoebe looked at Reggie, imagining him modeling the thongs, and her face flamed. She grinned broadly, and Reggie responded though she wondered if he would have if he had known what she was thinking.

"Ummm...fine," she murmured. "Just taking more time than I thought. See you in a little while." She turned the phone off and handed it to Reggie.

"It's called a phone, a cell phone, a mobile phone."

Reggie set the shoes down and studied the phone.

"We communicate with it. Like I can call Annie back at the apartment."

"Fascinating," Reggie murmured. "Is it possible to call England? Perhaps not as it is so far away."

"Sure, I can call England...for a price. But who would we call, Reggie?"

Reggie's smile faded, and he shook his head. "I know no one in England now, do I?" His shoulders drooped almost imperceptibly as he handed the phone back to her.

"Oh, Reggie! I'm sorry. I can't imagine what you must be feeling." Phoebe took a seat on the bench next to Reggie. She covered his hand as it rested on his knee.

"It seems impossible that Samuel and my father no longer live. Unthinkable."

He placed his free hand over Phoebe's, and she forgot what they were talking about for a moment. Then he lifted his chin.

"It is of no consequence. I shall see them soon enough. As interesting as I find it here in your America, I feel certain this is only a temporary sojourn, and that I will return in due time."

Phoebe pulled her hand from his and rose quickly. "Well, let's try those shoes on before you have to leave." His words stung though she knew it wasn't his intent.

Reggie looked up at her, startled. He rose hastily. "Forgive me, Phoebe, if I said anything to cause you distress. I am most appreciative of everything you have done for me, I truly am. I did not mean to imply that I was desirous of hastening back to my own time just yet."

"I understand," Phoebe said, slightly mollified. "Sit down and try your shoes on." She gave him a small smile. "Here." She showed him how to lace them. The shoes fit perfectly, and Reggie delighted in walking around in them.

"I do feel like a sneaker," he said, "silent and stealthy. Wonderful invention, these."

Phoebe pressed her lips together again to hold back a laugh. There was a boyishness to Reggie that she found utterly charming, and she wondered if he seemed so ingenuous in his time or whether it was because his naïveté was exaggerated in her modern world. She watched him for a few moments. His tall, well-built physique was all man though.

"Come on, sneaker. Let's go change into the rest of your clothes. You might as well just leave the shoes on so you can wear them out of the store. I can't imagine what you'd look like with the jeans stuffed into your tasseled Hessian boots." Phoebe grabbed his boots, located the men's fitting room and pushed him inside with the clothing and underwear. "You can figure how to put those on yourself," she said. "Take your time."

She made her way over to the checkout desk to face the saleswoman.

"Look, I know this is really unusual, but my...uh...boyfriend is going to wear his clothes out of the store." She held up a hand as the woman raised her brows. "Don't ask. Anyway, here are the tags, the box for the shoes and two packages of the same underwear that he is trying on. So, if I could pay for all of these. Oh, and do you have a shopping bag that I could use to carry his *costume* out to the car? Job as a doorman gone wrong. I can't explain, really."

"I'm not asking," the woman said with pursed lips.

"I appreciate that. He's from out of town."

"Yes, I think he must be." The saleswoman rang up the tickets, and Phoebe paid. She took the large plastic bag from the saleswoman, dropped Reggie's boots inside and returned to the fitting room area. The store was quiet at this early hour, and Phoebe hoped no one else was inside trying on clothes.

"Are you doing okay in there?" she whispered at the entrance.

"As well as can be expected," Reggie called out. "I am grateful for the depiction of the male model on the packages you gave me such that I was able to don some of the clothing correctly, I believe. However, there is one complication, and I am afraid it is insurmountable."

Phoebe's heart dropped.

"What's that?"

"There is a metal device on the trousers which I cannot comprehend."

"The zipper!" Phoebe said. No zippers in the Georgian era?

"Zipper," Reggie repeated. "Are there no trousers with proper buttons?"

"Probably, somewhere, but let me show you how to work the zipper." Phoebe, with a furtive glance over her shoulder, darted into the men's fitting room and located Reggie in one of the stalls. Luckily, he was the only man inside. He had buttoned his shirt and left it untucked and hanging loose over his jeans. Phoebe thought he looked wonderful in the long-sleeved white shirt with thin blue stripes that she had grabbed off the rack—a lucky find. The light color accentuated the darkness of his hair. But then, she couldn't imagine Reggie looking anything less than gorgeous!

"Miss Warner! I am not dressed," Reggie protested.

"I know, but you're never going to finish getting dressed unless I come in and help you. I'm sorry this all has to be so difficult in our time, Reggie. What I think are simple things must seem very complicated to you." She noted the underwear sat neatly on a bench in the fitting room stall, but bits and pieces of the plastic wrapping were strewn all over the floor. "I suppose I should have explained how the plastic wrapping works."

Reggie looked down at the floor. "I apologize for the disarray. Though the material resembled glass in that it shined and could be seen through, it was quite, quite fragile."

Phoebe nodded. Plastic! Who knew?

"Okay, can I see this zipper?"

"Miss Warner, Phoebe, I really do not think that would be seemly."

"How about if you look up at the ceiling, which you are so fond of doing, and I zip them up real quick, and you'll never know." Phoebe paused and bit her lip. "No, that won't work because you'll have to unzip them again to go to the bathroom."

"Phoebe!" Reggie protested

"Reggie!" Phoebe countered. "We say bathroom all the time. *That* you'll have to get used to. We have an expression known as 'suspend disbelief,' maybe you all do, too. If you don't, I'm sure you can imagine what that means. Is there any chance you can *suspend your shock* for a while? Because you're going to be shocked often, Reggie, a lot."

"I must try," he acknowledged. "If you demonstrate the technique, I will attempt to master it. Proceed," his martyred self said.

Phoebe rolled her eyes, but her hand shook as she lifted his shirt. "Here, hold your shirt up."

Reggie held his shirt and looked down at his waistline as Phoebe grabbed one edge of his jeans with a shaking hand and quickly pulled the zipper up. She took a step back.

"See? And then you button the top. You know, the button you wanted."

"Yes, I do see. I shall practice when I am in private."

The image made Phoebe's lips quiver, but she held the laughter back.

"Yes, you do that. Now, do you want to wear your shirt in or out? It doesn't matter for breakfast, but it would if you were going out at night or something. You would tuck it in. Oh, wait, we didn't get you a belt. Do you wear belts?"

"Suspenders, actually. These trousers feel very secure upon my person. I think I may dispense with suspenders or a belt for now. How would you prefer that I wear the shirt, Phoebe?"

Phoebe blushed. In, out, on, off—she didn't care. Everything about him was perfect, even the way he made her laugh without trying.

"Out would be fine for this morning. I think it probably looks a little odd to tuck a shirt in without wearing a belt."

"I see you have as many conventions regarding clothing in your time as we do in ours. I will wear it as you wish. It is my desire to please you."

Phoebe stared at the Georgian-era man standing in front of her. Oh, couldn't she keep him? Oh, please?

CHAPTER SIX

Reggie stepped out of the dressing room, appreciating the lightness of his shirt and the freedom of the open collar.

"Shall I require a cravat or a frock coat? I think the top hat is to be dispensed with, is it not? I did not miss the curiosity on the saleswoman's countenance when she regarded my hat as if it were some sort of oddity. And I saw no other gentlemen on the street in similar hats." He opened the bag to show the hat stowed inside.

"You don't need a cravat or a top hat, Reggie. And it's warm enough out that you don't need a coat right now, but we should get you a jacket later this morning when we come back shopping with Annie. It's late spring, and it could get cold again."

"I am concerned about the extent of your expenditures on my behalf, Phoebe. I mean to recompense you at the earliest opportunity."

"I know," Phoebe said. "I know. Are you ready? Got your shoes on?"

"My sneakers," Reggie grinned. "Yes, I think I am fully dressed. Is there aught about my appearance that is amiss?"

"Not a single thing," Phoebe said with a smile. Her cheeks brightened as they had done several times that morning.

"Good! I value your opinion."

Phoebe dropped her eyes, and he hoped he had not muddled his words of appreciation.

"We'd better go," she said. She led the way from the store, and Reggie followed, carrying his own 'shopping bag' like a groom. There appeared to be a paucity of servants either in New York City or in Phoebe's life. Was she so terribly poor? She did not appear to live in squalor but enjoyed a comfortable home at the whim of her wealthier cousin, and yet she was forced to seek employment and had no

54

companion or servants to care for her.

Reggie ruminated on Phoebe's circumstances as they walked. If her cousin, Miss Annie Warner, were wealthy, why did she not at least settle a small living upon Phoebe and provide her with a modest staff? He sighed inwardly. Such was not always the case in England either. Often, those with ample means were miserly and ignored their poorer relations.

Reggie looked down at the top of Phoebe's head. Golden highlights in her brown hair gleamed under the morning sun. How delightful to see lively hair bouncing upon a woman's shoulders rather than confined into tight curls at the back of one's head.

It had been some time since she had unceremoniously grabbed his hand as she was wont to do, certainly not since departing the clothing shop. He missed the spontaneous gesture, the feel of her skin against his, the surprising strength in her small hands. But he could not simply possess himself of her hand at his whim. It was not done. He would never admit as much, but he deliberately allowed his left hand, nearest her person, to dangle loosely and freely. He had even dawdled upon their departure from the shop, fully expecting Phoebe to take his hand, but she had not.

He mentally abjured himself to avoid dwelling overly much on the intimacy of the encounter in the "fitting room," yet he could not help remembering. That Phoebe had fastened his trousers as if he had been a child shocked him, but had seemed to cause her only mild embarrassment. It would seem that the social niceties were vastly different in the twenty-first century. His lips now twitched at the memory, though he had not thought it amusing at that moment. The look in Phoebe's eyes when she regarded him after the incident had not been that of a mother regarding her child, but of a woman looking at a man. He cleared his throat.

"And what sorts of foods might we find in this establishment?" It was impolite to walk in silence.

"Oh, lots of different stuff. You can have lunch food and probably some things on the dinner menu, as well, if you want." Phoebe stopped at a silver metal and glass door and pulled it open. Reggie reached to grab it, dismayed that he failed once again in his gentlemanly duty to assist her with such efforts. Although, quite honestly, she never awaited his assistance.

They entered a busy room filled with people seated in various arrangements. Some were seated on benches facing each other with small tables between, others on red-cushioned stools along a long trestle table that seemed to face the kitchen directly.

"It is unusual to see servants dining with their masters," he said in a low voice. Phoebe gave him a startled look.

"What?"

He nodded toward the long table near the kitchen.

Phoebe laughed. "That's the counter, Reggie, just another way of sitting. We don't really have servants here in America anymore. We have employees, and they can eat anywhere they want in a diner."

Reggie tried to ignore her perpetual laughter at his expense, but he must have failed to guard his face.

"I'm sorry, Reggie. I keep doing that, don't I? I don't mean to make fun of you, and I'd smack the first person who did."

He lowered his eyes to see her repentant countenance. "I would not wish that upon anyone," he murmured.

Phoebe grinned. "There's Annie in a booth." She waved to her cousin, seated at one of the tables flanked by red-cushioned benches.

As they approached, Annie's eyes widened, and Reggie followed her gaze. So comfortable was his clothing, he had almost forgotten he wore modern sneakers, shirt, and 'jeans.'" Self-consciously, he reached for his bare and unadorned neck. Without a properly tied cravat, he felt somewhat undressed.

"Well, you clean up nice," Annie said. Phoebe slid onto the bench across from Annie and indicated Reggie should take the seat next to her. She took the bag from him and placed it on the ground beneath the table. Reggie slid in beside her.

"Thank you, Annie," he said in formal tones.

"So, how did it go?" she asked. She handed Phoebe and Reggie large shiny documents, which were shown to be menus.

"Oh, fine. Slow though."

"How did you find time to change? Did you go back to the apartment?" Annie asked.

"Oh, um, Reggie had left some clothes at the office."

Annie raised her eyebrows and shook her head.

"I don't get it. Well, anyway, I've got some news! I'm going to take off for Hawaii tomorrow, and guess who's meeting me there?"

"Johan?"

"Phoebe! How did you guess? Yeah, he called me and said he missed me. We're going to try to work it out. He's never been to Hawaii, so..."

"That's wonderful news, Annie! I'm so happy for you."

Reggie remained silent. Matters of the heart were not discussed so freely in his home, if at all, and he had nothing to offer.

"So, I'm off again, and you can have the apartment back to yourselves."

"Oh, that reminds me," Phoebe began. "I have to deposit the rent check today."

"I don't know why you keep doing that, Phoebe. I've told you that you don't have to pay rent. I don't need the money."

Phoebe cast a glance in Reggie's direction, and he lowered his head discreetly to study the menu.

"I'm not going to live off you, silly," she said.

Clearly, Phoebe took employment so she could pay her own way in the absence of parents or a brother. She seemed to have no other expectations, no inheritance, perhaps not even a dowry. And yet she insisted upon paying rent to her wealthy cousin for her lodgings. Were it within his power, he would provide for her himself. However, not only could he not provide for her at the moment, he was a burden, a drain on her meager resources. The thought unmanned him, and he desired nothing more than to return to his own time. Were he to wish upon the moon again, he would make sure to do so with a pocketful of money. If only he had worn jewelry or carried coins in his pocket when he had left his father's house in anger.

Reggie, struggling with the humiliation of his dependence upon a young woman, remained silent throughout the meal. He was not unaware that Phoebe cast sideways glances in his direction, but his manners failed him, and he could not offer comment during the meal other than to respond that yes, he did indeed enjoy the food.

The young woman serving them deposited a small scrap of paper on the table, and Annie reached for it.

"My treat," she said.

"Let me pay for ours," Phoebe said.

"No, no. I got it," Annie replied.

Reggie's face flamed. He should have been able to wrest the blasted paper from both of them and lay the coins upon the table himself. He longed to rise and leave, yet that would have been in worse form than staying and offering nothing in the way of compensation for his meal, as he now did.

The bill paid, they rose and left the "diner."

"So, now we go shopping," Annie said with a grin.

Reggie longed to plead a headache or some other missish ailment and return to the apartment—anything to avoid the prospect of watching Phoebe spend yet more money on him. But he could not bear to see the disappointment on her face should he do so, and he feared he would disappoint her or perhaps make her look foolish in front of her cousin.

They returned to the same shop.

"I'm going to look for some summer stuff for Hawaii. I'll be over there," Annie said, nodding in the direction of an array of colorful garments on metal stands.

"Okay, we'll be here."

As soon as Annie moved away, Reggie spoke.

"I cannot allow you to purchase anything further for me, Phoebe. I simply cannot. I am appalled at my dependency upon you, and am reduced to begging you to believe that I am indeed a man of means. It is humiliating. When you and your cousin negotiated who must pay for the meal, what did I do? Remain silent. Wish myself elsewhere. Anything but do the gentlemanly thing and pay! This clothing that you have already purchased is new. It is durable. It will suffice for some time until I can find a way to procure funds. I would be much better served if I were to spend my time seeking out my family's fortune, *my* fortune, in order to access it."

Phoebe's face colored, but Reggie would not be dissuaded by her mortification.

"I do not wish to discomfit you, Phoebe, I truly do not. You must know that I hold you in the highest esteem. But my own esteem is suffering, and I cannot take anything else from you. As it is, I must continue to depend upon your for shelter and food for the foreseeable future. It is intolerable!"

"I understand what you're saying, Reggie. As you probably heard at breakfast, I don't actually have to pay Annie rent, but I insist on it, even if it's much lower than she could get from someone else. I don't want to owe anyone anything." She shrugged. "I know you would pay me back if you could, Reggie. And maybe someday you will," she said with a smile. "There are really only two things that can happen. You'll return somehow or you'll stay. If you stay, you'll either find your family's money or you'll get a job."

A job? Did she mean employment? Reggie lifted his head at the notion. For a moment, he imagined himself delivering coal or serving as a valet or a groom. He glanced at the bag in his hand. It seemed he was already well on his way toward the latter occupations.

"Yes, employment. A job, as you say." Reggie couldn't imagine such a thing, but he was hesitant to express his thoughts to a lady who was herself employed by necessity.

"I'll just go tell Annie that we're leaving," Phoebe said. "You'll really need a change of clothes, but I'll leave that up to you. It's a good thing Annie has a washer and dryer in the apartment."

"Aha! So, you do have people to attend to your clothing. I shall be pleased to have them wash my clothing."

Phoebe fell into another fit of unbecoming riotous laughter, doubling over in the most unladylike manner. Reggie noted several passersby looked her way and then passed on.

"Phoebe! Please compose yourself. I assume I have said something humorous yet again."

She clutched at her side and waved a vague hand. "Sorry! No, no people who wash and dry. Those are machines! Let's go tell Annie we're leaving."

Reggie pressed his lips together. Machines. How was he to know?

They found Annie in a section if the shop with a sign which read "Misses" above one wall.

"Hey Annie, Reggie decided he would rather wait until his stuff arrives from England than buy a whole new wardrobe, so we're going to take off. Are you all right here?"

"Oh, sure," she said, holding aloft a long yet scanty dress of bright red adorned with large white flowers.

Reggie raised a brow at Phoebe's inventiveness. He presumed "wait until his stuff arrives from England" was a reference to having his clothing sent from England.

"What do you think about this dress?" Annie asked.

"Very nice. Buy it." Phoebe said.

"I think I will. I'm going to go look at bathing suits. I'll see you guys later." Annie strode off in another direction, and Reggie followed Phoebe out of the store.

"So, what would you like to do?" Phoebe asked.

"I would like to find my money," Reggie said. "Perhaps we could visit a banking institution? Make inquiries?"

"I have a better idea, Reggie. Let's go to my office and get on the computer. The Internet is the first place to start looking for you or your family. I would say 'let's go home,' but Annie will probably show up there soon, and I don't want to have to explain what we're looking for. I doubt if anyone will be at my office. It's Saturday."

Though Reggie kept his eyes on Phoebe's lips, lovely as they were, he was not able to decipher all of her words.

"Pewter? A net? I fear I do not understand your meaning or what one might have to do with the other."

"I am not going to laugh. I am not going to laugh," she chanted breathlessly. Her lips twitched, but to her credit, she pressed them together. Reggie did not know if he could tolerate one more episode of rowdy amusement, especially on the street in full view of passersby.

"Thank you, Phoebe."

"*Com*-puter. *Inter*-net. These are new *inventions* that help us manage information. In your case, we are going to look up references to your family, your estate, even your bank to see if it still exists. We should probably look up time travel and the phases of the moon while we're at it." Phoebe grinned and took his hand as they stopped at a crossroads. Reggie relaxed at her touch. At last!

A large silver metal pole festooned with a red light which changed to green seemed to beckon them as the group of people surrounding them surged forward. A white light depicting a small man striding could be seen.

Reggie rotated his wrist such that he now held Phoebe's hand in a firm clasp. Phoebe cast him a quick glance, but he kept his eyes on the busy street.

They stopped in front of a tall brick building and entered another large glass and silver metal door. Reggie prided himself that he was quick enough this time to pull the door open for Phoebe. After an enjoyable ride in yet another elevator, Reggie followed Phoebe out of the door into a hallway. She produced keys from her bag and unlocked the door of an establishment noted to be "Sinclair Publishing, Inc."

Sinclair! It seemed only yesterday that Reggie resented that name. William Sinclair, his step-brother, who had married the lady of his dreams, Matilda Crockwell. Looking down upon Phoebe's lovely brown locks, he thought he could not remember the color of Miss Crockwell's hair at the moment.

However, that was England almost two hundred years in the past. The name Sinclair was common enough as was his own. He imagined the name was merely a coincidence.

Phoebe flipped a switch on the wall and soft lighting flooded the entrance. She led the way down a tan-carpeted hallway and stopped in front of a door. A metal holder held a small sign which read "Phoebe Warner, Copy Editor."

"You have an office of your own? I did not realize you held such an important position," Reggie exclaimed.

Phoebe chuckled. "Not me. But I am lucky to have an office. Here, take a seat." She pulled a wheeled chair toward a large glass-topped desk and took the other seat behind the desk. Reggie sat in the proffered chair and almost fell out of it, the back unexpectedly giving way as the sea spun around in a circle.

"Watch out!" Phoebe laughed before clamping a hand over her mouth.

"What in the—" Reggie jumped up and regarded the offending seat. "Is this a rocking chair?"

"No, no," Phoebe chuckled. "Well, kind of, I guess. It's just a desk chair. You know, the back relaxes, the wheels move, the chair rotates."

Reggie stared hard at the chair, almost willing it to behave. He'd had enough of appearing foolish in Phoebe's eyes. Better prepared, he gingerly retook his seat and settled into it, keeping a firm hold of the arm lest it move in some other unexpected fashion. When nothing happened for a moment, he crossed his legs and relaxed.

Phoebe had been pushing various buttons on a small machine, and he watched with interest.

"And what is that? The *Inter*-net?"

"No, this is the computer. We will get to the Internet through it. The Internet is a source of information, but you can't touch it, you can't feel it, you can't turn a page. It's like a huge book, but not."

Reggie shook his head, feeling particularly obtuse.

"Here," she said. "I'll type in Lord Reginald Hamilton."

Reggie tried to see the glass frame on the machine but could not.

"May I approach?"

"Oh, sure," Phoebe said.

He took a position behind her and leaned over her shoulder. He straightened quickly. Her scent caught him by surprise—a sweet, fresh smell of spring flowers. Reggie was not at all certain that he could behave with decorum under the heady influence of her nearness.

"Are you all right?" She asked as she looked up at him.

"Yes, indeed," he murmured. He took a deep breath and attempted to concentrate on the glass frame of the machine. The soft-appearing skin of Phoebe's exposed arms tantalized him. Her hair shone like silk under the overhead lights. Reggie straightened again and reseated himself in the chair. The struggle to prevent himself from touching her proved too much, and he needed distance.

"What's the matter?" Phoebe asked. Her cheeks held a decidedly pink tinge.

Reggie cleared his throat. "It is nothing. I think it best that I not encroach upon your person."

Phoebe smiled shyly, as if she knew what he was thinking.

"I see," she said. Did she? Could he be so besotted with a woman after so little time in her company? What of his sorrow over Miss Crockwell, now Mrs. Sinclair? Was his calf-love so easily forgotten? Did American women hold a particular appeal to him? And if so, why?

No, he thought not. He had fancied himself in love once or twice with English girls as a youth. It was not their country of origin. Not accent, nor the customs nor even the bold familiarity though he found himself charmed by it at times. It was almost as if the former Miss Crockwell and Phoebe shared similar mannerisms though they had been born almost two hundred years apart, and which could not be solely accounted for by the mere virtue of a common shared heritage.

"Oh, look!" Phoebe cried out. "Here's your name on a listing of British peers! This could be you!" She turned to him with an intent look in her eyes. "Reggie, if I click into this site, it could possibly show the date of your death...or maybe your disappearance, if you don't return. I don't want to know when you die, and I can't believe you do either."

Reggie struggled to comprehend how the glass screen could hold such information, especially that which had not yet occurred. He reminded himself that he had traveled in time to the future. The world held unknown potential.

"You are saying it is possible to ascertain whether I shall return to my own time?"

Phoebe nodded. She pulled her hands from the buttons on the machine and slid them under her lower limbs sit upon, as a child might. An endearing gesture.

She seemed loath to return her attention to the screen but kept her eyes averted.

Reggie was not certain he was prepared to know his fate either—certainly not the date of his death. Nor did he wish to know at this immediate moment whether he returned to the past for if he did, he most surely would never see Phoebe again. That was a future he did not wish to contemplate.

"I admit to some reticence to delve further into this investigation, Phoebe. I am not certain that I am ready to return home just yet." His cheeks heated, and he hoped she would not notice. "That is to say, there is so much to learn from your time. Is it possible to inquire into my accounts without obtaining any other information?"

Phoebe shook her head. "I don't see how, Reggie. I really don't. The Internet is pretty notorious for listing birth and death dates of almost anyone really, famous or not. And there is no way to filter that information out. If we start to dig into your family, there is the potential that you'll discover when your family passed away, whether you had descendents...or even whether you married. You'd know the entire course of your life...if you do manage to return." She shook her head. "I don't think we should do this. Or at least, I don't think *you* should do this. *I* can look it up and just not tell you what you probably shouldn't know in advance."

"You would edit my life?" He meant the comment only in jest but was taken aback when Phoebe swung her head toward him with large, luminous eyes. Several tears slipped down her face, and she shrugged her shoulders and raised her hands in a helpless gesture.

"That's what I do. I'm an editor."

Reggie covered one of her hands with his.

"Do not fret, Phoebe. I meant it only in jest and did not remember that your profession."

Phoebe's small fingers turned within his palm and clung to his hand with a tight grasp. He looked down at their clasped hands and raised them to his lips.

"Come! We shall trouble ourselves no further on this matter today. Show me your New York City." He rose and pulled her to her feet.

"Wait! I have to shut the computer down," she said. Reggie moved to wait by the open doorway. He spied a line of portraits on the wall across the hall, and he approached to peruse them. Lifelike, it was as if the men and women in them stood before him, their faces encased in frames with glass coverings.

"Almost there. Some program is running," Phoebe said. Reggie looked over his shoulder toward her. She stared at her computer impatiently.

He returned his attention to the portraits. Names were etched upon metal fittings on the frames. One name caught his eye. Thomas Ringwood, Editor-in-Chief. An elderly man gazed at him, white hair echoed in the color of his sideburns and mustache.

Reggie narrowed his eyes and stared at the portrait. It was not possible. Thomas Ringwood had indeed left for America only the year prior with his bride, Sylvie Sinclair. But the man in the portrait was much older than the Thomas he had known, and Thomas had not sported facial hair. He shook his head. No, not possible. Time travel was playing havoc with his senses. He thought every name he encountered was that of someone he knew in England. He imagined himself smitten by a young woman he had only just met. And he carried bags about like a groom. A groom he might soon be, if he could not find the bulk of his family's fortune without fixing his date of death.

"Are you ready?" Phoebe said. "Ah! The publishers' wall. Quite impressive, isn't it?"

Reggie nodded. "Yes, I thought I recognized a familiar name, but that is not possible. Still, tell me about this process of painting which renders the visage so lifelike."

CHAPTER SEVEN

Phoebe spent a glorious day with Reggie, showing him the sights of Manhattan—a day which she hoped to repeat many times. She delighted in his astonishment at the sights and sounds of Times Square, not the least of which was an underwear-wearing, guitar-playing cowboy. He marveled at the view from the top of the Empire State Building and insisted on riding the elevator twice. He pronounced pretzels with mustard from a street vendor to be his new favorite delicacy. He clung to the rails of the subway, his eyes widened at the speed of the train. A street market caught his eye, and he browsed for an hour, resisting when Phoebe tried to move him along with comments about how much more there was to see.

As dusk approached, they returned to the apartment. Phoebe had steeled herself to spend the next few hours trying to fool Annie, but she found a note on the console table just inside the entrance stating Annie had gone out to meet several old friends and would not be back until late. She noted that her flight left early in the morning.

Phoebe checked her cell phone, which had apparently been off since she went to bed last night. Annie had indeed texted the same information by phone.

"Annie won't be back until late tonight, so maybe I won't have to make up any more stories for a while. That's a relief."

"I noted that your skill with weaving tales appears to grow by leaps and bounds." Reggie grinned. He stood just inside the living room, as if uncertain of what to do.

"Funny!" Phoebe said with a smirk. "Have a seat. I think I'll order a pizza. I still didn't make it to the grocery store. Any chance you've had pizza before?"

"Peet-sah," Reggie repeated to Phoebe's amusement. "This is a bread dish from Italy, is that not true? I have heard of this food, from the streets of Naples. I have not eaten peet-sah though."

Phoebe could have kissed him. He was so darn adorable.

He settled himself on the sofa, his blue-jeaned legs seeming to jut out too far from the edge of the cushion. He tapped his hands on his knees and studied Annie's wall art.

Phoebe picked up her cell phone and called the local pizza joint down the street. Not the best pizza she'd ever had, but it was food.

"Would you like some iced tea? I don't have anything else to drink. Not like hard liquor or anything."

"Tea would be lovely. Did you say 'iced tea?'"

"Yes, I have some in the fridge. But if you want hot tea, I'm sure I can find some tea bags. I just didn't think hot tea and pizza would go together."

"No, I should very much like to try this 'iced tea.' I wonder if it is similar to our tea punch, although tea punch does include liquor as an ingredient."

"Nope, this tea is just straight. No punch to it."

"It will suffice."

Phoebe poured out two tall glasses and brought them to the living room. She sat down on one of the easy chairs opposite Reggie and watched him sip his tea. A smile lit up his face.

"Delightful," he said. He seemed to include her in his appreciation.

Phoebe smiled, inordinately pleased. She found herself suddenly tongue-tied, wishing the pizza would arrive and provide a distraction from Reggie's continued regard. He watched her steadily as if he was trying to memorize her face.

"Well, the pizza should be here soon," she said.

"How will it arrive?"

"They deliver it. Usually, they send a boy up with it. It's only a five minute walk."

"Would that we had such a hot food delivery service."

"Yes," Phoebe said. Having exhausted the pizza conversation, she struggled to come up with conversation. "Tell me about life in your time, Reggie."

"What would you like to know? It seems you know more of how my life has been conducted than I know about yours—from a historical perspective, that is."

"Well, how about courtship?" Phoebe rushed in. "You're what? Twenty-five?"

"I am not yet five and twenty." Reggie nodded, his eyes wary.

"When are you expected to marry? We don't really have those expectations anymore. I mean, people marry all the time, but it isn't a given, a requirement—at least, not here in the United States. It is in some other countries though."

Reggie shifted in his seat. "There is no requirement that I marry, of course, but it is, as you say, expected of me, especially since I am the heir to my father's estate. My father has recently begun to make rumblings about such things, especially in light of his own recent nuptials, and a rash of marriages at neighboring estates."

"But you don't have anyone in mind yet?" Phoebe couldn't help pushing the subject, though she suspected Reggie was uncomfortable. She had to know. "Wasn't there a lady? An American? What happened to her?"

"She married another," Reggie said, swallowing more tea. "And rightly so. I was but a boy, and she was no doubt very much in love with her future husband before I ever set eyes upon her, though I did not know it." He looked down at his glass. "You have certain colloquialisms in your speech which remind me of her."

"Really? Well, maybe that's because we're both American, although that's back in 1827 or so, right? I don't think our speech is at all the same as it was back then though. What do I say that reminds you of her?"

He shook his head and smiled. "I can think of no specific phrases. Perhaps it is the manner of your speech, the cadence, the accent. I do not know."

"Is it a good thing?" Phoebe asked.

"Yes, Miss Warner. It is a good thing." His grin broadened.

Phoebe blushed. "I wish I could visit your time with you," she said. "It must be so interesting."

"I wish you could as well," Reggie said. "Phoebe... I—" He was interrupted by the doorbell.

Phoebe rose to answer the door and pay the delivery boy. She took the pizza to the kitchen and set slices on plates. Reggie stood and followed her.

What had Reggie been about to say? Whatever it was, he seemed to have forgotten about it as he inspected the pizza with interest.

"Let's eat in the living room and watch the lights of the city. Ambience and all that," she said with a nervous chuckle. What she really wanted was the softer—and more concealing—lighting of the living room. She didn't want Reggie to see the look in her eyes—a look of adoration she didn't think she could hide under the bright white overhead lights of the kitchen.

"Ambience," Reggie replied. "We shall have a picnic in the living room."

They retook their seats.

"Oh, do you need silverware?" Phoebe asked. "We just usually pick it up with our fingers and eat it, but some people do cut it and use a fork."

"Like so?" Reggie said as he bit into the end of it.

"That's it," Phoebe laughed. She joined him, thinking that the previously lackluster pizza suddenly had taken on the best flavor in the world.

They ate with occasional snippets of conversation relating to the pizza. Phoebe delighted in watching Reggie study each section before he bit into it. At first, he tried to set the plate on the table and eat over it, and then after watching her, he lifted his plate and held it near his chest and below his chin. She suspected he'd never eaten so casually, and she wondered what his idea of a picnic really was. Tables? Linen? Crystal stemware?

"How was it?" she asked as she swallowed her last bite and set her plate aside.

"Wonderful," he said. "I shall instruct our cook prepare something similar upon my return."

Phoebe smiled faintly and rose to take the plates to the kitchen. She rinsed them off and set them in the dishwasher. Of course, there was no way Reggie could know how painful that was for her to hear—that she couldn't bear the thought of his return, of never seeing him again. Her very own, real-live historical Georgian gentleman.

She took a deep breath and returned to the living room. Reggie stood at the open window with his hands clasped behind his back, and she came to stand beside him. The lights of the city seemed to twinkle especially bright tonight.

"I misspoke again, Phoebe, did I not? It is as if my words regarding a possible return to my own time cause you pain."

Phoebe sighed as she looked at the windows of the building opposite. Why lie? It was disingenuous.

"I'll admit...it does hurt my feelings when you talk about returning, and yet, of course, you want to go home. So would I! I don't mean to be childish, Reggie. It's just... You just got here, and I haven't gotten to know you very well yet. It's stupid, I know."

"Not stupid, Phoebe. And you *do* know me well, as well as anyone with perhaps the exception of my brother. In the short time since my arrival, we have exchanged many confidences—you and I. You *do* know me well." He sighed. "I do not wish to hurt your feelings, Phoebe, and it is not as if I dwell upon my return...or possible return. I think I say these things without forethought."

Reggie, his eyes still on the view outside the window, reached for her hand, and Phoebe melted at his touch.

"The moon rides high and round in the sky yet again, though it cannot still be considered full," Reggie murmured.

Phoebe followed his eyes.

"I wish I could go with you when you return, Reggie," she murmured.

"And I most fervently wish you could return with me as well, Phoebe."

The moon shimmered, and Phoebe felt herself falling. She clung to Reggie's hand to break her fall, and he reached for her. Darkness descended, and she couldn't see anymore.

CHAPTER EIGHT

Phoebe sneezed and opened her eyes in the darkness. Groggy, she had the oddest impression that her face was planted in some sort of grass and dirt. Living in an apartment in the city, she hadn't smelled grass for a long time. She really needed to vacuum the carpet.

She lifted her head to the sound of leaves rustling overhead, as if she lay under or near a tree. *What?*

Phoebe scrambled to her knees, barely noticing how cool the night air was. Where was she? Not her apartment, that was for sure. The moon cast a gray light around her, and she spotted Reggie to her left. She grabbed what she thought was his arm and shook it. He appeared to be lying on his stomach, his face turned toward her.

"Reggie! Reggie! Wake up!"

A bleating sound in the distance startled her. What was that? She shook Reggie again, even more urgently.

"Reggie? Are you all right? Are you hurt? Oh, please tell me you're not hurt," she muttered. She leaned over him and ran her hands over his body for obvious injury, but she wouldn't have known what to look for anyway.

Another bleating sound broke through the quiet, this time at a lower pitch, almost human like. She jumped at the nearby sound, a shiver running up her spine.

"Is anyone there?" she called out.

"Sheep," Reggie said as he rolled over onto his back. "It is the sound of sheep."

"You're awake!" Phoebe cried. She touched his face for reassurance, and he covered her hand with his own and kissed it.

"Yes, I am awake, Miss Warner. Who could not be with your hands upon them in such a familiar fashion?" A faint gleam of white teeth accompanied his grin.

"Are you well, Phoebe? Not injured?" Reggie raised himself to a sitting position and stood, pulling Phoebe up beside him. He peered at her face.

"I'm okay," she said.

He nodded and turned to look around. She followed his head.

The moon glowed on the landscape, revealing they stood on the edge of a dirt road of some sort, flanked by small hedges. The road seemed to run between fields or pastures. Several sheep repeated their bleating as if to greet them. They stood near a large tree, the source of the sound of leaves rustling in the occasional breeze.

"I am home," Reggie said quietly. He took Phoebe's hand in his and turned to look at her. "We are in England."

"But when?" Phoebe asked. "What happened? How did we get here?"

"We both wished...at the same moment."

"And we wished for the same thing," Phoebe said quietly.

"Yes, I believe we did."

"But the moon wasn't full, was it? Can't it only be full one night?"

"It would seem not. It appeared to be full."

"I've got to remember to look up the phases of the moon," Phoebe murmured. She reached for his hand and looked around again. "Well, now what?"

"We stand at the very spot where I traveled forward in time. My horse does not await me, and I hope he returned to the stables. It is but a walk of several miles to my father's house. I could hasten to the estate to procure a carriage, but I do not like to leave you alone in the dark."

"I can walk. But Reggie, what if we haven't arrived back in your time? What if we ended up in the sixteenth century or even in my time, but in England?"

"It is not what we wished for, but if that does occur, I shall appeal to either my ancestor or my family's descendents for assistance. All will turn out well, Phoebe, do not fear." He grinned, and Phoebe thought she saw a new confidence in him. Of course! He was probably home.

"Shall we?" Reggie gallantly bowed and held out his arm to Phoebe. She took it and they set off down the road. "Take care with the ruts. They are as they were when I left, dried after the spring rains. The road will smooth out as we near Hamilton Place."

Phoebe, feeling as if she were hanging onto him, slid her hand down to his.

"Do you mind?" she asked. "It's easier to hold your hand as we walk along the road."

"Not at all," Reggie said. "I have become quite attached to this form of perambulation."

"So, where exactly are we, Reggie?"

"We're in the county of Bedfordshire in eastern England. This is the road leading from Hamilton Place to Wellston, the local village, where one can catch the post to London. The road upon which we now walk is part of my father's estate which extends all the way to the village."

"How far did you say it was to your father's house? And why do you call it your father's house? Isn't it your house as well?"

"Several miles. No, it is my father's house while he is master there. It is my *home* but not *my* house. Is it not that way in America?"

Phoebe shook her head. "Not really. Kids usually call where they live 'my house,' as in 'let's go to my house to play.' At least they do now. I don't know how they did things in America in 1827."

Phoebe tightened her grip, clinging to the strength in his hand, hoping it would sustain her in the coming hours or even days. If they *had* traveled back to his time, she didn't know how long she was going to be here. She supposed she could just stop Reggie and insist he join her in wishing her back to her time—if that were the way this time travel thing was working—but she didn't want to let go of him yet. And she didn't want to say goodbye. Not yet.

"What's going to happen when we get to your house, Reggie?" Phoebe's voice sounded small, and she felt very child-like at the moment. Dependent. Frightened, but she didn't want him to know how scared she was. Life in the early nineteenth century was considerably different than in the twenty-first century, especially for a woman, and for all the I.C. Moon books she'd read, she had no idea what that life in the era was really like. Not really.

Reggie tightened his hand. "I have given that some thought, Phoebe. I am not decided as to whether we should knock on the front door and reveal all, or whether I should devise some other story to explain your presence, *and* my absence, although when I left, I did state that they should not expect to see me again. If Sebastian returned to the stables, as I most fervently hope that he did, then my father may have sent some men to look for me, fearing me to be lying in a ditch somewhere, fallen from my horse, perhaps injured."

"You're not really going to tell them the truth, are you? Look, no one believes in this time travel thing in my time, and that's a couple hundred years into the future when we can fly into space and walk on the moon."

"Walk on the moon?" Reggie asked.

Phoebe looked up at the moon, wishing she hadn't said something. How to explain that? She tried briefly but ended up confusing Reggie.

"So, you are saying that although man can walk upon the moon, they cannot live there?"

Phoebe nodded. "Which doesn't help us figure out what we're going to do when we get to your house. Or at least what *I'm* going to do."

Reggie paused and turned to look at her. "You sound frightened, dearest."

Phoebe almost melted at the endearment. She nodded.

"I *am* frightened. Just as I imagine you must have been."

He raised a hand to her cheek, and she covered it with her own.

"I will not let any harm come to you, Phoebe, you have my word. As you cared for me, I shall care for you."

"I know you will. I trust you."

For a moment, Phoebe thought he was going to kiss her, but instead, he took her into his arms. She clung to him, wrapping her arms around his waist. She felt a tremor in his body, and he lifted his head and spoke with a shaky laugh.

"I seek only to reassure you, Miss Warner, not to press myself upon you when you are vulnerable."

"Either way," Phoebe murmured, pressing her face against his chest, warming to the thudding beat of his heart. "I wish we could stay this way forever."

"I might echo your words but for the still bright moon overhead. I cannot imagine the course of our lives attached to each other in perpetuity in this position. How might we eat? Dressing could be a most arduous task."

Phoebe chuckled. "You're right. I'd better be careful what I wish for."

"I know what my wishes are," Reggie said, "but I will keep silent lest they be opposite yours." He was silent for a moment, and Phoebe remained silent, savoring the moment.

"Come! I have thought of another scheme," Reggie said. "If you can mange, we shall make our way to the neighboring estate to seek out the aid of Mrs. Matilda Sinclair. She is the American I spoke of, and she is more likely to accept the presence of a strange young woman from America than my father or my stepmother would do. I bitterly regret now that I failed to purchase my own lodgings, my own estate, but it did not seem necessary as I was a bachelor."

"Sinclair? That's where I work," Phoebe mused.

"Yes, I know. It is not an uncommon name, I believe." He took her hand again and started walking.

"So, this is the lady you had the crush on, huh?"

Reggie didn't speak for a moment, and she hoped she hadn't offended him. She needed to stop harping on that.

"Yes, this is the young lady for whom I developed an infatuation at one time. It seems a long time ago now, and my interests lie elsewhere."

Phoebe grinned. She thought that was Georgian-era speak for "You're the one I like now." At least she hoped it was.

"Mine, too," she said with a squeeze of his hand.

Reggie returned her smile. "I am glad of it."

They walked on down the road with Reggie helping her sidestep some of the deepest ruts and apologizing that his father had not yet sent men out to attend to the road.

"I shall speak to him about it. No doubt he does not know the condition of the road as he has not traveled away from home lately. We approach the gates to Hamilton Place now."

Phoebe looked toward where Reggie pointed. Two stone pillars topped by lions sitting on their haunches flanked iron gates.

"Well, that's impressive."

"A folly of the fourth earl in the eighteenth century. My father is not fond of them, but feels he must preserve them for his descendents."

"That would be you," Phoebe chuckled. "Do you like them?"

"They bother me not at all. I am fond of ostentation. Were I not, I could not live at Hamilton Place. It is a very ornate manor"

They passed the gates and kept walking. Phoebe craned her neck to peer down the entrance, but could see very little other than another long road.

"You will see it soon enough, Phoebe, perhaps as soon as this evening if Mrs. Sinclair is not able to assist us."

"Exactly what do you mean by 'assist us?'" Phoebe asked with growing suspicion. "You're not planning on leaving me there, are you?" She stopped walking and pulled against his hand, forcing him to stop as well. "Because I'm not going if you are. I'm staying with you." She faced him with narrowed eyes.

"I cannot stay with you, Phoebe. It simply cannot be done. My plan is to ask Mrs. Sinclair to give you shelter. I will know better when I speak with her whether I shall attempt to tell her the truth or devise some other story, though at the moment, I can think of nothing plausible to explain your form of dress. It is my fervent hope that, since you share a common heritage, she will help us. But there is no possible excuse for me to stay, not when my own home is just next door."

"Reggie! Please don't leave me there. Can't I stay in your stables or something?" Phoebe knew she was being unreasonable, but she couldn't bear to be parted from him. Not now. Maybe not ever.

"Phoebe, dearest, please try to understand. Of course, I would take you to my home if I could, and I am not afraid to make the attempt, nor would anyone in my home deny you shelter. But I do not wish to subject you to the possibility of my father's ill graces or my stepmother's censure. Mrs. Sinclair has always been kindness itself, and I believe your reception at her house will serve you better." He lifted her hand to his lips. "Stables indeed! Although I might find myself sleeping in the stables tonight."

He tugged at her hand gently, and she allowed him to pull her farther down the road. Phoebe didn't mind meeting the American woman, Mrs. Sinclair, but she really had no intention of staying in a strange house somewhere in Georgian England—not if Reggie wasn't staying with her.

In fact, she knew within an hour of meeting Reggie that she never wanted to be further from him than the next room. She'd fallen hopelessly in love with him, and she wished with all her heart that she could stay with him forever. She glanced up at the moon and kept her mouth shut—just in case Reggie had other wishes. Though she hoped he didn't.

Twenty minutes later, they approached another gate, this one a little less ostentatious than the lions. No animal perched on top of the stone pillars that stood about six feel high. She wasn't quite sure what the gates were for. She hadn't seen any fences to keep anything in or out. Perhaps they were just a statement or even a marker. "Make a left when you reach the stone lions and you've arrived."

They turned into the entrance and walked down a well-maintained path flanked by trees. She couldn't tell what kind they were in the dark.

"I have never walked down this path but always ridden across the estate or taken a carriage here with my father and brother. How odd it feels."

Phoebe dragged her feet, unwilling to face what might come. Maybe this Mrs. Sinclair would boot them out of the door. That would be nice, Phoebe thought. Well, embarrassing, but preferable to Reggie leaving her.

"Come, Phoebe. You will like Mrs. Sinclair. I do not know how she will receive us unannounced at this hour, but I trust she will be kind. I have never known her to be otherwise."

"I'm sure she's a fine person."

"Ah! Then you lag because you are worried about my imminent departure."

Phoebe gulped. Not departure. If he only went to the neighboring estate, it wasn't really a departure, was it?

"Yeah, but don't you think we should stay together? What if you accidentally travel forward in time again...and I'm not there? What then?" Hah! She was right. They needed to stay together.

"I think we must wish for the same thing to effect the time travel, and at the moment, I do not believe we share the same wishes. I wish for your safety and comfort, and you wish to sleep in a stable. I do not fear that I will travel in time."

"What about me? What if I wished hard enough and I returned? But you didn't know it. And then you would look for me, and you'd be worried when you couldn't find me."

Reggie paused to look at her. Before he could speak, she grabbed the lapels of his jacket and pulled him against her. She looped a hand around his head and brought his mouth to hers. Startled at first, he wrapped his arms around her and returned her kiss with warmth. Phoebe clung to him, her knees weak.

"That was just in case we get separated," she murmured against his mouth. "I don't want you to forget me."

Reggie lifted his head and studied her face. "I could never forget you, Phoebe, not if I lived for another two hundred years. We will not be parted, I promise." He bent to kiss her again then dropped his hands from her waist. "With the exception of your lodging arrangements." He grinned.

"You'd better promise," Phoebe muttered.

They turned and headed farther down the path. The trees opened up and moonlight shone on a huge house—just like one of the English country mansions one always saw in magazines.

"Wow!" Phoebe exclaimed.

"This is Ashton House," Reggie said. "Come, there is nothing for it but to knock on the front door. I think I will settle you on a bench in the garden until I am certain Mrs. Sinclair is at home and will receive us. I do not know what she will make of my garments." He looked down at his jeans.

They approached the house. Phoebe knew nothing about architecture, but she thought the house resembled one of those fabulous mansions one saw used for the movies based on I.C. Moon's books—at least three stories, seemingly hundreds of windows and numerous chimneys. As they neared, she noted thick, lush ivy growing up the sides of stone walls. Several windows on the third floor showed flickering lights, but in general the house seemed dark and shut down for the night. Lamps on either side of the main entrance glowed softly, a bit like nightlights. She wondered what time it was. Having foregone a watch in lieu of the clock on her cell phone, she had no idea how late it might be.

Apparently knowing his way around, Reggie veered off from the front of the house and led Phoebe along a path around the left side of the house that ended in a garden of some sort. Luckily, the moon gave them enough light to see several benches scattered throughout. He seated her on one of them.

"Do not be afraid. I know it is dark, but there is nothing here to harm you." He looked up. "The moon will watch over you."

"Fine job it's done so far," Phoebe mumbled. She resisted letting go of his hand, ashamed of her fear—the fear of somehow losing him. She lived in New York City. She wasn't afraid of a quiet English garden at night.

"It has brought us together," he murmured. He brought her hand to his lips. "I shall return as soon as possible."

He strode away toward the front of the house, and Phoebe, too keyed up to sit still, jumped up to survey the house and gardens. Moonlight reflected off several of the darkened windows on the side of the house. The sound of a fountain tinkled nearby. Although she couldn't see the colors of the flowers bordering the path, the alluringly sweet smell of flowers filled the air. Spring had arrived in England, it seemed.

She couldn't say she was exactly *surprised* to find that time travel was possible—not since finding Reggie on her apartment floor—but she had no earthly idea that it would ever happen to her. It made sense, of course. If one could travel forward in time then one should be able to travel back in time. And weren't so many romance novels written about that very thing? It was just that, as far as she knew, time travel had not been proven to be possible. So, why should it happen to her? Or to Reggie?

Phoebe imagined a scenario where she returned to New York City, announced her discovery and experiences, and wrote a best-selling book followed by rounds of talk shows and public appearances. She would buy an English mansion—maybe one like Ashton House—with her newfound wealth. The image of curiosity seekers and tourists knocking on her door by the busloads and asking her to tell her story in person threw a kink into the rosy future—as did the Reggie's absence in her scenario.

Where would he be? In the past? Lost in the future? And wouldn't he be subject of intense media scrutiny a la movie star? His life would be horrible. No wonder she couldn't imagine him in the scenario.

That was if anyone believed her anyway.

She paced the path restlessly, listening intently for Reggie's return. Time travel to the past was one thing—frightening, surreal, even seemingly impossible—but time travel to the past without Reggie's presence was unimaginable.

Footsteps approached. Phoebe turned in their direction and steeled herself for the unknown, remaining silent in case it wasn't Reggie.

Reggie appeared out of the darkness.

"Forgive me for leaving you here, Phoebe." He took her hands in his. "Much of the house was abed, but Mr. and Mrs. Sinclair were not, and they await you in the library."

"Oh, geez, Reggie. Isn't there some other way? In the library? Like *Mrs. Plum* and *Colonel Mustard*?"

"There are no persons here by that name. The Sinclairs have no guests at the moment. I understand your fears, truly I do, but this is the best possible course of action at the moment. Mrs. Sinclair is most anxious to meet you, a fellow American."

Phoebe had forgotten that Miss Crockwell/now Mrs. Sinclair was an American. She relaxed—a tiny bit.

"I still wish you could stay with me," she said.

"Of course he's going to stay the night, aren't you, Reggie? You can't just leave her here with strangers," Mrs. Sinclair said from the darkness behind them.

CHAPTER NINE

Reggie and Phoebe swung around at the unexpected voice.

"Mrs. Sinclair! I thought we were to meet you in the library. William! You too?"

William followed his wife, carrying a lantern that he held aloft. Both were fully dressed, having only just retired for the night, as they had reported.

"Reggie, surely you know that your message of bringing an unfortunate young woman from America to stay for an indefinite period was not conducive to Mrs. Sinclair waiting patiently in the library, nor is your unusual manner of clothing. To my wife's credit, she did stand there for a full minute before rushing out of the door behind you."

"Hi, I'm Mattie," Mrs. Sinclair said with a shocking lack of formality. Reggie eyed Mattie Sinclair as if she had gone mad. He had hoped for recognition from a fellow compatriot, but was astounded to see Mattie clasp Phoebe's hands in her own as if they were indeed friends of long acquaintanceship.

"Phoebe," his own dear one said on a whisper. He moved closer to her as if to protect her.

"Wow, are you a sight for sore eyes!" Mattie said.

Reggie looked from one woman to the other in confusion. What the deuce was occurring? Was he the only one not to understand? He turned to William.

"Nothing is amiss," William said quietly. "All is well."

"Mrs. Sinclair? Mattie?" Phoebe whispered in a voice of confusion. "Are you like me? Did you travel...?"

"Let's get you inside," Mattie urged. "It's cool here in the garden." She took Phoebe's hand in her own. "Come on, Reggie. Stay close. She's going to need you."

Reggie could do nothing but attempt a reassuring smile as Phoebe threw him a concerned look over her shoulder. William clapped an arm around his shoulder and guided him toward the house.

"You can have no idea what a happy occasion this is for my wife, Reggie. All will be made clear to you very soon."

They entered the house, and John, the Sinclair's footman, closed the door behind them.

"Thank you, John. If you could just bring us some tea to the library, that will it for tonight," Mattie said as she escorted Phoebe toward the library. Reggie did not think he had ever been in the library of Ashton House before, and he surveyed the lovely room, paneled in dark wood with the requisite number of books on shelves lining the walls. A settee of royal blue and matching gilt-edged chairs faced the hearth.

Mattie settled Phoebe onto the settee and seated herself beside Phoebe.

"Would you care for something stronger than tea, Reggie?" William asked.

"Yes, thank you." He took the glass of port William offered.

"And you, Miss Warner? Tea or something stronger?"

"I think you should stick to tea at the moment, Phoebe," Mattie counseled. "You're going to need to keep a clear head for now."

"Tea," Phoebe said in a small voice. She stared at Mattie then allowed her gaze to sweep the room to encompass William and himself. Reggie could not begin to fathom what was afoot. Americans seemed such an informal lot. He had always admired Mattie's lack of ceremony, but had never known the extent of her familiarity until now—perhaps because she had often much been in William's company.

"Gosh, do you know what this means, William?" Mattie asked as she gazed at Phoebe.

"I can only begin to imagine, my love. But I do believe that Miss Warner and Reggie would appreciate some explanation as well."

"I'm just waiting for John to come and go, and here he is!"

John entered with a tea service and set it on a mahogany table in front of the settee.

"Thank you, John. See you in the morning," Mattie said. The footman bowed and left the room, and she poured out several cups of tea. Reggie waited impatiently. That which had begun as a plea for help had evolved into a puzzling mystery to which only Mattie and William now held the answers. He did not like to think what might have happened had he attempted to take Phoebe to his father's house first, and he thanked his lucky stars—or the moon—that he had chosen to seek Mrs. Mattie

Sinclair's assistance.

"Well, I don't know where to start," Mattie said with a broad smile as she studied Phoebe's bewildered face. "Reggie, you'd probably better take a seat."

Reggie complied, all eagerness to hear Mattie's words. She addressed herself first to Phoebe.

"I'm Mattie Crockwell...Mattie Sinclair now, and I'm like you, Phoebe—a time traveler." Mattie's eyes swung toward Reggie. "And I guess like you too now, Reggie, if those jeans of yours are anything to go by."

Reggie cast a startled eye upon her for a moment before turning toward William who nodded.

"It is true."

"I do not know why I did not previously recognize you as such," Reggie murmured. "Of course, that explains much." He eyed Phoebe who remained silent for the moment. He knew her too well to suspect she would hold her tongue for long. He was right.

"And you're still *here*?" Phoebe asked Mattie abruptly. William, standing by the fireplace mantle throughout, moved restlessly, and Mattie threw him a bright smile, which served to set him at ease. He seated himself in a chair opposite the settee and swallowed his port.

"Do you mean, am I still here by choice or am I still here because I couldn't get back?" Mattie asked.

Phoebe bit her lip. "I'm sorry. I didn't mean that to come out so rudely. What I meant to ask is...so it's possible to stay in the past? Or the future? There's no time limit?"

"I don't think so." Mattie looked to William as if for confirmation. "I'm still here. I've been here for two years now. But I did end up going back for a month...accidentally."

"And you, William? Did you travel forward in time? Is it not a wondrous thing?" Reggie asked.

"I have not," William replied. "Until tonight, I did not know it was possible for one of our time to go forward. I think I must not chance it. I will rely upon the three of you to share your exploits."

"So, you liked it, Reggie? I can't imagine the scene. What happened when you traveled? Was it the moon?" Mattie asked.

Reggie's nod of affirmation echoed that of Phoebe's.

"We think it's the moon. Is that what happened for you?" Phoebe asked. "Was it full?"

Mattie nodded, casting a decidedly unfashionable but devoted look of affection in William's direction. "Yes, we wished on the moon. We think that wishing on the moon for the same thing at the exact same time initiates the time travel." She looked from Reggie to Phoebe. "How on earth did you travel forward though, Reggie? What was your wish?"

Reggie felt his face redden. "I do not like to say, but it sufficed to send me to New York City in the year 2013. I did not wish for that particular year though or any particular year for that matter."

"Well, I think you both must have been wishing for the same thing. And you traveled back at the same time. Was that planned? Or an accident?"

Phoebe chuckled, and Reggie delighted in the sound which suggested her fears of being left at the Sinclairs were eased to a degree.

"No, it was definitely an accident. I would have been better prepared if I had known I was going to show up in the late Georgian era, and Reggie would definitely have changed back into his clothes."

"So, he appeared in his pantaloons and waistcoat?" Mattie smiled broadly, and William joined her response.

"Mrs. Sinclair! Please," Reggie said faintly.

She laughed. "I hope you know something about the Georgian era, Phoebe, because the customs take some getting used to. Like what you can and cannot say without embarrassing someone. Isn't that right, Reggie?"

"We must not tease Reggie so in front of his guest, my dear," William said. Reggie heard his chuckle as he pretended to chide his wife.

"Reggie switches to 'Miss Warner' when I say something that shocks him," Phoebe with a smile. "I've read a lot of historical novels—mostly romance, I have to say—so I can guess at some of the customs."

She turned to William.

"In fact, I work at a publishing house. Sinclair Publishing. What a coincidence, huh?"

Mattie gave William a startled look. "Really? That's odd." She seemed about to speak further but pressed her lips together.

"Will you have another, Reggie?" William asked, gesturing to his glass of port.

"Yes, I think I must," Reggie replied.

"I think it wise that you brought Miss Warner to us, Reggie," William said as he rose to pour him a drink. "Since my mother is now mistress in your house, given the marriage of our parents, I can safely say that she would not be overly pleased to receive yet another strange woman into her home. She has only just now begun to accept Mattie following the birth of our child, her first granddaughter. It was most difficult for Mattie when she first arrived, and I would not wish to see Miss Warner undergo the same difficulties. As you are not master in your father's house, you may not be able to employ the same measures as I did—that is, the right to insist on having my guest treated with civility."

"William. Don't be too hard on her," Mattie protested.

"No, I must speak. I know my mother, and I love her, but she did her best to dissuade Mattie from marrying me, and I do not forgive anyone for that."

He resumed his seat, and Reggie regarded him with renewed admiration. He had always looked up to the older boy who lived on the neighboring estate, but as William's junior by several years, he had never felt completely at ease with him. As a red-faced youth, Reggie had sought to emulate him.

"I often forget that we are now stepbrothers. It is not often remarked upon," Reggie murmured.

"And since you are, I think you can just as easily stay here as at our house," Mattie said. "We have plenty of room, and I know Phoebe wants you to stay. I heard her say so in the garden."

"Yes!" Phoebe exclaimed enthusiastically. Reggie's lips twitched. These modern women seemed to practice little restraint.

"If I am invited to visit awhile with my stepbrother and his wife, then I humbly accept," Reggie said. "I am most grateful. I shall have to send for clothing as soon as possible in the morning."

"I shall see to it," William said. "We must send a note around to your father as early as possible in the morning to assure him of your safety. Your father sent a groom over just this morning to ask after your whereabouts when your horse returned to the stables without you."

"Sebastian! I am relieved to hear he arrived home safely. I assumed my father would have sent out a search party. Although I left the house in anger, vowing not to return for some time, the arrival of Sebastian, riderless, would have elicited concern."

"Did you have an argument with your father?" Mattie asked.

"It was nothing. I related that I wished to remove to America for some time—as did your sister, William, and Stephen and Louisa Carver. He was adamantly opposed to it, fearing I meant never to return."

"Yes, I can see his concern," William said. "You are heir to the estate."

"So, let me guess. You left the house, rode out on your horse, wished on the moon to be in the States, and there you were, right?" Mattie exclaimed.

"Succinctly, yes, that is what occurred."

"Hah! That's it! And I don't have to ask what you were wishing for, Phoebe. It's kind of written all over your face."

Reggie watched as Phoebe looked first to him with brightened cheeks, then covered her face with her hands, allowing only her eyes to remain visible.

Mattie laughed and patted Phoebe's knee. "It's okay, Phoebe. Same thing happened to me. I loved my romance novels, and look where I am now! Right in the middle of one."

Reggie looked to William for his reaction, but he only smiled fondly at his ebullient wife. Reggie thought he understood the smile and the sentiment behind it as he himself felt the same affection for Phoebe, now dropping her hands and glancing sideways at him. His own dear Phoebe.

"So, what are your plans, Phoebe?" Mattie asked. "Are you thinking about staying? You can stay here with us as long as you want, of course. No need to worry about anything. I'll loan you some clothing in the morning."

"I don't know," Phoebe said with a guarded glance in Reggie's direction. "I have no idea. I have a lot of questions as you can imagine."

Mattie nodded. "Yes, I *can* imagine. I did, too. We'll tackle them in the morning. You guys look worn out. Let's get you to bed." She rose and addressed herself to both Phoebe and Reggie. "Remember though! No wishing on the moon. No wishing. No moon. Don't even look at it. Unless you plan to go back right away." She smiled. "And I hope you'll at least visit for a while. I'd love to hear what's going on in the States."

"No wishing," Phoebe echoed.

"It shall be as Phoebe wishes," Reggie said with a smile.

Phoebe turned to him with a roll of her eyes and a wry smile. "Very funny," she said.

Reggie inclined his head and followed the party out of the library and up the stairs.

William escorted him to one bedroom, and Mattie took Phoebe to another.

"I hope you will be comfortable here," William said, surveying the well-appointed room, the furnishings comfortable and in good taste. "I will send word to your father as soon as possible in the morning. We must prepare for a visit from him though, and the inevitable questions about your disappearance. What will you say?"

Reggie shook his head. "I had not thought of that." He mused for a moment. "I suppose I could say that I was struck on the head and, rendered unconscious, was found by a tenant and nursed to health until I regained my senses."

"He will wonder why you have chosen to stay here. Mattie may believe there will be no questions regarding your stay given our new family connection, but I think your father and my mother will have doubts. Your father may even suppose you to still be angry with him."

"I cannot deny that I am still displeased with him. He vowed to cut me off if I emigrated to America. Though I made clear that emigration was not the object of my desired travels, but only an extended visit, he did not appreciate the difference. I was forced to remind him that I have my own income from my mother's inheritance."

"I am sorry to hear that he has issued such threats. He must be frightened of never seeing you again."

Reggie shrugged. "Perhaps. And perhaps I was too hasty with my anger."

"I do not think he can disinherit you in any event as the estate is entailed to the firstborn son."

Reggie shook his head. "No, he cannot, but if he feels the better for saying it, then I suppose I must allow it. Did you never wish to go to America, William? Or for that matter, attempt to travel to Mattie's time...to the future?"

William nodded. "Yes, I did contemplate it when I could not foresee a future here with Mattie, when I thought she would not stay. Although she was returned to her own time for a month, quite by accident, and I desperately wished to join her there, I could not leave my family or the estate. As you may imagine, once my mother married your father, and my sister married Thomas Ringwood, I might have been free to travel forward in time, but by then, Mattie had returned to me, and we were expecting a child. Now that we have a child, the question is unthinkable. We cannot be separated from each other—not I from my wife or child, and not my wife from her child or me."

"I feel much as you do, William. I cannot bear to lose Phoebe."

"So, it is as Mattie suspected. You have developed a fondness for Miss Warner."

"I am completely enamored of her," Reggie said with a smile.

"Do you intend to make her an offer?"

Reggie nodded. "Yes. I would need to purchase a home as I would not with to reside with my father, but yes, I do intend to make her an offer. As to whether she will accept, I cannot say. Her immigration involves not only life in a new country, but a journey of nearly two hundred years. It is much to ask."

William nodded. "Yes, it is. I do not envy you the uncertainty of your situation, Reggie. You may rely upon me to assist you in any way that I can."

"Thank you, William. Of course, there is always the chance that she will have me, but upon her terms—in her time and in her country. I do not worry about the estate as you must have done. Father lives, and Samuel could assume the inheritance in my permanent absence. There is no one to care for—no sister, no mother. Lady Hamilton, your mother, would have no concerns. It is possible that I could seek to return to the future with Phoebe, and if so, I would entrust the management of my mother's inheritance to you."

"Is that your desire?"

Reggie shook his head. "I do not know. It is wonderful in the future— comfortable, even luxurious, but one must have money or seek employment. I would prefer to have my own income and debate the possibility of employment if I should so desire." He looked around the bedroom, not really seeing it. "But this is my home, and I would miss England terribly."

Reggie gave a short laugh and continued. "I have not yet asked Phoebe for her hand, therefore, I do not know if my musings are just that, and not simply a means of torturing myself."

"I hope she will consent. When will you ask?"

"In the near future, I think, but I must give her time to adjust to her present circumstances."

CHAPTER TEN

Phoebe looked over her shoulder to see Reggie follow William into a room down the hallway. Reggie caught her eye and nodded with a reassuring smile. And Phoebe was reassured.

She followed Mattie into a large bedroom that looked remarkably like one of those photographs she'd seen on historical architecture. Mattie used her candle to light several candelabras in the room.

"This was the bedroom I first stayed in when I got here, so I thought I'd bring you to this one." Mattie grinned and opened her arms expansively as if to display the bedroom. "So, what do you think? Feels like a fairytale, huh?" She laughed, surveying the room as if with fresh eyes.

A high-ceilinged room, the walls were painted pale green. Dark green velvet drapes covered the windows. The coverlet of the velvet-curtained, four-poster bed was white, mirroring a lighter color found in the rose and moss green Oriental carpet. A green velvet settee and several chairs flanked the fireplace.

"It's stunning," Phoebe breathed.

"I can't tell you how frightened I was when I got here, but you seem to be handling it pretty well."

"Am I?" Phoebe mused. "Maybe because I came with Reggie. You must have felt very alone."

Mattie shrugged and led Phoebe to the settee. "Sometimes, but only when William wasn't there. I fell in love with him the moment I met him. It sounds hokey, I know, but I felt like I already knew him when I met him. It's a long story."

"I'd be interested to hear it sometime while I'm here."

Phoebe, now better able to focus than when she first arrived, studied

Mattie's empire-waisted silk gown of brown. The colors accented the brown specks in her hazel eyes. Small ballet-like slippers peeped out from beneath her skirt. Mattie's auburn hair was pulled up behind her head into a chignon, with curls allowed to escape around her forehead and cheeks.

"While you're here," Mattie repeated. "What are your thoughts on that?"

"What do you mean?"

"Well, I can't really say 'what are your plans,' because I don't know if you really have control over your future right now, but what are your expectations? I could probably sit here and tell you my experiences, what I've learned and haven't learned about living here, whether I had to stay here, if I could return, but it would probably be easier if you told me what you want to see happen."

Phoebe closed her eyes and tried to imagine her apartment in New York. She bit her lips as she thought of Annie's frantic search for her.

"My cousin, who was staying in the apartment for a few days, will call the police. She'll worry about what happened to me."

Mattie nodded. "Yep, I'll bet she does."

"I feel bad about that."

"I know. I had a friend from work who called the police the first time I disappeared, but I was able to leave her a message the second time I went back, so I'm hoping she didn't that time."

Phoebe nodded. "About this going back thing..." She waited hopefully.

Mattie grimaced. "It was an accident, and one I didn't want. I was already in love with William by then, and although I swore I had to go back—couldn't live in the 1800s—when I was accidentally transported forward in time, all I wanted was to return to be with William. Luckily, I managed to get back."

"So, there's a possibility of going back and forth?"

"Well, yeah, you can see that it happened to Reggie. I wouldn't risk it again, of course, because I have a child now, a toddler. There's no way I would go back. William and I actually make wishes every full moon that we can stay together forever...just to make sure." Mattie smiled softly for a moment then sobered.

"But what about you? Would you be interested in staying in the nineteenth century? You have to give up a lot."

Phoebe shook her head. "I don't know, Mattie."

"What about Reggie? What do you think of him? He was such a cute kid, but I can see that he's grown up a lot in the past year or so. I hadn't noticed before."

"Reggie is...great! He's wonderful. It's embarrassing to admit, but I'm half in love with him now, and I've only known him for a couple of days."

"I know what you mean. Same thing happened to me." Mattie grinned and patted Phoebe's hand. "Well, I don't know if this helps or hurts, but I think he's more than half in love with you. They way he looks at you reminds me of the way William looked at me, the way he still does—that kind of steady, face-searching, loving gaze that feels like they're reaching into your heart and pulling on it."

"The ole tugging at your heart trick?" Phoebe smiled tenderly.

"That's the one. I don't know how these Georgian guys do it. Not to mention they are so handsome and dashing in their outfits."

"Love the pantaloons," Phoebe whispered.

"Oh, yes!" Mattie said. "And the cutaway coats? The way they broaden the shoulders and narrow at the waist?"

"Reggie has the broadest shoulders...ever."

"He does, doesn't he?" Mattie said with a chuckle. "All grown up now."

"He used to have a crush on you, didn't he?" Phoebe's cheeks heated.

"I don't think so," Mattie said. "Why would you say that?"

"There's something in his voice when he mentions you."

Mattie grimaced. "Oh, I remember now. Yeah, I think there was this small infatuation when I first showed up. But he was young then. Two years has really matured him. He *never* looked at me the way he looks at you."

"I don't know how I could do without him. His original plan was to ask if I could stay with you—because you're American—and he would stay at his house. You probably heard me in the garden begging him to not to leave me."

"I did," Mattie said with a nod. "And I know how you feel. Here's what I think about this moon time travel thing. I think that we've traveled in time to be with the one we love, or the one we were meant to love. That they happen to live in another century is inconvenient but not insurmountable. In fact, it's probably part of the reason we love them. So, whatever you decide—whether you're going to try to return or stay—keep that in mind. I don't think it's random."

Phoebe rubbed her temples. "No, it doesn't feel random to me either. It feels like...oh, gosh, can't believe I'm going to say this...destiny."

"Destiny. Yes, I would agree," Mattie nodded. "Well, listen, I'll let you get some sleep. I'll be back in the morning. The baby gets me up early."

"A baby," Phoebe murmured.

"Yup, my own Georgian baby. She'll grow up in the Victorian era, poor thing. Lots of corsets."

"Not with you as her mother, I'm sure."

"You're right about that!" Mattie laughed. "Oh, that reminds me. I'd better get you something to sleep in. I'll be right back." Mattie sailed out of the room and returned within a minute.

"Here you go." She handed Phoebe a soft white cotton garment. "No nylon or cotton jammies yet. By the way, there's a bathroom through that doorway. Flushing toilet. Oh, you know that's the first thing I got done when I decided to stay!" Her face softened. "Well, William did it for me. I love that man!"

Mattie turned and headed for the door. "See you in the morning, Phoebe. Sleep well, and don't worry about anything. Everything will turn out the way it should. I really believe that."

"Night," Phoebe called out to the closing door. She turned away and laid the nightgown out on the bed. A visit to the bathroom revealed a cozy room with a white porcelain claw foot tub, a sink, and a toilet, just as Mattie had said. Phoebe used the facilities and washed her face and hands with the lavender-scented soap. She had just returned to the bedroom when she heard a soft tap on the door. She opened the door to find Reggie on the other side.

"Are you well, Phoebe? I could not close my eyes until I discovered how you fared."

Phoebe, her heart racing unexpectedly, stepped back and opened the door wider. "Come in," she said.

Reggie laced his hands behind his back and straightened. "I cannot. It is not proper, and I am returned to England. Neither do I wish to offend our hosts with such improprieties."

Phoebe cocked her head and studied him. Though he still wore his long-sleeved shirt, jeans and sneakers, he had somehow recaptured the Georgian-era essence.

"I understand," she said with disappointment. "I'm fine. Talking to Mattie has been like talking to someone from home. And *you're* here." She smiled. "Thank you."

Reggie's cheeks bronzed, and he looked down at the floor before raising his eyes again to her face. "We have not been apart for more than a few moments during the last two days. I feel the loss of your company acutely."

"Me too, Reggie." Phoebe looked over her shoulder. "I see a bench at the foot of the bed if you change your mind."

Reggie flashed a bright smile. "Would that I could, Miss Warner. Sleep well. You know where my room is if you need aught during the night."

Phoebe nodded. "I'll see you in the morning. Good night, Reggie."

He bowed, still a dashing gesture even in his modern day clothing.

She watched him traverse the hallway to his room, and she waved as he looked back over his shoulder. Closing the door, she crossed over to the bed and dropped onto it. The mattress was surprisingly comfortable, and she relaxed into it.

The late Georgian era, Reggie, Mattie, William Sinclair, green velvet curtains, a horse named Sebastian. The words swirled around in her mind like a chant as she drifted off to sleep. The last word she remembered was *Reggie.*

****

"Phoebe?"

A voice caught her attention, followed by a touch on her shoulder. Phoebe opened her eyes with difficulty, feeling as if she'd been drugged.

Mattie stood by the bed, looking down on her.

"You didn't even make it into bed, did you?"

Phoebe shook her head and yawned. "No, I must have fallen asleep the minute I laid down. Very comfortable bed. My compliments to the hostess."

Mattie laughed.

"I hope you were warm enough. Central heating is next on my list of things to figure out. No chance you brought the schematics for such a plan, did you?"

Phoebe shook her head. "No, sorry. I should have thought of that." She smiled, sat up, and scooted to the edge of the bed.

"Here are some clothes for you," Mattie said. "*I* don't mind if you traipse about in your jeans and T-shirt all day, but the servants might have a heart attack, and I think Reggie's father is coming this morning. William already sent a note over to their house and got a very flustered response."

Phoebe jumped up. "Oh! Well, I'd better get dressed then." She paused. "Unless... Well, he doesn't have to even know I'm here, does he?"

Mattie shook her head. "Don't bother. You can't hide in England in the 1800s. He'll know you're here. And it's possible that Reggie will want to introduce you. I haven't seen him yet this morning. William was looking for some clothes for him as his haven't arrived yet. Luckily, they're both tall."

"Okay." Phoebe took the clothing Mattie handed her and eyed a beautiful lawn gown of rose. "This is gorgeous!"

"I think it will look nice on you. If you're anything like me, you'll be a bit bashful about me staying, but you will probably need help getting dressed. Better me than a maid, I'm thinking."

"Oh, sure!" Phoebe said. "Let me just wash my face. Great bathroom, by the way!" she called over her shoulder. She washed and returned to the bedroom where Mattie had laid out several other articles of clothing in addition to the dress.

"You'll have to get used to drawers because they don't have any underwear here, but I've modified mine so that they don't have the opening between the legs. I couldn't deal with that." She handed the bloomers to Phoebe. "And here are some stays, stockings, a garter to hold them up, a chemise, and some petticoats. I don't know if you want to wear the stays. They're not really like corsets, but they do 'lift and separate' as my mother used to say. I've had to start wearing them because I'm a little bit bigger on top than before I had the baby."

"If you wear them, I will." Phoebe said with a smile. "Okay, so which order do these go on?"

"The pantaloons, the garters, stockings, chemise, stays, petticoats, and dress. I'll tie anything that needs tying."

Over the next half hour, Mattie helped Phoebe into the various garments—thick white stockings held up by a satin garter, which hung from her waist, a chemise that felt like a soft white cotton dress and satin stays, which served as some sort of bra. Mattie tied Phoebe's petticoats at the back of the waist and helped her slip into the lovely morning gown. They studied Phoebe's reflection in the mirror.

"That wasn't so bad," Phoebe murmured. "I thought there would be more."

"There usually is," Mattie said. "I think most of the ladies around here wear three or more petticoats. It depends on the thickness of the dress and how clingy you want it to look. Did you want something to cover your top?"

Mattie indicated Phoebe's neckline. Phoebe slid her eyes toward Mattie's more generous proportions.

"I don't think I need it. Nothing is showing."

"Lucky you," Mattie said. "Okay, let's see, what else? Shoes and hair. I brought a pair of slippers for you, but I don't know...you're feet look bigger than mine."

Phoebe eyed the small slippers and shook her head. "Too small. Lucky you! I'll just have to wear my athletic shoes until I can round some slippers up. Do you think anyone will notice?"

Mattie chewed on her lip and eyed Phoebe's feet. "If you sit down, yes. But maybe not if you stand up. We can probably trot into the village later and pick up some slippers, but I'm worried that Reggie's father will be here this morning and what we should do about your shoes for now."

"I'll stand when he's here." Phoebe seated herself to tie her athletic shoes.

"Okay, well, we'll figure that out when it happens. Sit down, and let's do your hair," Mattie said. "You'll get the knack of doing it yourself in no time at all. It's pretty simple, not like a Gibson or anything. Just pull it up and drop a few curls."

She pulled Phoebe's hair on top of her head and deftly twisted it into a bun before slipping a few pins in to secure it. She pulled a few curls out from around the temples.

"There! Lovely! You make a beautiful Georgian girl...just like you were born to it."

They surveyed Phoebe again in the mirror. She did have to admit that the clothing suited her, and it was comfortable—at least for the moment. She didn't want to think about the mechanics of going to the bathroom or climbing into a carriage, but for now, it felt fine.

"Pull your skirt out a bit so the tips of your sneakers don't show," Mattie said.

Phoebe complied. The stance was a bit awkward, but she thought she could manage for a while if she had to stand.

"Are you ready? It's time for breakfast, and I want you to meet my little girl."

They made their way downstairs, and Phoebe followed Mattie into a large room. Reggie wasn't there, and Phoebe tried to hide her disappointment.

A long gleaming mahogany table dominated the high-ceilinged room. Olive-green silk drapes framed large windows and contrasted with the small-print yellow wallpaper. A fireplace on the opposite end of the room sported a white mantle and, above it, one of those large restful field-and-stream paintings depicted in pictorial essays of English country homes. Silver chafing dishes had been set up on one of the mahogany buffets placed along the wall.

"I know what you're thinking. Ostentatious! But it's home." Mattie said as she followed Phoebe's eyes around the massive room. "I don't see the point in changing things just to change them. Besides, everything is really quite beautiful, isn't it?"

"Oh, yes," Phoebe breathed. "Just like the pictures in those coffee-table books."

"There you are, Reggie," Mattie said, turning toward the entrance. "Good morning. You look well."

Phoebe swung around to see Reggie enter the dining room. Dressed once again in Georgian-era clothing, he wore beige pantaloons, a forest green cutaway coat, a corn-colored waistcoat and a bright white shirt complete with cravat. Brown boots encased his lower legs. His dark hair gleamed as if he had just washed it. Phoebe's heart thudded in her chest. William's clothing fit Reggie very well, it seemed. Very well indeed.

Reggie bowed. "Mattie. Phoebe."

He eyed Phoebe pointedly with a warm smile, and she dropped her eyes. She hoped he found her attractive.

"There you are, baby girl!" Mattie cooed as William carried a carrot-topped toddler into the room and set her down. She ran to her mother who scooped her up. A tiny clone of her mother, complete with a matching white dress, she was adorable.

"Mia, this is Miss Warner. And Uncle Reggie. This is Amelia."

Mia Sinclair thrust out a hand and reached for Reggie's cravat.

"No, no, baby," Mattie said. "We don't mess with the men's cravats. Can't do it."

Mia, easily diverted, reached instead for his hair, and Reggie allowed her to pat his head in a kindly fashion.

"She will break many hearts, I fear," Reggie said with a laugh. "I have not seen her for many months. She has grown much."

"Yes, she has," Mattie cooed. She handed Mia back to her father. A young blonde woman in a cap and pale blue dress had followed him in, and William handed the baby to her.

"Thanks, Jane. I think Reggie's father is coming over this morning, so I'll come get her in a little while."

"Yes, mum," Jane replied with a curtsey. The baby laughed and waved bye-bye to the room in general as Jane carried her out.

"So that's my baby," Mattie beamed.

"Good morning, Miss Warner. You look very well. Our era becomes you," William said gallantly.

"Indeed it does," Reggie said.

Phoebe blushed.

"Just help yourself to whatever you want. It's a buffet," Mattie said. She urged Phoebe forward and handed her a porcelain plate. Phoebe took a few things that looked recognizable and returned to the table with them. John poured tea, and another footman poured juice at the place settings. Phoebe suspected that William must be very, very wealthy.

She hesitated until Mattie pointed to a chair next to her. Reggie took the seat on Phoebe's right.

Mattie dismissed the footmen with a smile "Thank you, John. We'll serve ourselves." She waited until they left before addressing William.

"So, what time do you think Reggie's father is coming? Did you send for some clothing for him as well?"

William pulled a pocket watch out of his waistcoat. "I should say quite soon. His message said he would wait upon at half past ten. And yes, I did direct his valet to send some of his things. I hope you do not think that too presumptuous of me, Reggie. You look splendid in my clothing, but I am sure you would much rather have your own things. I presume your valet will wish to attend you as well, and he will no doubt present himself at the earliest opportunity."

Phoebe watched the two men with fascination. The intricacies of social customs and dictates—who did what or whom did what and when and how—was all quite mesmerizing to watch. She noted that her favorite books by I.C. Moon seemed to accurately depict the era so far, even to describing the interior furnishings of an English country estate similar to Ashton House.

"Yes, thank you, William, that was most kind of you." Reggie turned to her "And how do you find your first morning in 1827, Phoebe? Did you sleep well?"

She looked up to see Mattie and William smiling at her and awaiting her response. She blushed and nodded. It wasn't quite like talking to Reggie in private.

"Yes, thank you. I slept very well. The bed was *exceedingly* comfortable."

Mattie hooted. "Oh, you *are* going to fit in!" she cried. "*Exceedingly* indeed!"

Phoebe grinned. "You like that, huh?"

Reggie looked toward William. "What is it that they find so amusing, pray tell?"

William laughed. "You will find that my wife finds it tiring to speak in our vernacular, Reggie, and she rarely does so in private. She does, however, attempt to conform when in the company of strangers who do not know her particular circumstances. It seems she is amused to find that Miss Warner is able to conjure up some particularly 'old-fashioned,' I think Mattie might say, colloquial speech as well. The women seem to be kindred spirits as well as compatriots."

Phoebe and Mattie grinned and chuckled.

"I just had to channel some of those historical romance novels I loved so much. The lingo gets easier the longer I'm here though," Mattie said. "I can't remember if you said you read, Phoebe. Do you?"

"Oh, yes," Phoebe replied. "I love historical romances."

Mattie nodded. "I thought you might. So, who was your favorite historical novelist?"

"Well, Jane Austen, of course, but I absolutely love the works of I.C. Moon. Have you ever heard of her?"

Mattie's fork clattered to her dish and she swung her head in William's direction with a rounded "oh" shape to her mouth. William's eyebrows shot up.

"I.C. Moon? Are you kidding? How did—" Mattie began. She was interrupted by John who knocked on the door and stepped in.

"Lord and Lady Hamilton have arrived and await you in the drawing room."

CHAPTER ELEVEN

Reggie rose abruptly and straightened his waistcoat.

"If you wish to finish your breakfast, Mattie, I can attend to my father."

"No, no, we'll come. It might be better if we did. I didn't know your mother was coming, William. Are you ready, Phoebe?"

Phoebe gulped and nodded. She had a sense of foreboding about this encounter, a feeling that the unexpectedly soft and lovely sensations of the Georgian era would soon be put to the test.

She followed Mattie into the drawing room. The men brought up the rear.

"Lady Hamilton. Lord Hamilton. How nice to see you. Will you stay for tea?" Mattie said.

"Yes, thank you, Mattie," Lady Hamilton, a tall svelte blonde, said. "I should also like to see Amelia while I am here. Perhaps before we leave?"

"Certainly. I am sure she would love to see you as well." Mattie pulled a bell rope near the wall.

William kissed his mother's cheek and led her to the settee.

"Reggie, my boy!" Lord Hamilton boomed as he pulled his son into an embrace. He shared his son's height, though his frame was bulkier. "I thought you had made good on your threat and left for America, but when Sebastian came home without you, I knew something was amiss. William was good enough to send me a message saying you were discovered yesterday late and brought here. Were you injured?"

Reggie shook his head. "No, Father, only rendered unconscious for a short period." He gestured to Phoebe, who had been hiding by the door, to come forward. She approached on leaden feet.

Mattie jumped in.

"And here is my cousin, Miss Phoebe Warner, come to visit us from New York City." She fixed Lady Hamilton with a challenging eye.

Lady Hamilton drew in a sharp breath and stared hard at Phoebe.

"I am delighted to meet you, Miss Warner. A cousin?" Phoebe couldn't remember if Lady Hamilton knew that Mattie had traveled in time, and she hesitated to answer.

"Yes, she is, Lady Hamilton," Mattie said with a straight face. "On my mother's side."

Lady Hamilton slid her eyes in Lord Hamilton's direction with an almost imperceptible shake of her head. Phoebe deduced that Lady Hamilton knew about Mattie, and therefore now Phoebe, but Lord Hamilton did not.

"Welcome to England, Miss Warner," Lord Hamilton said almost dismissively. "And where have you been then for the past two days, Reggie? Why did you not return home last night?"

"I was found by a field hand, and he and his wife saw to me until I was well enough to travel again. They delivered me here...in their cart."

"What field hand, pray tell?" Lord Hamilton bellowed. "Do not say they did not know who you were. Everyone knows you are my son. Why would they not return you to our house for proper medical attention? Give me his name at once, and I shall rectify this."

"Nonsense, Father. I am well and recovered. Please say no more about it."

"What is this nonsense of having clothing brought here? Your valet was packing as we left the house."

"I am of a mind to sojourn with my brother, William, and Mrs. Sinclair for a while, Father."

John arrived with the tea, and the room quieted. On his departure, Lord Hamilton blustered a bit more. Phoebe thought she saw genuine love and grief on the older man's face, and perhaps hurt—hurt that Reggie wanted to leave in the first place, and hurt that he wasn't returning home right away. She blamed herself. If she hadn't begged Reggie to stay, he would have gone to his own house. That had been his original plan.

"Come, Jonathan, please sit and have some tea," Lady Hamilton said. "Reggie is a grown man, and must do as he likes. Your *other* brother, Samuel, would like to see you, Reggie. He desired me to tell you he would visit you in the afternoon if that is convenient for you."

Reggie's cheeks bronzed. "Yes, of course. I would have come to see my brother as soon as possible."

Phoebe dropped her eyes to the floor. She could have smacked herself. And she was keeping him from his brother as well. How selfish could she have been, whining about her fears and pushing to get her own way? She looked up to see Lady Hamilton studying her.

"Will join me on the settee, Miss Warner?" she asked.

Phoebe moved forward automatically, but as she walked she noted the tips of her sneakers popped out. She hesitated and moved to stand behind the chair in which Mattie sat.

"I hurt my back somehow and have to stand today. Thank you though."

"A pity," Lady Hamilton said. Mattie, no doubt in support, rose to stand beside Phoebe.

"Yes, we believe she injured herself traveling."

Lady Hamilton gave Mattie a wry look, and Mattie gazed at her innocently.

"Traveling can be fraught with peril," Lady Hamilton murmured. "And how *did* you travel to England, Miss Warner?"

"By ship, of course, Mother," William replied with a warning lift of one eyebrow. He too looked toward Lord Hamilton, who seemed unaware of any undercurrent in the conversation.

"Well, of course," Lord Hamilton agreed. "How else would she arrive, my dear?"

At his words, Lady Hamilton recollected herself, as if she had forgotten he was there.

"How long will you be staying, Miss Warner?" Her eyes slid to Reggie with a speculative glance.

"We do not know, Lady Hamilton. Perhaps a long while." Mattie replied.

"I find it somewhat disconcerting that everyone feels they must answer for Miss Warner. Are you bashful, Miss Warner?" Lady Hamilton with a faint smile.

Phoebe took the bait.

"Just a bit, Lady Hamilton. I am not sure how long I will be staying."

"When did you arrive?"

Phoebe glanced at Mattie who gave a slight shrug.

"Yesterday."

"And then Reggie was found. What a busy day for the Ashton House, to be sure," Lady Hamilton said dryly.

"Yes, indeed," William said with a lift of his lips.

"Then it follows that Reggie and Miss Warner met yesterday? Or this morning?" Lady Hamilton asked.

Phoebe looked at Reggie who watched his stepmother with narrowed eyes.

"Yesterday," Reggie said tersely. "A most felicitous event. I was very pleased to meet the cousin of my sister-in-law."

"Yes, I think that must be true. And an American, no less," Lady Hamilton said, again with a dry note in her voice.

"Yes," Reggie agreed.

"American," Lord Hamilton repeated. "Yes, I am sure you are pleased, Reggie, given that you have stated you wish to emigrate there."

Reggie sighed. "Not emigrate, Father. I said I wished to *visit* for an extended period of time. Not emigrate."

"And are your plans still fixed in that direction?" he asked.

Reggie's eyes narrowed. "I think this conversation might not be of interest to others, sir. Perhaps we could discuss this at another time. In answer to your question though, I shall remain in England for the present."

"Good!" his father said. "Miss Warner, please find a happy medium between describing your country enough to satisfy my son's curiosity, but not in such glowing terms that he must continue to harbor this desire to move to America."

"Father!" Reggie sputtered. Lady Hamilton smiled but sobered on Lord Hamilton's next words.

"Do not 'Father' me, my boy. Lady Hamilton has already lost her only daughter to America. We cannot continue to lose our children to foreign countries."

"I think we have belabored this conversation long enough, particularly in front of a guest," Reggie said firmly.

"Yes, I think so, too. Let's bring Mia down to see her grandparents," Mattie said.

"Capital!" Lord Hamilton said. "A jolly child."

Lady Hamilton smiled, a genuine smile of affection unlike the unfailingly polite smile she'd worn up to now.

Mattie rang for John and asked him to have Jane bring Mia down.

Reggie startled Phoebe by moving quickly to her side. "I think we must leave the grandparents to visit with their grandchild. Would you care to take a walk in the gardens, Miss Warner?"

"Yes, thank you."

Phoebe grabbed his arm and, ignoring Lady Hamilton's sharp look, sailed out of the room with him. Once outside the door, she let her mouth drop and stared at Reggie, who grinned, but put a finger to his lips.

"This way, Miss Warner," he said as he led her out the front door.

"Oh, my gosh, Reggie," Phoebe said on a nervous giggle as soon as they cleared the house. "That was nerve wracking. She knows."

"My stepmother? Yes, it would appear that she has correctly surmised that you are a time traveler like Mattie. William told me last night that Lady Hamilton knew about Mattie. This is all so novel to me, and yet I discover that the notion of time travel was not unheard of in this family. I am dumbfounded."

They walked around the front of the house, which in daylight, still looked like one of the mansions in the I.C. Moon movies with its walls of golden sandstone. Was it possible they had filmed one of the movies here? She couldn't remember. A myriad of windows with white-painted sills faced the front and sides, flanked by the ivy she'd noted the night before—emerald green now in daytime. The sun shone gently as she had imagined an English sun would.

Reggie led her back to the garden where she'd waited for him the night before. The wonderful smell she had previously noted emanated from roses, lots and lots of roses in bloom. A small fountain did indeed trickle in the middle of a circular stone pond.

Reggie bypassed the benches and continued to stroll along the garden path. Phoebe lifted her skirts and petticoat to keep them off the ground. She'd always wondered what women did with the hems of their dresses outside. Just let them trail in the dirt?

"Phoebe, do you still wear your sneakers? How is it that you may continue to wear your sneakers and I may not?" Reggie laughed.

She dropped her skirts.

"Oh, man, I've got to remember that I've got them on," she said. "That's why I was standing in the drawing room, couldn't sit down. Mattie's slippers are too small, so I had to keep wearing these. Cute with the dress, don't ya think?"

"As cute as a button," Reggie said with an admiring glance in her direction.

Phoebe's heart brimmed with love.

"I sought an excuse to see you in private, Phoebe," Reggie said.

"Is something wrong?" Phoebe asked. "Did I mess up in there?"

"No, not at all. You comported yourself very well, especially in light of my stepmother's interrogation. I simply wished to be with you, that is all. As we were—without an audience."

Phoebe tucked her arm in tighter and pressed closely to his side. "Me, too. Everyone has been so kind, but I feel happiest when I'm with you...alone."

He covered her hand with his own. "Just so," he murmured.

"Do you think your father knows? About the time traveling?"

Reggie shook his head. "I do not. My father could not remain silent regarding such knowledge. He is not a particularly discreet man, as you may have noticed."

Phoebe laughed.

"No, but I'll bet you're never left in doubt about his feelings. He's pretty open."

"Open," Reggie muttered. "Yes, that is a good word."

"I have to say I prefer that to the polished front that Lady Hamilton puts on. She worries me."

"In what way, Phoebe? For all her high-handed ways, my stepmother would never seek to harm you."

"No, no, I don't think she would do that. But..." Phoebe paused. "She doesn't really seem to accept Mattie, and I think she probably won't accept me...not that she needs to, of course."

"But she most assuredly needs to accept you...as the woman whom I most admire in the world. For if it is within my power, if I can will it to be so, I will you to stay with me. I am completely besotted with you, Phoebe. I love you most dearly, and I do not wish to be parted from you...ever."

Phoebe forgot all about Lady Hamilton as she felt herself swept up into an embrace. Reggie held her firmly but kissed her tenderly, and she returned his kiss with love.

"I love you too, Reggie. I really, really do," she whispered against his lips. "No, I can't be apart from you either. I just can't imagine."

Reggie lifted his head and smiled at her. "Miss Phoebe Warner, would you do me the honor of—"

The sound of a child's laughter caught their ears, and they sprang apart. Mia toddled into the garden followed by her father, Mattie, and Lord and Lady Hamilton.

"Ah! You have found our guests, Mia," William said. "Forgive our boisterous intrusion. Amelia insisted on running out to the garden, to the point of pounding on the front door. It is quite her favorite place on the estate."

Phoebe caught Reggie's eye and smiled regretfully before turning her attention to the group near the fountain. Mia reached over the basin of the stone fountain and splashed the water with her tiny hands, giggling and stomping her baby feet as she did so.

"Here you are, Reggie," Lord Hamilton said. He came to stand beside his son.

Lady Hamilton looked from Reggie to Phoebe with narrowed eyes before seating herself on the bench to watch Mia play with the fountain. William, a knowing smile on his face, turned his attention to Mia, and Mattie joined him.

Thankfully, Mia became the center of attention for the next fifteen minutes as she played, and Phoebe was able to collect her thoughts with an occasional glance at Reggie. Had he been about to propose to her? After only two days? What was she supposed to do? Say?

Everything seemed so surreal in 1827—the palatial mansion in front of her, the clothing, the mannerisms, a proposal of marriage. Did things really move so quickly here? Shouldn't she and Reggie "date" for a while? Get to know each other better?

She watched Reggie as he spoke to his father. She was crazily in love with him, there was no doubt about it. But she didn't really know him very well. What if her Georgian hero had a dark side, a violent streak? What if he hid a crazy wife somewhere or a mistress? What if Reggie had a disease, not curable in the nineteenth century—tuberculosis or a venereal disease? Not everything in the nineteenth century was a pleasant Jane Austen novel. The Bronte sisters had already been born, if Phoebe's memory served her correctly, and were well on their way to depicting gloomy, forbidden romances. Phoebe thought she remembered reading that they themselves had died of tuberculosis.

A shiver ran up her spine. She knew nothing about Reggie at all, and yet she felt so incredibly close to him—as if he were the other half of her. What she knew of him, she loved. But to give up her entire life to a virtual stranger?

She eyed Mattie who seemed very happy with her William. Reggie, similar to William in his aristocratic bearing and dashing looks, seemed wholesome and harmless. But two days?

Maybe she could avoid the subject for a while, stall if and when he brought it up. Besides, for all she knew, he might have been inviting her for a drive in his carriage. Perhaps she was overreacting. The tightness in her throat eased. Reggie—diseased, dishonest, dishonorable? Never!

Lady Hamilton rose and announced they would depart. As the group turned toward the front of the house, Reggie held out his arm and Phoebe took it. He bent his head to speak to her.

"We must continue our conversation at the earliest opportunity, my love. I wished most particularly to ask you a question."

Phoebe bit her lip. "Umm...sure," she replied.

She should have known Reggie would be attuned to every inflection in her voice. His brows came together.

"Is aught amiss, Phoebe? I watched you while the child played at the fountain. Your face registered many emotions, some of which I could not decipher. I hope that I have not frightened you with the ardency of my affections."

Phoebe couldn't help herself. "I love you, Reggie. What I know of you," she whispered. "But we don't know each other very well."

He didn't answer at first, and she looked up at him. They approached the front door after the others had entered, and he paused to look down at her.

"You wish to take time to think about your response? Is that correct?"

"Oh, shoot, I don't know, Reggie!" Phoebe exclaimed. "I'm probably going to start spouting something like 'this is all so sudden,' but that's kind of how I feel. I hope you understand."

"I do," Reggie said quietly. "I shall say no more on the subject."

"Not even about love?" Phoebe knew she was being unreasonable. She wanted his love, but she also wanted to make sure he didn't have a mad wife in the attic, or a tendency to lie in a pathological way, or even a gambling problem.

"Love and marriage go hand in hand, Miss Warner. I will let you have your time, if you decide to stay."

"Don't you 'Miss Warner' me, Reggie Hamilton! I love you. Nothing is going to change that. I just don't know you well enough to marry you, and you don't know me well enough to ask me!"

Lord and Lady Hamilton emerged from the house, and Reggie stepped away from Phoebe to say goodbye to his father. Having rapidly grown used to tucking her arm in his, she felt her hands dangling uselessly at her sides, empty, and her throat began to ache. She curtsied awkwardly, mumbled goodbye and ran inside the house.

CHAPTER TWELVE

Reggie bid his father and stepmother farewell and turned to see Phoebe disappear inside the house. Rather than follow her in, he turned and walked toward a small grove of trees on the right side of the house.

Phoebe was not incorrect. The brief span of their acquaintanceship dictated that they could not possibly know each other well. Yet, he felt he knew her as he knew himself. Perhaps he was not yet familiar with the vagaries of her temperament or her particularities, but he recognized a kinship with her, an affinity, as if their fates were meant to be intertwined. His attraction to her had been instant and comprehensive—from the delightful upturn of her lovely face to her maternal instincts, though he had resented feeling like a helpless small boy at times. He loved her dearly, and he wondered now that he could ever have thought his youthful attraction for Matilda Crockwell Sinclair to be anything other than an infatuation.

He stared at the ground unseeingly as he strolled in the grove with his hands clasped behind his back. Phoebe had not refused his offer out of hand for which he was manifestly grateful. She simply needed more time to know him—a period of courtship, not at all unusual. But how to court a woman who might or might not disappear at any moment—into the future? How long could he depend upon the generosity of the Sinclairs to house her? And how long could he himself "visit" William when his own house lay not a half mile across the fields—without raising even more undue suspicion or unwelcome speculation from his father and stepmother? Or the neighbors.

It was not possible to avoid contact with the local gentry, nor was it advisable to try to do so. Such social isolation would be cruel to Phoebe. She should experience gaiety in the form of dinners and dances. Was he to lock her away in a stone tower, never to be heard from again? Reggie chuckled at such an image. He could not imagine her going quietly into such an arrangement.

The image, however ludicrous, served to remind Reggie that he needed to set about procuring a house for himself. His father promised to outlive them all, and if Phoebe consented to marry him in the future, he would need to have his own home.

Reggie returned to the house and sought out William. John directed him to the library where he found William at his desk.

"William, I wondered if you knew of any land agents or solicitors who might seek out a house for me."

"A house?" William said as he leaned back and surveyed Reggie with a lift of one brow. "Did you make Miss Warner an offer?"

Reggie sighed and dropped into a chair. William rose to pour him a brandy.

"Here, I think you must need this."

"Thank you. Well, I was at the point of uttering the words when you, Mattie and Mia, as well as my father and stepmother arrived, and I was not able to finish. Phoebe preempted any further efforts on my part by informing me that she does not know me well enough to marry me...yet."

"Yet," William repeated. "That is certainly encouraging."

Reggie nodded. "I believe that we share the same affection for each other, but she wishes to proceed more slowly."

"But that is the point of an engagement, I should think. To become better acquainted before marriage."

Reggie nodded. "I thought so as well, but I have no experience with this. As you well know, my education regarding women has been sadly lacking in the absence of a mother. I believe my father found my naiveté amusing, along with that of my brother, and the source of much entertainment."

William chuckled. "Yes, I think he must have. But you have matured now, even more so than when I saw you only last month. I suspect it is due in large part to your encounter with Phoebe and your experiences in the future. Women can either make men or boys of us, and it would seem that Phoebe has made you the former."

Reggie laughed and sipped his drink. "When she is not playing the mother to me, that is. She has a strong maternal instinct and devoted herself to protecting me while I was in the twenty-first century."

"Is there much danger there?" William asked.

"Not that I saw, but the pace seems very fast, especially in New York City. Phoebe worried that I might injure myself more than be injured by another. She fretted about cars, traffic—"

"Cars? Describe these to me. Mattie has attempted to tell me of the future, but she is hindered by the fact that she never lived in the nineteenth century. Or I am too obtuse," William smiled. "Tell me about your journey."

For the next hour, they discussed Reggie's experiences.

"Yes, I understand more clearly now. Fascinating! As you know, I once thought I would have to travel to the future to remain with Mattie, but the difficulties inherent in leaving the estate gave me pause."

"Had she not come back, would you have gone forward, William?"

William nodded. "Yes, had it been within my power, that is, had Mattie and I wished at the same time—though hundreds of years apart—for the same thing, then I would have followed her to the future. I love her," he said simply.

Reggie nodded. "I understand the sentiment. Though my love for Phoebe is in its infancy, I cannot imagine a future without her."

"Is she willing to stay here or must you go forward?"

Reggie shook his head. "I do not know. However, I think I must have my own lodgings. You were going to direct me to your man of business? I think I shall seek out an agent in the village as well."

"Yes, yes. Here is his address." William dashed off an address on a card, handing it to Reggie as he rose. "Come, let us find the ladies and have some luncheon."

****

At the end of a delightful repast, Reggie asked Phoebe if she cared to take a walk on the estate grounds to which she agreed, much to his relief.

"I must confess I was concerned you might seek to avoid me after our conversation of this morning," Reggie said as they strolled the lane on which they had arrived, now bathed in pleasant sunshine.

"Reggie!" Phoebe said. "Of course, I would walk with you. I want to be with you all the time. *All* the time," she muttered. "And frankly that worries me. Here, in your time, we can't hang out together any time we want. We can't be together whenever we want. It's a little freer in my time. But that doesn't mean we should get married right away either."

"No," Reggie agreed, trying to follow her tumultuous thoughts. "We *have* been together much over these past few days, it is true, but it is not the accepted practice, especially not between men and women who are not married. During the course of a normal day, I believe gentlemen attend to matters of business or pursue their interests, and ladies visit or sew or..." Reggie shrugged with a wry smile. "Frankly, I do not know what ladies do. I do not remember much about my mother's daily ritual."

Phoebe straightened her eyes after rolling them. "Visit and sew. Oh, gosh, that sounds mind numbing. So, are you telling me that if we were to marry—and I can't believe I'm even saying that after having known you for two and a half whole days now—that I'd never see you during the day? Well, I suppose that would be just like back in the States where we work all day and see each other at night. And then what? Dinner together, right? Weekends together?"

Reggie chewed on a corner of his lower lip. He could see that he was not presenting her possible future to advantage.

"How would you wish to conduct your daily activities, Phoebe?"

"Ideally? If we were married and living in your time? Assuming you worked at home, which I'm sure you actually do. We'd have breakfast together, you could do some work in the morning, then we'd have lunch, take a walk or a ride, have dinner together, read together, sleep together, and then get up and start the day all over again. And maybe travel." She looked up at him with a grin and a sparkle in her eyes.

"Reggie, you're blushing! Ohhhh, the sleep together thing. Silly! Everyone sleeps, Reggie."

"Yes, quite so," he said as he cleared his throat. "The scenario you described has much togetherness in it. People would comment. The servants would gossip."

"Tell them not to," Phoebe smirked. "Make them sign confidentiality agreements." She chuckled.

"I do not know these agreements," Reggie said with a shake of his head.

"Never mind," Phoebe said. "They wouldn't be binding. So, what do you mean, 'people would comment?' Like neighbors? Your father and stepmother?"

Reggie nodded. "I am not concerned for myself, but I must worry about your reputation."

"How would wanting to be with my husband hurt my reputation?"

"It simply is not done, not to my knowledge."

Phoebe, who had been smiling, sobered and paused to stare up at him. She pulled her hand from his arm.

"Are you saying we couldn't spend time together because of what people might think? Even if we're married? Reggie, tell me you're not serious!"

"It is the custom, Phoebe." His lips curved into a grin. "However, I am not averse to spending every minute of the waking day with you as well. I can think of no other activity I should like so much."

Her brow smoothed and the dark look in her eyes lightened. "But not the nights?" she said coyly.

"And the nights," Reggie agreed, willing back the warmth which flooded his cheeks.

She slipped her hand in his again and resumed walking.

"Good. I'm thinking about it."

"Which?" Reggie said with a teasing glint in his eye.

"All of it," Phoebe laughed. "Why, Reggie!"

"Yes, Madam?"

"I'm surprised at you."

"May not two play that game, Miss Warner?"

"You know you're only 'Miss Warner'ing' me because you're embarrassed."

"You *do* know me well, Miss Warner."

"Perhaps," she grinned. "But I'm still waiting to find out if there's a wife in the attic."

Reggie opened his mouth to protest, but the sound of a horse's hooves caught their attention, and they looked up to see a rider approaching on the lane. Reggie recognized the dark head underneath the top hat as his brother.

"It is Samuel, come to visit as my father said he would! I had forgotten."

"Oh!" Phoebe straightened her bonnet and peered forward. "What should I do? I'll just run back to the house and leave you two together."

Reggie pressed her arm against his side. "Nonsense! You must meet my brother. He is a sensitive sort and might take it amiss if you were to scramble away. I wish to introduce you to him. He is a very amiable fellow."

"Okay," Phoebe acquiesced.

They waited as Samuel slowed his horse and dismounted, holding the reins lightly as he bowed to Phoebe.

"Brother," he said in a quiet voice. "Father reports that you fell from your horse and are back from the brink of death or some such account. You look well enough."

Reggie laughed and urged Phoebe forward.

"I am well, Samuel. May I present Miss Phoebe Warner of New York City? She is visiting her cousin, Mrs. Sinclair, from America."

Samuel, a tall young man, similar in color and appearance to himself, bowed. Phoebe curtsied charmingly, but then Reggie thought she did everything with charm.

"Miss Warner. I am pleased to meet you," Samuel said. "My father spoke of you."

She looked uncertainly to Reggie.

"Samuel, you would have Miss Warner think she was the subject of much discussion." Reggie forced a laugh. He hoped that had not occurred.

"Not at all," Samuel replied. "He merely mentioned Mrs. Sinclair had a heretofore unknown cousin from America staying. Lady Hamilton said little on the matter."

"Would you care to continue to stroll with us or would you like to return to the house for tea, Samuel?" Reggie asked.

"Do not let me interrupt your walk. I only came to see that you were in good health. Sebastian does well, but I believe he misses you."

Reggie turned to Phoebe. "It has been my habit to ride every day, Miss Warner. I have been remiss in tending to my horse."

"It is a mystery to me why you are staying here though, Brother," Samuel said. "Father expressed his discontent as well. I think he fears you mean to leave the house for good. If not for America, then to William's house as a permanent guest."

Reggie threw Phoebe a quick look. This was not the way he had hoped to broach the subject with her.

"Although I have revised my plans to travel to America for the present, I am of a mind to purchase a house of my own, Samuel."

"What?" Phoebe asked.

"I beg your pardon?" Samuel echoed.

Reggie turned to face them, both of whom had stopped walking to stare at him.

"I wish to procure my own lodgings. Father will be long-lived, Samuel, and I wish to have some autonomy, some privacy, particularly if I should choose to marry."

Reggie kept his eyes on Samuel's face, but Samuel's eyes darted toward Phoebe before returning to Reggie.

Phoebe, in a gesture that brought a twitch to Reggie's lips, appeared to study the clouds in the sky as if she had never seen clouds before.

"I see," said Samuel.

"Yes, I thought you might." Reggie nodded. Samuel knew full well that to bring a wife into the home now presided over by his stepmother would be an unhappy state of affairs. Lady Hamilton liked to have things her way, and Samuel and he had already noted changes in the running of the house that were not to their liking.

"Perhaps I should come with you," Samuel said.

Reggie had not thought of it before, but noted the idea had some merit.

"Yes, perhaps you should. I have the address of William's man of business, and I will write to him today to make inquiries. Further, I will look out the land agent in the village as soon as possible and visit with him."

Reggie tried to ignore Phoebe's sharp intake of breath, but Samuel did not.

"You do not approve of my brother's plan, Miss Warner?"

"Me?" she asked with a hand to her neck. "I'm sure it's not my business."

"No?" Samuel asked with a small smile.

"I cannot lie to my brother, Miss Warner," Reggie said. "Although I have not known Miss Warner long, I have asked for her hand in marriage. She has not immediately agreed, and so I am courting her. Therefore, my place of residence is her concern. I hope it is, at any rate."

Phoebe turned wide eyes to him, and Reggie gave her a wry smile.

"Ah!" Samuel said. "Now, I understand Lady Hamilton's single observation regarding her meeting Miss Warner. 'Why cannot Americans stay home?' she said."

Reggie laughed, and even Phoebe joined him. Of course, to them, the words signified much more than a simple matter of an American traveling to England.

"Did she now?" Reggie asked.

Samuel nodded. "If you do find a house, I would be pleased to keep you company there until such time as you do marry. Forgive me, Miss Warner, if I speak openly, but our new stepmother is a strong-willed woman, used to having her way, and she has turned our comfortable, if slovenly, home into a pristine museum. She states I must re-shelve my books in the library rather than stack them about my room—as if it is any of her concern."

Reggie laughed again. "Yes, dear brother, you may most certainly reside with me, and you may stack as many books in your room as you choose."

"I'm sure Reggie will let you stay there even after he gets married," Phoebe said, joining in the laughter. "Whenever that is."

"You have a delightful American accent and manner of speech, Miss Warner, much like Mrs. Sinclair's. Very informal."

Phoebe glanced at Reggie from under her eyelashes.

"Thank you, Samuel."

They had reached the gates at the end of the lane.

"Since we are already here, I shall return home," he said. "My books await me. It was a pleasure to meet you, Miss Warner. I hope to see you again soon." He turned to his brother. "I am glad to see you well, Brother."

Reggie clapped a hand on his back. "Thank you. I shall send word to you when I have found a suitable house."

"Yes, I look forward to it. Until then," Samuel said. He mounted his horse without assistance and trotted down the lane toward home.

Reggie was not surprised when Phoebe turned to him.

"You're buying a house? When did you decide that?"

"In all probability, before I ever traveled in time. I would as soon leave Hamilton Place to Lady Hamilton while she lives and find my own dwelling. And I see that Samuel feels the same. I wonder that I did not think of it sooner."

"Oh! So, you're not buying a house because you...because we...because you asked..." Her cheeks grew pink, and she dropped her eyes to the ground.

Reggie took pity on her.

"Because I asked you to marry me? Yes, that is one of the reasons, but do not be alarmed. Even should you choose not to marry me," he swallowed hard, "I would have found another house in which to reside. My father will be most upset, I fear, but he has Lady Hamilton to console him."

Phoebe looked up at him. "You're being sarcastic, aren't you?"

"I am," Reggie said. "Does it become me?" He smiled at her tenderly.

"Kind of," she said with a small grin. "Just don't turn it on me."

"I will not."

They returned to the house where Mattie awaited them impatiently in the drawing room.

"I forgot to tell you. We're having company for dinner. Some people are coming down from London."

"Oh!" Phoebe said. "Well, I can stay in my room."

"No, no. You and Reggie will join us. I asked my maid to put some fresh clothes in your room. You may want to take a bath."

"Am I acquainted with your guests?" Reggie asked.

"No, I doubt it. They're a couple of publishers, actually."

"Publishers?" Phoebe exclaimed. "Really?"

Mattie seemed almost to hang her head.

"Yes. I'm going to start writing."

"No way!" Phoebe exclaimed. "I think that's a great plan! I can edit them...if I'm still here."

Reggie groaned inwardly. Must she insist on adding that caveat?

"Wow! That would be great!" Mattie said. "I don't even know how to start."

"I'm not a writer, but I know how it works. I'll help you!"

"It is most unusual for women to write novels, Mattie, though not unheard of, I think," Reggie said. "Will you use a pseudonym?"

Mattie sighed. "I'll have to. William's reputation, you know. I'll be writing under the name I.C. Moon."

CHAPTER THIRTEEN

Phoebe gasped. "*What?*"

"Oh, you don't like it?" Mattie asked with a scrunch of her nose and a wry smile. "It's kind of goofy, isn't it? You get it though, right? I.C. Moon...I see moon? Hah!"

"*You're* I.C. Moon?" Phoebe asked. She stared hard at Mattie. Well, of course, she was. Why hadn't she figured that out sooner?

"I love your books," Phoebe said. "Love them. I work at Sinclair Publishing. You probably don't even know this yet, but your husband is going to open up a publishing house, and publish your books!"

It was Mattie's turn to draw in a sharp, audible breath. "*You* work at Sinclair Publishing? *Our* Sinclair Publishing? I know he's going to open up a publishing house, and I know I'm going to write because I read it on the Internet when I returned that time. It's kind of inevitable, and who am I to mess with destiny?"

"Then Thomas Ringwood does become publisher of the New York office. That was indeed his likeness I saw on the wall at your office, Phoebe," Reggie said.

"It must have been," Mattie said. "A painting? Photograph?"

"Photograph," Phoebe replied, still stunned. "I can't believe I looked at those pictures every day and didn't know. *Your* photograph isn't in any of the books," she said almost accusingly.

Mattie chuckled. "Well, it's a little early for cameras."

"Oh, that's true! I can't wrap my head around this," Phoebe said with a shake of her head. "It's dizzying, trying to think in two different centuries."

"I know," Mattie agreed.

"What sorts of novels shall you write, Mattie?" Reggie asked.

"Romance novels, Reggie. Want to be in one of them?" Mattie giggled, and Phoebe joined her.

Reggie pressed his lips together. "Certainly not," he replied.

"Don't worry, Reggie. I'll change your name, but I'll probably have to use you in one—you and Phoebe. I can't make William the hero in every book. Someone will figure out who he is."

William approached.

"Do I hear my name?"

"William! Phoebe works as a copy editor at Sinclair Publishing in New York City. You haven't opened it yet, but you know you will. That's why the publishers are coming for dinner tonight," she said to Mattie and Reggie.

"What a coincidence!" William said, eyeing Phoebe afresh. "A copy editor, you say. Do I pay you adequately? Should you be promoted to assistant publisher?"

Phoebe laughed. "Well, sure. Just write me a note, and I'll take it back with me."

At her words, Reggie's smile dropped, and Phoebe bit her lip.

"Well, *if* I go back," she amended. Phoebe had the worst feeling that she might not have any choice in the matter. Could she really avoid the moon every month for the rest of her life? Would she need to if she finally got up the gumption to marry Reggie? Mattie and William celebrated the moon and wished on it once a month—to stay together. Hopefully, they never wished on it when they were mad at each other.

She let her hand brush against Reggie's, and she squeezed his fingers lightly. If Mattie wrote books, and Phoebe edited for her, maybe a lifetime of "visiting and sewing" wouldn't be in her future. Reggie responded with a squeeze of his own before releasing her to clasp his hands behind his back.

"Then I shall count upon your advice and counsel when we meet with the publishers, Miss Warner, for you already know the outcome," William said.

"Oh, I don't know how the publishing house got started, William. I've only worked there for about a year."

"You know much more than we do at the moment, Miss Warner."

"I just don't want to do anything that might affect the future," Phoebe said. "What would happen if I did?"

Mattie nodded. "I have wondered the same thing, Phoebe. If by knowing the outcome of the future—what happens—could I inadvertently affect it in some way?"

"It certainly poses an interesting question, does it not?" Reggie mused. "Phoebe felt it best we not research my family on the 'Inter-net' on the chance that knowing the date of my death might distress me. And yet, had I known my future, would I now take steps to avoid or even promote the outcome of that future?"

Although her intentions had been good, Phoebe now wondered if she should have at least looked to see whom he married, if that information was available. And knowing whom, would she try to change or promote the same outcome herself? She had a feeling that if it weren't her, she'd be very, very unhappy.

"I know what you mean," she said.

"There is no way of knowing, is there?" Mattie said.

"Enough speculation," William said. "It will drive us all mad. Tell me as much as you know of the publishing house, Miss Warner. In this case, I may use your knowledge to negotiate with the publishers who come to visit. For the foreseeable future, I must use their expertise to delve into the business, but knowing that the company will be long-lived, even beyond my time, will help me make some decisions."

For the next hour, Phoebe, Mattie, and William discussed the publishing house...or as much of it as Phoebe understood. Mattie asserted that she didn't want to hear about her books, how many she would write, or anything about them in case the knowledge inhibited her writing in any way. Phoebe agreed that was a good plan.

"I've heard one editor say that nothing can block a writer as much as their own expectations of themselves. So, I agree, you shouldn't know anything about the books you'll write."

"But *you* do," Mattie grinned.

"Oh, yes," Phoebe said. "I know almost all of them. I'm a diehard fan!"

Mattie blushed. "Aw, a fan already! I'm touched!" She chuckled, and Phoebe laughed.

"Well, listen, I'm going into the village this afternoon to do some shopping, and I think you'd better come with me to see the local seamstress, Phoebe. That is, if you're staying. Otherwise, you can borrow my stuff," Mattie said.

"I don't have any money to pay for clothes." Phoebe bit her lower lip. "Is it all right if I borrow yours for a little while longer?"

"I will purchase clothing for you, as you have done for me, Phoebe," Reggie said. "I insist."

"No, no," Phoebe protested. "It doesn't make sense to have a seamstress make a bunch of dresses if..." She left the words hanging. Oh, why had Mattie brought the subject up?

"If you will not stay?" Reggie said in a quiet voice.

Mattie and William looked from one to the other.

"Well, we'll leave you two to discuss it. You decide," Mattie said. "I'm leaving in about fifteen minutes. I could use the company if nothing else, Phoebe."

"I'll come with you," Phoebe said. Mattie and William left the drawing room, and Phoebe looked to Reggie.

"I'm sorry, Reggie. I didn't mean to hurt your feelings. I just don't want to waste anyone's money...or the seamstress's time."

"She will be glad of the work," Reggie said. "It is not every day a seamstress in the village is commissioned to sew dresses for a lady of quality. The local ladies normally acquire their clothing in London. As for my 'feelings,' as you call them, they do continue to sustain bruising, but that is not unexpected. You have been placed in a very difficult situation, and I must remain sympathetic to your plight. You have been forthright with me in desiring more time with which to make a decision regarding marriage to me and, consequently, whether you will stay."

"I love you, Reggie, no matter what," Phoebe said with a tremulous smile.

"Then why must you ponder a decision?" Reggie asked in a harsh voice.

Phoebe opened her mouth to speak, but Reggie threw up a hand.

"No, no, forgive me," he said, rubbing his hand over his brow. "My world is much simpler than yours. If a gentleman is enamored of a suitable lady, he asks her to marry him. If she responds in kind and is also suitable, she accepts. And the deed is done."

"Am I suitable?" Phoebe asked with a tender lift of her lips.

"To me, you are," Reggie said. He stood and took her hands in his, pulling her into his arms. "Imminently suitable."

Phoebe smelled the clean scent of soap on his coat as she laid her face against his chest. His heart beat steadily against her ear. She couldn't imagine ever loving anyone more than she did him.

"I accept," she whispered, pressing her face harder against his coat.

His heartbeat started thudding, and he set her from him to search her face.

"You accept?"

Phoebe swallowed hard, ignoring her fears—the fact that she barely knew him or whether she would ever return to her own time. She nodded.

"Yes, I accept."

"Oh, my love," Reggie whispered as he pulled her back into his arms and kissed her with a fervent warmth that made her head spin. "You have made me the happiest man in the world."

Phoebe clung to him and kissed him back. "I love you, Reggie," she muttered. "That's the only reason I'm marrying you."

He lifted his head to look at her with a raised brow. "But that is the best reason of all, my dear girl. Do you not agree?"

Phoebe nodded. She regretted the silly words and wasn't quite sure why she'd said what she did. She suspected she meant that despite the myriad of complications inherent in loving a man from 1827, she believed love would conquer all. She truly hoped it would.

"Just promise me you don't have a wife hidden in an attic," Phoebe muttered.

Reggie laughed. "The wife in the attic again?" He shook his head. "Oh, my poor love, what novels *have* you been reading? There is no wife in an attic. And since I shall purchase a new home for us, you may be the first to inspect the attic. Will that ease your fears?"

Phoebe chuckled and shook her head. "It's a metaphor, Reggie, for the things I don't know about you. But you can bet I'll be checking the attic."

A knock on the door startled them, and they pulled apart.

Mattie stuck her head in, a charming bonnet trimmed in silk roses on framing her face.

"Anyone going to the village with me? We should at least get you some slippers."

"Yes, I'm going," Phoebe said. "How about you, Reggie? Since you're footing the bill." Phoebe surprised herself with the ease to which she transitioned from diffident stranger to money-sharing fiancée.

"Footing the bill?" Reggie laughed. "Yes, I will indeed accompany you."

"Did I miss something?" Mattie said, eyeing the two with a widening smile.

Reggie bowed his head formally. "I have the happy pleasure to announce that Miss Phoebe Warner has consented to become my wife."

"Phoebe!" Mattie exclaimed moving forward into the room to hug her. "Congratulations!" She turned to hug Reggie, who looked taken aback at the intimate gesture. "Oh, this is great! Now, you'll stay!" She turned back to Phoebe with a furrowed brow. "You are staying, right? Or are you planning on taking Reggie back with you...if you can."

Phoebe shook her head. "No, we're staying. Although I don't know if I could have made that decision before I met you and saw that you are surviving."

"I am, my dear, I am," Mattie said. "The best of both worlds would be a machine that can transport us back in time like a plane, but in the meantime, I'm content to stay here. I really didn't leave anything behind."

Phoebe thought of Annie worrying about her disappearance, of her beloved job at the publishing house, her favorite books she must leave behind. She looked at Mattie. The author stood in front of her. And one of the heroes of her books, Reggie, stood right beside her. What more could a girl want? Chocolate? That had been served at breakfast.

After passing the news of the engagement to William, Mattie, Phoebe and Reggie set out in the carriage to visit the village. Phoebe had ridden on a stagecoach once in a touristy Midwestern town, but she'd never been in a carriage. The feel of the ride wasn't very different from the stagecoach—lots of rocking and jostling. Reggie had taken the seat opposite them facing the rear as Mattie professed to get "carriage-sick" if she rode backward. Phoebe suspected she would feel the same.

Reggie kept his eyes on her—his expressions ranging from loving affection to tenderness to happiness. Phoebe blushed at his steady gaze and dropped her eyes. Could she live up to the love in his eyes? Would she disappoint him in some way? Did he love an idealized version of some sort of woman from the future? She put the thoughts away and prepared to enjoy her first ride in a carriage and her first sight of an English village—in any century.

Hardly what Phoebe would call a village, the small town of Wellston sported a wide main street, albeit of hard-packed dirt, fronted by rows of three-story brick buildings. A large church with its iconic spire dominated one end of the street. The carriage pulled up to a large red-brick building fronted by a charming white-trimmed bay window. Several small carriages, and one vehicle that looked a lot like her stagecoach, lined up in front of the building as if loading or unloading passengers.

"This is the Village Inn," Mattie said. "We'll just park here and make our way around town on foot. This is the largest staging inn in town. Lots of coaches come through here to and from London. I'm trying to remember how I saw things when I first arrived. I was pretty dazzled. Wild, isn't it?"

Phoebe nodded as Reggie stepped out of the carriage and helped them down.

"We'll have tea here before we return to the house. You may not need it, but Reggie is used to having tea. We won't have dinner until much later."

Mattie spoke to the driver, and the carriage moved away and turned right as if to go behind the building.

Reggie offered them his arms, and they moved away down the street, stopping at the wooden door of a first-floor shop over which hung a sign "Ladies Dressmaker."

Mattie lowered her voice before they went in. "Now, this lady is the daughter of a local preacher who died some years ago, so she's had to open up a shop. As is usual, he didn't leave anything for her, and there's no welfare system to help anyone."

"I was unaware of that, Mattie," Reggie said.

"Well, no, I don't know why you would be."

The door suddenly opened, and Samuel stepped out. He jumped back when he saw them, then bit his lips and nodded.

"Reggie," he said as he closed the door behind him. "Mrs. Sinclair, Miss Warner. I did not know you were coming to the village, Reggie."

"I must say I think it highly unusual to find you frequenting a ladies dressmaker, Samuel," Reggie grinned. "We are come shopping for Miss Warner who seeks some clothing of English design. And what do you do here?"

Samuel looked over his shoulder at the closed door. "An errand for Lady Hamilton. Nothing more."

The door opened, and a lovely dark-haired woman in her mid twenties, Phoebe guessed, greeted them.

"Mrs. Sinclair! How do you do?" She curtsied. "Please come in."

The blush on the woman's cheeks and matching redness in Samuel's face needed no explanation—at least not to Phoebe. She suspected Mattie summed up the situation at the same time by the way her eyes darted from the seamstress to Samuel. Reggie bowed, seeming to notice nothing.

"Miss Tollerton...Sarah, this is a cousin of mine from America, Phoebe Warner, and you may know Samuel's brother, Reggie Hamilton?"

"Lord Hamilton, Miss Warner, welcome. Please come inside." She held the door wide, avoiding looking at Samuel. Although Mattie had not introduced Reggie by his title, it seemed that the dressmaker knew of his family. From Samuel, no doubt.

"With your permission, Mrs. Sinclair, Miss Warner, I shall visit with my brother while you ladies do whatever it is you do in dress shops. Miss Tollerton, please direct the bill to me at Mrs. Sinclair's address."

"Certainly, Lord Hamilton." She nodded, keeping her eyes respectfully averted.

Reggie bowed and left with his brother, who threw a look over his shoulder that only Phoebe seemed to notice.

Phoebe entered the small shop, hardly more than several rooms, really. Several worn velvet-covered chairs rested beside small scratched tables against one wall. A counter presided on the other, cloth spilling over the edges.

"May I offer you some tea?" Sarah asked.

"No, thank you, Sarah. We are having tea at the Village Inn in a bit. We have come to purchase some dresses for Miss Warner."

Phoebe noted that Mattie's speech had taken on a formal note. Had she not known her, she would have thought she was born in the early 1800s, although in America given her accent.

"Oh!" Sarah said with a blush. "Dresses? I would be most delighted. What would you like?" She turned to Phoebe who looked to Mattie.

"Miss Warner is new to England, and she would like to try some English fashions. Could you make some morning dresses, a walking dress or two, a few dresses for evening and several Spencers for cool days? Let's see. What else? Oh, could you make some unmentionables, petticoats, several chemises?"

Sarah nodded with wide eyes.

"Do you have a preference for colors? Would you like to look at some samples? I fear my cloth may not be as nice as that which you might find in London. I could send for some cloth."

Phoebe spoke up. "Whatever you have is fine," she said. "I like what Mrs. Sinclair is wearing. The fabric is lovely." Mattie wore a plain cotton dress of lavender that looked stunning on her for its simplicity.

"And if you have some silk, you can make some evening dresses from that. I do not think Miss Warner is particular about color, are you, Phoebe? With her hair and skin, she can obviously wear anything." Mattie grinned. "We need to have some of the clothing as soon as possible, Sarah. Miss Warner's luggage got wet on the crossing from America, and her things are ruined."

"Oh, certainly. I could have a morning dress and an evening dress ready within three days? Would that be sufficient?"

"That's fine for a start. Thank you, Sarah."

"I need to take Miss Warner's measurements." Sarah pulled out a tiny silver container containing a blue cloth tape and measured Phoebe from head to foot.

Phoebe tried to pull her white athletic shoes inside the dress but failed to conceal them completely. Sarah paused in her measurements for a moment when she saw them, but she looked up quickly, smiled, and continued.

Phoebe shot Mattie a look. Mattie waggled her eyebrows and shrugged as if to signal there was nothing they could do, and that Phoebe shouldn't worry.

"Oh, that is cute, Sarah. Where did you get that?" Mattie asked, spotting the small filigreed tape measure that Sarah used.

Sarah blushed and kept her eyes on what she was doing.

"It was a gift, Mrs. Sinclair."

"Mattie. Please call me Mattie. Mrs. Sinclair is my mother-in-law. Well, no, not really, she's Lady Hamilton now, but still...you know what I mean."

"Mattie then," Sarah said with a smile. "In private. It would not do for me to call you anything other than Mrs. Sinclair in company." She rose and jotted down Phoebe's measurements on some thick paper.

"I have everything I need, Miss Warner," she said.

"Oh, that was quick," Mattie said. "Ummm...Sarah?"

Phoebe thought she knew what was coming.

"Are you and Samuel...you know...seeing each other?"

What sounded like a fairly harmless question to Phoebe turned Sarah to stone. Her cheeks blazed, and she dropped her eyes to the floor.

"Oh, Mrs. Sinclair. Please do not tell anyone you saw him here. His brother was suspicious enough as it is. I saw it on his face. If Lord or Lady Hamilton discover..." She wrung her hands and shook her head.

Mattie moved quickly to her to take her hands.

"Oh, Sarah! I'm so sorry. I didn't mean to upset you. I promise I won't say anything to them. I promise."

Sarah threw a shame-faced glance in Phoebe's direction, and Phoebe looked down at her hands. She was obviously embarrassed to discuss the matter in front of a stranger.

"No one must know. I told the foolish boy to go away, but he does not go." She shook her head but smiled tenderly. Phoebe recognized the look. Those Hamilton boys! How did they do it? Charm the caution right out of a girl?

"Well, of course not," Mattie murmured. "Why wouldn't he be interested in you? You're beautiful, you're sweet, you're intelligent."

"But poor," Sarah said with a wry smile. "Too poor to marry."

"I can see that could be a problem. I take it Samuel doesn't have his own money?" Mattie looked toward Phoebe as if she knew.

"Reggie does, but I don't know about Samuel," Phoebe said. "I can't believe that would be a problem though. Couldn't he find some work?"

"Work?" Sarah whispered. "Oh, I do not think so. He told me he once mentioned becoming a solicitor, but his father would have none of it."

"I'll talk to Reggie," Phoebe said. "Maybe he can help out. I take it you all want to get married?"

"No! Please do not say anything to his brother, Miss Warner. I could not bear it if they disagreed on this matter. Samuel worships his brother. I think he fears his brother's displeasure more than that of his father, but he has not said so in words."

"Okay, okay, don't worry, Sarah. I won't say anything," Phoebe soothed. "I don't see why Samuel and Reggie would disagree about your marriage, but I'll keep quiet."

The opening of the door startled them, and they swung around. Reggie entered alone, a broad smile on his face.

"Have I returned too soon, ladies?" he laughed. "Your countenances show varying ranges of dismay. A gentleman could feel unwanted."

Phoebe grabbed his arm. "No, no. We're done. Thank you, Sarah. We'll see you soon." She pulled Reggie from the shop while Mattie stayed behind.

"So, you and Samuel had a good visit?"

"Yes, we did. I spoke to the local land agent, and he is aware of several houses for sale. I should like to visit those as soon as possible. I will need you at my side, of course, for the final decision must be yours."

"Mine?" Phoebe squeaked. "You're going to make me pick a house? What do I know about historic houses?"

Reggie patted the hand tucked in his arm. "Not all the houses will be historic, my dear. Not in 1827."

"No, I guess they won't," Phoebe said with a grin. "We'll choose together. How about that?"

"Delightful! See how well we get on?"

"Mmmm hmmmm," Phoebe murmured with a lift of one eyebrow. "Only the attic will tell."

CHAPTER FOURTEEN

They returned to the inn in good time for tea, with a stop at a cobbler's shop to procure slippers for Phoebe with an order for several more. The innkeeper saw them to a table, and a serving girl brought tea and sandwiches.

Reggie's heart overflowed with joy, and so elated was he that he could not say with any degree of confidence how the tea or food tasted. Marriage! A wife! *His* wife! Phoebe had consented to become his wife. He thought he understood her concerns—that they did not know each other very well, but there could be nothing about Phoebe to which he would object strenuously.

"And was the seamstress able to accommodate your needs?" Reggie asked.

Phoebe looked to Mattie before responding. "Yes, she was. She'll have some dresses ready in a few days. Meanwhile, I'll keep borrowing from Mattie."

"Excellent!" Reggie said. What could be other than excellent this day? "She seems a very nice sort of young woman. I cannot imagine that Lady Hamilton should send Samuel to the dressmaker on an errand rather than her own maid, but it was pleasant to see him again today. He is alone too much, reading in the library."

Phoebe and Mattie seemed to exchange glances again, almost secretive, and Reggie's heart missed a beat. There was a look of hesitance on Phoebe's face, of caution. He prayed that she had not changed her mind. He did not think he could bear it.

"Is there aught amiss?" he asked, dreading the answer. He directed his question to Phoebe, who looked down at her tea as if to divine her fortune in some way.

"No," she said. "Not with me." She directed a sideways glance at Mattie, who turned to survey the room with studied interest.

"I wonder if those two gentleman are the publishers who are coming to dinner tonight. William said they were going to stay here."

Phoebe was quick to follow her eyes, and Reggie tore his gaze from her with reluctance. Something *was* amiss. Phoebe, his own dear love, normally guileless with him to the point of indiscretion, hid something from him. He was certain of it!

Reggie turned to see two well-dressed gentleman seating themselves at a nearby table. Their attire was fashionably correct, most certainly obtained in London, yet subtle and discreet, which suggested they were men of business and not leisure.

"I could make inquiries, if you wish," Reggie said without enthusiasm. "Their names?"

"Oh, let's see. Thompson and Duncan, I think. Mr. Thompson and Mr. Duncan."

"Very well, I shall ask. Do you wish them to join us for tea?"

"Oh, sure!" Mattie said.

Phoebe, having looked at him while he spoke to Mattie, dropped her eyes again when he turned to her. He pressed his lips together, longing for a private moment in which to speak to her.

Reggie approached the men and discovered that they were indeed publishers and scheduled to dine with Mr. and Mrs. Sinclair that evening. He invited them to the table and introduced them.

"Mrs. Sinclair, allow me to present Mr. George Thompson and Mr. Ian Duncan, of Milton Publishers in London. Mrs. William Sinclair and Miss Phoebe Warner."

"Welcome," Mattie replied with a smile. Phoebe nodded politely.

The gentleman bowed and took the two available seats at the table.

"Such a pleasure to meet you early, Mrs. Sinclair," Mr. Thompson, a short thin man of middle age and graying hair, said. "Mr. Duncan and I look forward to meeting Mr. Sinclair this evening."

"Yes, indeed," Mr. Duncan replied. "Is that an American accent I hear, Mrs. Sinclair?" A tall, dark-haired young man of handsome features, Mr. Duncan appeared to have a sparkle in his eye for the ladies.

Mattie laughed. "Yes, I'm from America. So is my cousin, Miss Warner."

Reggie listened to the conversation with half an ear as he wondered what could possibly have changed Phoebe's mind about marriage in the past few hours. Had someone said something that gave her pause? Mattie? Unlikely. Mattie had seemed quite happy when he announced the impending marriage. The dressmaker? He did not know the woman.

Or had he badgered Phoebe with his pleas of marriage such that she accepted with reservation and, in the light of day and in his absence, found opportunity to review and revise her decision?

"Yes, from New York City," Phoebe was speaking. "I work at a publish—" She paused. "My father works at a publishing house there."

"Aha!" Mr. Duncan. "Which one? I am certain we would have heard of it."

"Oh, I don't think so. It's very small, a small press really."

"Nonetheless, we in the publishing business know each other very well," Mr. Duncan pressed. "I am sure I will have heard of it. The name?"

Phoebe's face took on a harried expression.

"Miss Warner is not mistaken. I have been to the publishing house. It is very small. You will not have heard of it," Reggie said with finality.

Mr. Duncan quirked a dark eyebrow but ceased the line of questioning. Phoebe gave Reggie a grateful look, but he turned his face away lest she see his unhappiness.

"Oh, you have been to New York then, Lord Hamilton?" Mr. Thompson asked. "A vast new market for books. I envy you."

"I am not in the business of publishing books," Reggie said. "But I did enjoy New York City. I was only there for a short while."

"I hear a note of regret in your voice," Mr. Thompson said. "A pity you could not stay longer."

"Yes, perhaps," Reggie said. It was not regret for the brevity of his visit to New York that Mr. Thompson heard, but a lament for the intolerable situation in which he now found himself—engaged to a woman who most likely did not wish to marry him.

The remainder of their time at the inn was spent conversing on the merits of publishing in England and abroad with Reggie involved not at all as his mind was elsewhere. Phoebe took very little part in the conversation as well, seemingly equally distracted with occasional glances in Reggie's direction. Mattie listened intently while Mr. Thompson and Mr. Duncan spoke.

"Well, we should be going if we are going to make it back in time for you to come to dinner," Mattie said with a laugh. "I will see you at eight o'clock, gentlemen."

Farewells were made, and the carriage was brought around for the short journey home. Reggie caught Phoebe's eyes on his face occasionally, and he smiled briefly and turned his attention to the scenery outside the window.

On arrival at Ashton House, Mattie hurried inside after Reggie handed her out, and Phoebe lingered until the carriage had pulled away.

She looked up at him questioningly.

This was the opportunity for private conversation that he had longed for, and yet now that it had arrived, he found himself tongue-tied.

"Is anything wrong, Reggie?"

"I do not think so," he replied, his hands clasped behind his back. "Is all well with you?"

"I'm fine," she said. "You asked me that earlier."

"I did, did I not? And your answer was the same."

Phoebe hesitated and reached out to touch the lapel of his coat. Reggie steeled himself for her next words.

"When do you want to go house-hunting?" she asked softly.

Reggie drew in a sharp breath and stiffened. Her words were not what he had expected to hear.

"Do you still wish to accompany me?" he asked in a husky voice.

"Of course I do. Why wouldn't I? Unless..." Phoebe dropped her hand and took a step backward.

"Unless?" Reggie prompted.

"Unless you've changed your mind," she said in a strangled voice. "You have, haven't you? You've changed your mind."

"About the house? No, I have not."

"About me?" she cried.

So taken aback was he by her reaction that he could do nothing for a moment but stare at her without words.

"Oh, Reggie!" Before he could stop her, Phoebe grabbed her skirts and ran inside the house. He turned to follow her but did not catch her before she ran up the stairs. He could not simply chase her down, nor he could he with any degree of decorum pound on her door and ask for an explanation of her whimsical changes in temperament.

In a house not his own, he was not even free to sulk in the library, and he had no intention of retiring to his room to brood. He longed to ride Sebastian, but there did not seem to be enough time to hurry over to his own home and saddle him.

Reggie turned from the house and made his way to the wooded area at the side of the house, there to ponder the mysteries of women, love, and marriage—not necessarily an inclusive package as he was discovering.

"I hear you are to be congratulated," William said as he approached.

Reggie looked up, stricken. He shook his head. "I do not think so, William. Perhaps this morning, but I cannot think that Miss Warner desires to marry me."

William looked taken aback, and Reggie did not blame him. Could this have been the shortest engagement in the annals of history?

"Come, come, Reggie. What has gone awry? Mattie told me only a short time ago that you and Miss Warner were engaged. But now I find you brooding in the woods, and Miss Warner apparently locked in her room."

"I cannot say." Reggie shrugged. "One moment I am made the happiest man in the world and in the next, I am brought lower than I thought possible. Phoebe did agree to marry me this morning and all seemed well, but at some point during our visit to the village, she seems to have rethought her decision."

"Did she say so?" William asked.

"Not in so many words," Reggie shrugged. "But there was a hesitation about her when I met them at the dressmaker's shop, a reluctance in her demeanor that gave me pause. She could not face me directly as she had only hours before, and I knew that I had pressed her too hard to marry me...that she had regretted accepting my proposal. You will remember that she did not wish to marry me at this time, claiming she did not know me well enough. That she agreed so suddenly this morning delighted me beyond words, but it should have been suspect, and I was too blinded by joy to allow myself to see it. I do believe she holds me in the highest regard, perhaps even loves me, but I do not think she is reconciled to marriage...or perhaps even to life in the nineteenth century."

William sighed. "I think you may have been hasty in your assessment of the situation, Reggie. Did you ask her whether she still wished to marry you?"

Reggie shook his head. "No, I did not ask the specific question." He scuffed the ground with the toe of his boot. "I was seized with a misery which tied my tongue and clouded my mind."

"And perhaps your judgment. I hear naught in your words to suggest that she wished to end the engagement," William said. He pulled out his pocket watch. "I must change for dinner, as should you. Mattie rarely entertains at home given that she did not grow up accustomed to such society, thank goodness, and I wish things to go as pleasantly for her as possible."

"Of course, William!" Reggie said. "I will be on my best behavior at dinner. I am grateful to you for sheltering us, and I wish only the best for Mattie. You are a very lucky man."

William clapped an arm around Reggie's shoulders. "I am a fortunate man, but my happiness was not achieved without suffering. It is possible that may be your path as well."

"If the end of the trial is a life with the woman I love, then I can endure anything," Reggie said quietly.

"Well said, Reggie."

****

As he promised, Reggie set himself out to be a gracious guest, although he was not overly fond of Mr. Duncan. He found Mr. Duncan to behave too familiarly toward Phoebe next to whom he was seated. Reggie had been seated on the opposite side of the table and forced to watch the tall dark-haired man attempt to charm Phoebe. Had Reggie introduced Phoebe as his betrothed, that might have put to rest the man's fatuous smiles toward her, but Reggie had been wounded at the time and had withheld that information—prophetically as it seemed.

Phoebe's face was drawn, and her nose tinged pink suggesting she had been crying. His heart ached for her, but he could not be certain he had it within his power to lift her spirits. Although, as William said, perhaps he had been hasty in his assessment of the situation that morning.

However, Phoebe averted her eyes from him, and he had no opportunity to talk to her privately that evening. In short, she avoided him, and there was nothing he could do about it at present.

The Sinclairs and Mr. Thompson discussed the possibility of investing in a publishing business. Mr. Duncan, when he could be bothered to draw himself away from Phoebe, joined in. At those times, Phoebe kept her attention on the discussion, and Reggie watched her.

He loved her dearly, of that he was in no doubt. But if she wished to return to her time, then perhaps she had better do so. The moon was still high in the sky that night. If she thought their joint wishes could help her return home, then he was prepared to do that for her. He did not know how much longer the moon would be full. He vowed to ask her what her wishes were before she retired to her room for the night.

The hours passed slowly, and the interminable, though well-prepared, dinner finally came to an end. William did not delay at the table but joined the ladies immediately. Reggie attempted to catch Phoebe's eye on entering the drawing room but failed. She kept close to Mattie. He noted Mattie watched them and exchanged troubled glances with William. Reggie shrugged when William looked his way.

Reggie moved closer to Phoebe and leaned near.

"A word in private before you retire, Phoebe," he said in a low voice.

"No," Phoebe whispered in a harsh note. "I don't want to talk about it anymore." She moved away to stand on the other side of Mattie as she talked to Mr. Thompson and Mr. Duncan.

Reggie stiffened and straightened. That was her answer. She did not wish to discuss the matter further. His chest ached, and he wanted nothing so much as to rush out of the house and hop upon Sebastian to ride out into the night—which, of course, was the thing that had brought him to his heartache.

And he had promised William he would do his best to make the evening a pleasant one for Mattie. He could not leave early, could not plead a headache or whatever it was that young misses did when they were unhappy.

Fortunately, the Sinclairs and the publishers concluded their business, and those gentlemen bid them goodnight. Mr. Duncan lingered overly long with Phoebe's hand in farewell, and Reggie contemplated raising a fist to the man's chin but held back and clasped the offending hands behind his back.

As the front door closed, Phoebe bid them good night and hastened up the stairs to her room. Mattie and William looked at Reggie, who pressed his lips together and said his good night as well. He climbed the stairs slowly and waited in his room until he heard the sounds of doors closing and the house quieting. He changed out of his eveningwear and into more comfortable clothing, grateful that a bag had been delivered for him that morning.

Reggie inched the door open and heard no sounds. He stepped out into the hallway and listened. Nothing. He approached the door to Phoebe's room and listened carefully. No sounds of stirring. A faint light showed below the threshold of the door. It seemed that Phoebe did not yet sleep. Reggie took a deep breath.

CHAPTER FIFTEEN

Reggie rode out on Sebastian early the next morning to meet with the local estate agent. His late night jaunt to Ashton House to ride Sebastian had been at once stealthy and yet liberating. Unable to force himself to knock on Phoebe's door as he longed to do, he had instead sought solace in the company of his horse. Contrary to his previous outing on Sebastian, he had not ridden pell-mell into the darkness in anger but had sedately allowed Sebastian to feel his way down the lane of the estate. They had retraced their steps to where Reggie had fallen in the dirt, lingering there a while to no particular purpose other than to dwell on memories.

The moon seemed to waver as it shone down on him, glowing less brightly than when he had last looked upon it. Was it still full? If Phoebe wished to return to her time, she must decide soon. He pitied her and pitied himself, indulging in a few moments of unadulterated wallowing before reining himself in.

Now, the next morning, Reggie determined to find himself a house regardless of whether Phoebe wished to marry him or not. He no longer cared to live in his father's house, but desired his own home. He had thought to ride over to Hamilton Place early in the morning and invite Samuel to accompany him since he had promised his brother he could have a home, but Reggie decided to investigate alone. If Phoebe could not accompany him as they had originally planned, then he wanted no other. Samuel could, of course, live in his home, but he would have no say in the selection of it.

He met the estate agent in the village, a tall, thin man of indeterminate age named Mr. Hart, and he followed him to an estate several miles from the village. In such close proximity to his own home, Reggie had indeed heard the name of the family who had previously owned the estate, the father a banker, but he had never met them.

Mr. Hart drove his small carriage while Reggie followed on Sebastian, preferring to be solitary. They soon approached the unassuming gates of the estate and entered to follow a wide lane toward the house. The trees parted and a charming castellated and turreted house festooned with multiple white-trimmed windows appeared before them.

Reggie's first impression was that Phoebe would have loved the house that had the look of a small castle. Having just been built in the late 1770s, the house appeared new and yet medieval with its many turrets. He half expected to see a moat surrounding it, but they arrived at the circular entrance without crossing any such thing.

"I should like to see the gardens of the house before entering it, if you please, Mr. Hart." Reggie dismounted and tied Sebastian to a post.

"Certainly, Lord Hamilton. I think I know something you will enjoy. This way." Mr. Hart led him around the side of the house and toward the back where they climbed onto a wide stone terrace that overlooked a pastoral scene of green fields as far as the eye could see with cows grazing along the side of a dazzling stream of azure blue. Trees dotted the landscape. The gardens just below the terrace sported masses of colorful flowers. He turned toward the house. Two large bay windows, as tall as the door they flanked, overlooked the vista behind him. He imagined evenings watching the sun set in the distance across the plains.

Without seeing the inside of the house, Reggie knew he had found the one. Phoebe would have loved it, and he knew he would love it as well whether she ever lived there with him or not.

"I will take it, Mr. Hart," Reggie said, his heart thudding as it had when he proposed to Phoebe. "When may I take possession?"

"Do you not wish to see inside, Lord Hamilton?"

"Yes, of course, Mr. Hart, but that will not change my decision. Shall we discuss the details while we walk?"

"Oh, certainly!"

They retraced their steps and entered the house while they discussed price and availability. The house, although furnished, was available, and Mr. Hart thought the owners might be willing to let the furnishings go with the house. It was available immediately.

The inside of the house, as promised, did not dissuade him from his decision, nor was there anything about it that was not wonderful. The layout was elegant yet informal, the furnishings festive and colorful. Phoebe would have delighted at the interior of the house. Perhaps she could still one day see the house before she returned to her own time, if that was her intention. He could not imagine that she would choose to stay for any other reason...unless it was impossible to find her way back.

Reggie returned to Ashton House. Mattie ran out the door as soon as he cleared the trees, and Phoebe hung by the doorway.

"Where have you been?" Mattie called out as he rode up. "And when did you get your horse?"

Reggie dismounted and handed Sebastian to a waiting groom.

"I am almost too mortified to admit that I went for Sebastian last night." He kept his gaze on Mattie.

"After dinner? Are you serious?"

He smiled awkwardly. "I am serious. I wanted to ride."

"Well, that's what happened to you last time, and look where you ended up." Mattie said. She turned to look at Phoebe by the front door watching them. She lowered her voice. "Look, Reggie, you need to fix this. I don't know what happened between you two, but she's miserable. When she found out you'd gone this morning, she burst into tears. You nineteenth-century guys! Heartbreakers, all of you!"

Reggie wished he could smile at her quip, but he could not. "I believe we are no longer engaged, Mattie. It seems as if Phoebe had a change of heart yesterday, or perhaps her heart was never in it."

"Oh, nonsense!" Mattie cried. "What do you mean? She's head over heels for you. What happened?"

"I do not know," he said, swallowing against the renewed ache in his throat. "When we met for tea, she had changed. You saw it, I believe. She was secretive, uncertain, reluctant. She could not meet my eyes. I knew then that I had pressed her too much and forced her to accept my suit."

Mattie's eyes widened, and she sighed and shook her head. "I think I know what this is about. It's not what you think, Reggie, I promise. Did you ask her about it?"

"I tried to talk to her last night, but she said she did not wish to discuss the matter. Unfortunately, she believes I have changed my mind. I believe she changed hers."

"You two!" Mattie muttered. "Phoebe, can you come here a minute?"

"Mattie, do not!" Reggie said harshly. "Do not press Miss Warner any further."

Phoebe moved forward reluctantly, as if she were headed for the guillotine. She came to stand beside Mattie, her eyes on the ground.

"Look, you guys. I'm kind of a wannabe matchmaker, so I can't let this sit. Reggie thinks you're hiding a secret, Phoebe—that you don't want to marry him. Reggie, Phoebe just cries and cries, say's it's over and won't talk about it." She stepped back and made a gesture of washing her hands. "You two figure it out. But trust me, Reggie, nothing happened in town yesterday that would affect how Phoebe feels about you. I know. I was there." She turned on her heels and reentered the house, leaving Phoebe and Reggie to face each other.

"I'm sorry I blew you off last night, Reggie. I should have tried to listen. I was just too scared to hear what I didn't want to hear. You can tell me what you need to now." Phoebe's voice was leaden.

Reggie gestured toward the garden. "Shall we walk, Phoebe? Whether you wish to marry me or not, I hope we shall always be friends."

Phoebe's head shot up and she stared at him for a moment before turning in the direction of the garden. He followed her. The lilac gown she wore suited her fair complexion and brought forth the golden tints in her brown hair. She wore no bonnet, and he wished he were free to run his fingers along the silky curls at her neck. Her ramrod straight back, however, suggested that would be out of the question.

She seated herself on the bench and turned to look at him.

"Would you sit down, please? I can't have you hovering over me that way."

Reggie realized he had been indeed hovering nervously, and he seated himself.

"So, what did you want to say, Reggie?" Phoebe asked in a quiet voice.

"I bought a house," Reggie said, the first thing that came to his mind. "I know you will probably never live there, but I wish you to see it."

Phoebe swung her head in his direction. Her face grew bright red, and her mouth worked but she uttered no words. She turned away, and Reggie swallowed hard. Tears rolled down her cheeks, and he fished in his coat for his kerchief.

"Phoebe, Phoebe, forgive me. I meant no injury to you. Please do not cry."

She began to cry in earnest, and he waved the kerchief ineffectually.

"Do not cry, my love. Do not cry," he murmured. He pulled her toward him, she resistant at first then yielding, and he held her as she sobbed. He murmured inconsequential words against the sweetness of her hair.

"I do not mean to hurt you. I am a beast. I sought only to share my find with you. You would adore the house. You truly would."

"You were supposed to take me with you," Phoebe wailed against his chest.

"But I thought you would not wish to go, Phoebe," he said. "You seemed so...reticent yesterday."

Phoebe began crying anew. "I wanted to go. You promised," she sobbed.

Reggie knew he had little enough experience with women, but he certainly had no experience with women from the twenty-first century.

"I could not speak to you last night. I thought you were angry with me."

"I was," she said. "I *was* mad at you."

"There! What am I to think? Yesterday morning, I was overjoyed, but then you retreated from me, and I suspected that you had changed your mind and could not find a way to tell me. Your acceptance of my proposal, while the most fortunate event of my life, was unexpected both for you and for me."

She nodded against his chest. "I know. It surprised me, too. I wanted to wait until I knew you better, but I realized I'll never love anyone as much as I love you no matter how well I know them."

Reggie wondered if he heard correctly. Her words were too wonderful.

"Did you say that you loved me?"

She nodded, her face rubbing against his coat. "I told you that before. *I* haven't changed."

"Oh, my love, I am so sorry to have hurt you. I should have waited to find the house. I was confused. I did not understand. Perhaps I do not know you well enough either. Why then did your temperament change yesterday morning? Was it an unexpected shyness on the occasion of our betrothal?"

Phoebe lifted her head and looked at him. "I can't tell you."

"You cannot tell me? Why ever not? What could you not tell me? Do we not love one another?"

Phoebe nodded. "I love *you*, I know that."

"And I love you too, my dearest girl. So then what?"

"I can't tell you," Phoebe shook her head again.

Reggie released her and rose abruptly. "What? Are we to begin our lives together with secrets and distrust? What can you not tell me?"

Phoebe jumped up. "It's not my secret to tell. I promised I wouldn't." Her voice was strident.

"To whom does the secret belong then? Is it Mattie? What secret could she have that would affect you and I?"

Phoebe shook her head. "No, not Mattie."

"William then?"

Phoebe shook her head. "Stop fishing, Reggie. It doesn't matter. I can't tell you."

"Well, it certainly cannot be that odious Mr. Duncan who fawns upon you. I hope we have seen the last of him, but I fear it is not to be if William intends to enter into business with them, and you and Mattie choose to work together."

Phoebe's lips twitched. "Not the *odious* Mr. Duncan," she said. "He wasn't that bad, Reggie."

"His behavior was reprehensible. Certainly to a betrothed woman." Reggie drew his brows together.

"Well, he didn't know I was engaged. I don't think we mentioned it. I think it was kind of up in the air at the time."

"Nonetheless, to openly flirt with an unmarried young lady in the home of his host. Appallingly bad behavior."

"Reggie," Phoebe murmured with an affectionate tone of reproach.

Reggie was not repentant. "Nonetheless," he stated to no purpose other than to have the last word.

"Tell me about the house. How is the attic? Anybody up there?" she said.

"You seek to change the subject."

"I do," she said. "It's like this. I love you, Reggie. I can't tell you what the secret is. I wish I hadn't acted the way I did yesterday, but you seem to have a knack for being able to read my expressions, so I can't hide anything from you. Whatever the secret is, it doesn't affect me."

Reggie took Phoebe's hands in his and kissed the backs of them. "I study your face often, my love, and do not miss many of your expressions which you show in abundance. However, I am not always able to interpret your emotions. If the secret does not affect you, then it does not affect me, and so I am content to let it be. I apologize for haranguing you on the subject."

Phoebe's eyes flickered, and her smile wavered.

"Alas, I see by your expression that my words have not rung true. Then if the secret does not involve you, it involves me. Is that correct?"

Phoebe sighed and would have removed her hands from his, but Reggie kept them in a gentle grasp. "Technically, I would by lying to you to say that it doesn't involve you, however remote. And I don't want to start lying to you."

Reggie heaved a sigh. "But it does not affect you, and that is my main concern. Who must I ask about this secret?"

Phoebe shook her head. "I can't say. You might try Mattie."

Reggie quirked a brow. "Then it is Mattie's secret. How it might concern me is beyond my comprehension."

"I'll bet," Phoebe said. "So, about that house."

"We should have luncheon then I shall borrow William's carriage, and we shall set out to see the house together this afternoon. I will need to obtain the keys from the land agent."

An hour later, not only did Reggie and Phoebe set out to see the house, but William, Mattie and their child joined them.

As Reggie had predicted, Phoebe loved the house, commenting effusively on how "new" it looked for a historic home. He reminded her that it was only approximately fifty-five years old, not at all historic in the true sense of the word. His hopes were realized when Phoebe sang the praises of the terraced view of the river and pastures beyond.

"Oh, Reggie, this is beautiful! Just beautiful. You picked well."

"You are pleased then?" he said as he held her hands.

"Oh, yes," she breathed. "It's perfect. It's like a castle!"

"A castle indeed," he said with satisfaction.

"I'm heading for the attics," she said with a broad smile.

Phoebe and Mattie, carrying Mia, continued on to explore the inside of the house while William and Reggie stood on the balcony and watched the river beyond.

"An excellent choice, Reggie," William said. "This will make a magnificent wedding present. I assume that you and Miss Warner have resolved your differences?"

"A misunderstanding, no more. I apologize if I seemed melodramatic. I felt quite despondent yesterday."

"I am pleased to see that you were able to speak to each other," William said. "Truthfulness is vital to a good marriage, I believe. Truthfulness, trust, and love."

"There is an element of the misunderstanding about which Phoebe is not able to be quite truthful though," Reggie began. He hesitated to broach the subject, but Phoebe did say he should ask Mattie, and Reggie deduced that what Mattie knew, William also knew.

"Oh?" William turned to him.

"Phoebe tells me she is in possession of a secret that does not affect her but does affect me. She came upon it yesterday at some point, and she states that Mattie is privy to it. I think you and Mattie share every confidence if I'm not mistaken, and I wonder if you could not tell me what it is. You can imagine what it is like to know there is a mysterious matter about one's self which one cannot know about."

William nodded and resumed his perusal of the river. Reggie thought he meant to dismiss the topic out of hand.

"I am conflicted," William began. "Mattie did speak to me in confidence, but she did not release me to speak to you. She and Miss Warner were sworn to secrecy. That is all I can say at this time. Let me speak to Mattie regarding the matter, and I will let you know her decision. It is not something that will *harm* you, Reggie. It is not something that should really overly concern you, in my opinion."

"Does it affect Phoebe in any way?" Reggie asked, ignoring an uncomfortable thump of his heart in his chest.

"Not at all," William said. "Nor Mattie, nor me."

"Then it cannot be so bad," Reggie said. "I will await your decision."

The ladies rejoined them, and they returned to Ashton House in high spirits. Upon arriving at the front door, they found Samuel there dismounting from his horse and carrying a carpetbag. A groom hurried up, and John pulled open the door.

"Samuel!" Reggie jumped down from the carriage. "Have you come to call?"

"I hope to come to stay if William and Mrs. Sinclair will have me. Hamilton Place is intolerable in your absence."

CHAPTER SIXTEEN

Phoebe, helped down from the carriage by Reggie, turned to look at Mattie, who seemed unfazed by Samuel's arrival.

"I don't blame you, Samuel," she said. "Not one little bit. Of course, you can stay here."

The groom took Samuel's horse, and John took his bag.

"Up to the blue room, John. Thank you," Mattie said.

"This is most kind of you, Mattie," Reggie said, wrapping an arm around his brother as they all entered the house.

Jane came downstairs to take Mia for a snack. "Could you ask them to bring some tea to the drawing room, Jane?" Mattie asked. "Thanks."

"Come on into the drawing room, Samuel," Mattie said.

Phoebe marveled at Mattie's ability to switch between a more formal speech pattern when speaking to strangers, and her modern-day Americanisms when speaking to family or her staff. Though Samuel probably didn't know she was a time traveler, she seemed unworried about possible discovery by him. Phoebe wondered if she would ever be able to transition between the two eras as well as Mattie seemed to be doing.

Reggie took her hand in his and pulled her gently by his side.

"Samuel, please congratulate me. I had the honor to ask Miss Warner for her hand in marriage, and she has accepted."

Samuel's eyes widened and his jaw dropped.

Reggie waited, and Phoebe thought she could feel a slight tension in the grip of his hand. She hadn't realized his brother's opinion was so important to him.

Why didn't Samuel say something? Was he worried he couldn't come to live with his brother as they'd talked about?

"You can still come to live at the house, Samuel! I wouldn't stop that," Phoebe blurted out. Reggie squeezed her hand.

Samuel's face reddened, and he bowed his head. "Many felicitations, Miss Warner. Reggie. Forgive my delayed response. I was taken aback, that is all."

"It is as Miss Warner says, Samuel. You shall come to live with us. I have this day purchased a house, and there is ample room for all of us...and more." He turned an affectionate eye on Phoebe who blushed.

She had no doubt he meant children. She hoped they looked like him.

"That is kind of you," Samuel said.

John arrived with the tea, and the awkward moment was broken as Mattie busied herself pouring. They seated themselves and settled into a discussion of the new house and grounds. Phoebe noticed Samuel, standing by the cold fireplace, stared at her then at Reggie, and she wondered what he was thinking. She tried smiling at him when she caught him watching her, and he responded with a faint lift of his own lips, but she sensed that he didn't really see her. She had a feeling something else was on his mind—not the news of his brother's marriage and not the house.

Was he thinking of the dressmaker? Sarah?

A glance to her left showed that Reggie, seated next to her on a settee, studied Samuel as well with a frown on his face. Phoebe hoped she wasn't coming between them.

John opened the door.

"Lord and Lady Hamilton," he announced.

Phoebe noted with a pounding heart that everyone in the room jumped up as Reggie's father and stepmother entered the room with the exception of William who remained calm and rose to bow in a leisurely manner.

"Samuel! We did not think to find you here." His father boomed. "I wondered why we did not see you for luncheon."

Phoebe exchanged glances with Reggie. Didn't he tell them he was leaving?

"Tea?" Mattie murmured. Her cheeks were bright, and she looked tense. William resumed his seat beside her and covered her hand with his own. Mattie calmed down almost instantly and turned a loving smile on her husband. Phoebe sighed.

Her own true love, Reggie, was speaking to his brother.

"Perhaps now would be a good time to advise Father of your plans, Samuel?"

"What plans?" Lord Hamilton asked with narrowed eyes. "Do not tell me you are now bound for America as well, Samuel?" He laughed but the laughter did not reach his eyes.

Lady Hamilton watched the discussion alertly, but she kept her expression neutral.

Samuel, maintaining his position at the fireplace, looked to his brother.

"Perhaps *you* should begin, Reggie. It would seem that my news might be superseded by yours in interest and importance."

"What news have you, Reggie?" Lord Hamilton barked. "And why, if both of my sons have news to impart, do they not visit me in my own house, begging the Sinclairs' pardon, of course."

"That would have been idyllic," Reggie said in a surprisingly calm voice. Phoebe stared at him with renewed respect. His father was a big man and a bit boisterous, but Reggie seemed to have no fear of him or of the news he was about to share.

"Nevertheless, since we are all gathered in Mr. and Mrs. Sinclair's home, I beg their gracious leave to announce the engagement between myself and Miss Warner." Reggie took Phoebe's hand in his, and she clung to him.

Lord Hamilton jumped up.

"What? What harebrained scheme is this? First, you decide to run away to America and now you are decided instead to marry an American of uncertain origins? And do you plan to return to America with her?" He approached Reggie and clenched his fists. Phoebe cringed. Was his father going to hit him?

Across the room, William rose. Reggie squeezed Phoebe's hand and stood, facing his father with an aloof, unyielding expression.

"Sir, I beg you to remember that you discuss my future wife," Reggie began.

Lady Hamilton rose swiftly and placed a restraining hand on Lord Hamilton. "Come, Jonathan, let us resume our seats. Certainly, there is much to discuss and many questions to be answered, but we must offer Reggie and Miss Warner felicitations."

Lord Hamilton, red faced, allowed himself to be guided back to his chair, and Phoebe eased out the air she'd been holding. Reggie, tense, his back ramrod straight, continued standing. Samuel's face was red as he watched the conflict, but he said nothing.

"Please sit down, Reggie. Your father was taken by surprise, that is all," Lady Hamilton said. "It might have been better had you advised your father in private of your intentions. Forgive us, Miss Warner, for our manners."

"My sincerest apologies. Bad form," Lord Hamilton muttered.

"Oh, I...uh...no problem," Phoebe said.

William resumed his seat as well and watched the discussion with narrowed eyes.

"And when do you plan to marry, Reggie? Has a date been set?" Lady Hamilton asked. Phoebe suspected she was none too pleased as well, but she masked her emotions much better than her volatile husband. If she had ever imagined loving grandparents for her own children, those images faded from her mind.

"Miss Warner and I have not as yet discussed the matter, but I hope it will be soon." He threw Phoebe a questioning look, and she gave him a slight nod with a smile. Reggie grinned. "As soon as the banns are posted then, I believe, in a fortnight."

"Such haste," Lady Hamilton murmured.

"And do you plan to remove to America?" Lord Hamilton asked.

"No, Father, no longer. Perhaps Miss Warner and I might visit one day after we are married, but we will live here. As it happens, I have purchased a house nearby."

"A house?" Lord Hamilton half rose, but Lady Hamilton caught him in time. "We *have* a house already! What do you mean you bought a house?"

"I would like to set up my own establishment, Father. Please do not distress yourself. I will not have gone far."

"But why can you not come home to live?" his father asked.

Phoebe suddenly felt sorry for the older man. He sounded hurt. She fervently hoped though that Reggie wouldn't change his mind.

"I am sorry, Father, but I wish to be master in my own home, and at the risk of offending you, Lady Hamilton, I wish my wife to be mistress in her own home."

Lady Hamilton nodded. "I understand," she said.

Phoebe, surprised, eyed her. She did seem to understand. Perhaps she wasn't so bad after all—from a distance.

Lord Hamilton looked to his wife, as if for reassurance, and she patted his hand.

"It is not unusual, Jonathan, for a man to want his own home, or for a lady to wish to be mistress in her own house. It does not mean that Reggie will abandon his inheritance or the estate. Samuel is still at home. You still have one of your sons with you."

Phoebe threw a look in Samuel's direction. This wasn't going to be good. Everyone in the room looked at Samuel in that moment, for various reasons.

"Do you wish me to speak, Samuel?" Reggie asked in a low voice.

Lady Hamilton turned a sharp eye on them.

"What is this?" she asked. "Samuel's news, I think. One hopes it is not as momentous as Reggie's," she murmured. "For your father's sake."

Lord Hamilton looked up, attempting to rally himself. "Let's have it then, Samuel. What news?"

Samuel half turned to Reggie as if for help, then seemed to steel himself.

"I have come to stay with William and Mrs. Sinclair for a spell, and then I will relocate to Reggie's house when it is ready."

Lady Hamilton didn't look surprised, but Lord Hamilton looked as if he were about to have a heart attack. He clutched at his chest for a moment.

Phoebe jumped up. "Lord Hamilton, are you all right?"

Reggie stepped forward quickly to peer at his father. William and Mattie rose as well. Samuel watched anxiously.

"It is nothing," Lady Hamilton said. She poured a fresh cup of tea and offered it to him. "Lord Hamilton has recently had some gastronomic concerns, and the doctor says he must avoid fatty foods. But he had a large helping of food at luncheon."

"Quite right," Lord Hamilton muttered. "A man enjoys his food, even if his children choose to eat elsewhere."

"Father!" Samuel spoke up. "It is not the food."

"Then why must you leave as well? Why are my children abandoning me? Have I not been a good father to you? Cared for you as best I could in the absence of your mother?"

"Yes, Father, yes, of course, you have," Reggie answered. He patted his father on the shoulder.

"Then why must Samuel leave as well?"

"I cannot answer for him, Father. Only Samuel knows that, but I will open my home to him for as long as he desires."

"Samuel," Lady Hamilton said. "Why do you wish to leave Hamilton Place?"

Samuel looked around with wild eyes. Phoebe wasn't sure he knew the answer himself, or if he did he didn't seem to want to share it.

"I see that Samuel has become suddenly tongue-tied," Reggie interceded. "You know, of course, that he has been keeping his own company overly much of late and is not now accustomed to gatherings even such as this, and certainly not speaking of highly personal matters in company. I asked Samuel to come to me here and to the new house because I wish to help him come out of the shell he has shut himself into."

Samuel stared hard at Reggie, his mouth working but no words came out.

Reggie gazed around the room as if daring someone to question him.

Lady Hamilton took on the challenge.

"We can help Samuel in that direction, Reggie. Samuel, you could have told us you tired of your life of solitude and reading. We thought you content. I would have been more vigilant about inviting you to accompany us on dinner parties. I could have hosted some dances or a ball. Is it that you wish to meet eligible young ladies? Are you also desirous of settling down?"

Samuel's face glowed bright red, and he continued to look around the room wildly as if he would bolt.

"Mother, pray do not begin matchmaking once again," William said. "Samuel is fully capable of finding a wife when he wishes to settle down."

Lady Hamilton shot William a dark look, but he watched her unfazed.

"Please, do not concern yourself with me," Samuel finally croaked out. "Reggie speaks the truth. He thinks I am too often alone, and he wishes to effect a change in that, albeit slowly and without balls and dances. Thank you for your concern, Lady Hamilton. I will enjoy my brother's company."

Phoebe knew he lied to support Reggie's story, but she had the worst image of Reggie and Samuel riding, fishing, and generally hanging out all day while she sat in the bay windows of the new house and longed for company, her sewing forgotten at her side. Was that how it was in 1827?

"Makes no sense. None at all," Lord Hamilton muttered. He rose slowly, his hand still at his stomach. "We must be off. I am not feeling well."

Lady Hamilton stood. "Forgive us. Lord Hamilton's stomach still pains him. This has been an eventful visit. Pray keep us apprised of your plans for the wedding. I wish to assist you in any way I can."

"Thank you, Lady Hamilton. Miss Warner and I have not yet discussed our plans, but you may be certain we shall call upon you for guidance if necessary." Reggie bowed his head. "Be well, Father."

"Yes, thank you. I have a tincture at home."

"Good."

They turned to leave, and Samuel strode toward his father and patted him on the back.

"I will visit often, Father. I am only just next door."

"Yes, my boy, I know," Lord Hamilton said with a sigh. "I shall probably see much more of you, I imagine, now that you will have left the library."

"Just so," Samuel smiled tentatively.

They left, and Samuel turned to the room. "Do you have something a bit more stout than tea, William? For I have news to impart."

"Certainly!" William rose and opened a buffet to reveal a decanter and glasses. He poured a drink for Samuel but declined to take one for himself as did Reggie.

All eyes followed Samuel as he took the seat recently vacated by his father. He swallowed his drink in two gulps.

"I must say, that was decidedly inventive of you, Reggie," Samuel said with a shaky laugh.

"I think not," Reggie said. "You *have* been buried in your books overly much, more so over the last year. I did not wish to say as much to you, thinking it to be your desire."

"And you have been buried with your dreams of moving to America. It was as if you had already left."

Reggie bit his lip and looked toward Phoebe.

"Yes, I think I have not been a good companion to you of late, have I? Forgive me. It is true. I thought I was dreaming of America, I admit it, but my dreams have been realized—not of America—but of the woman who will become my wife. That is what I dreamed of and wished for. My future wife."

Phoebe's cheeks flamed, and she smiled with a sigh. These men! So romantic!

Reggie gazed at her with love as if she were the only person in the world.

William cleared his throat. "You said you had news, Samuel?"

Phoebe snapped out of her romantic reverie and turned to see Samuel jump up to pour himself another drink and swallow it. Phoebe, Reggie, Mattie, and William exchanged concerned glances.

He retook his seat and scanned the room, pausing on Mattie and Phoebe before allowing his gaze to rest on Reggie.

"I suspect that Mrs. Sinclair or Miss Warner might have already deduced the nature of my revelation and shared that information with you."

Phoebe and Mattie exchanged glances. Uh oh. As if there hadn't been enough bombshells for one day, Samuel was about to mention he had a girlfriend.

"Not me!" Phoebe piped up. "We promised." She threw a look at Reggie, who stiffened.

"This *secret* then concerned my brother?" Reggie asked with narrowed eyes directed toward her.

Phoebe nodded and chewed her lip.

"You promised?" Samuel asked. "Not to me. I did not have occasion to speak to you on the matter. Did you speak to..." He left the words hanging.

"I'm afraid *I* did, Samuel," Mattie said. "I butt in where I shouldn't have. I should have known better."

"Dearest, I am afraid you will shock Reggie and Samuel with that particular colloquialism," William said with a broad smile bordering on laughter.

"*Butt* in?" Reggie said. "I can only assume you mean by 'butt in,' you mean *interfere?*" He looked from face to face. "But in what matter? Will someone please explain what is going on here? Phoebe?"

Phoebe couldn't stand watching Reggie in such an uncomfortable position. She was sure Mattie would have shared the news with William by now, as he didn't seem in the least confused. If Samuel didn't say something in the next two minutes, she was going to break her promise to Sarah. It wasn't worth watching Reggie struggle to understand something that everyone else already knew. She loved him way too much for that.

"Samuel, say something," Phoebe implored. "If you don't, I will."

"I was about to disclose all before I was interrupted. What I wished to announce, in the absence of Father and Lady Hamilton, is that I too have met a young lady, and I wish to be married as well."

CHAPTER SEVENTEEN

"You!" Reggie exclaimed. "But Samuel, this is wonderful news! Pray tell me her name. I am so pleased for you!" Reggie enfolded his brother in a brief embrace that astonished even him. They were not used to such spontaneous demonstrations of affection or congratulation. He supposed it to be the influence of his newfound love.

Samuel, cheeks bright, straightened his coat. "Please, Brother, desist with pawing at me. I fear you will not be pleased with my choice."

Reggie straightened his own coat and the smile faded from his face at his brother's downcast eyes. Was Samuel not happy? As happy as Reggie was now?

"What could elicit such a somber expression, Samuel? I am sure your choice of future wife will please me if she pleases you. Whom you choose should be no concern of mine," Reggie said. He looked to Phoebe whose eyes shone with love, and his heart fluttered at the pride he saw in her eyes.

"Very well," Samuel said as if in doubt. "Her name is Sarah Tollerton. She owns the dressmaking shop in the village."

Reggie thought he could not have heard correctly. A dressmaking shop?

"She what?" he asked.

"She owns the dressmaking shop in the village. You saw her only this morning when you took Mrs. Sinclair and Miss Warner to town. I assume they deduced almost immediately that my business there was not on behalf of our stepmother, but you did not."

Reggie shook his head as if to clear the cobwebs. He vaguely remembered a young woman opening the door to the shop, dark hair, a pleasing countenance. She seemed to know who he was, but he had not previously met her as he had never before had occasion to frequent dress shops.

"A dressmaker, Samuel? You cannot marry a dressmaker!"

"Reggie!" Phoebe cried out. She rose swiftly and faced him. "Why ever not?"

Samuel turned to Phoebe. "I am surprised you need ask, Miss Warner. As you must know, Miss Tollerton is deemed to come from another class of people, though her father was born of a respectable family. As the youngest son of a squire, he took orders and became a country parson. Upon his death, he left nothing for his only daughter and, because Miss Tollerton was forced into the trades, she is considered an unsuitable wife for the second son of an earl."

"Oh, for Pete's sake, Reggie's not like that," Phoebe said. "Maybe your father is, but Reggie doesn't think like that, do you?"

Reggie looked at his dear love who regarded him with a look of hope and trust in her eyes. He could tell her the truth...or he could lie, but he had sworn never to lie to her.

"It pains me to say this, both to you, Samuel, and to you, my love, but Miss Tollerton's situation in life renders her an unacceptable wife for Samuel. No children of the Earl of Hamilton have ever married someone in the trades. It simply is not done. Father would never countenance such a match."

Phoebe faltered and grabbed the edge of the settee, staring at him with wide eyes. Samuel turned away and headed for the buffet and a drink. Mattie wore an expression of disappointment and looked away to watch Samuel. Only William seemed to regard Reggie with anything resembling understanding.

"You've got to be kidding," Phoebe almost begged. Reggie understood she gave him an opportunity to retract his words, but to lie to her, to renounce everything he had ever understood about the nobility, forbade it.

"I do not jest, Phoebe. I think it must be different in your time."

She looked over her shoulder toward Samuel who stood by the buffet but apparently did not hear Reggie's accidental reference to "time."

"Well, of course it is." She jabbed a thumb unceremoniously toward her breast. "*I'm* different. *I'm* in the trades. *I'm* a nobody. How can you marry me but Samuel can't marry Sarah Tollerton? It's hypocritical!"

Reggie reached out a hand to her. "Phoebe, please. Let us speak of this in private. It is not the same."

"No, it *is* the same," she said as tears ran down her face. "I don't know why you can't see that, or were you marrying me *despite* what you considered to be a flawed upbringing? Sarah Tollerton and I are just alike—whether I work as a publisher or as a seamstress."

"Phoebe, please," Reggie said ineffectually. He did not know what he wanted. That she return the look of love to her eyes? That she desist in believing she and the dressmaker were of the same class? That the entire conversation had never begun at all?

Phoebe shook her head. "I don't know you at all, do I, Reggie? This is the wife in the attic, isn't it? This is the reason we can't get married." With that, she turned and ran from the room. He heard her footsteps pounding up the stairs.

Mattie rose to follow without a backward glance.

"Forgive me, Reggie," Samuel said in a now-slurred voice. "It was not my intention to upset Miss Warner when I revealed my news. Although I did accurately predict how you would receive the news, I did not imagine this would occur." He nodded over his shoulder toward the doorway.

"By this, do you mean the end of my engagement?" Reggie said in a strangled voice. He poured himself a drink.

William joined them. "I am at a loss for words, gentlemen. You both have my utmost sympathies." He poured himself a drink as well. "Let us remove to the library where we may speak in private. Surely, there is room for compromise."

Reggie followed Samuel and William into the library where the drink was more plentiful and more potent.

He slumped into a chair, unable to comprehend the ramifications of what had just occurred. Samuel threw himself into another chair, as morose as he. Reggie tried to find the wits to think of Samuel's misery and what he must have suffered for some time as he fell in love with Miss Tollerton. But at the moment, Reggie could only think of his own misery, the end of his dreams.

"Come, gentlemen. It is not as glum as all that. Love is a wondrous happy thing. It is only people who remove the joy from it."

Reggie stared at his stepbrother with a wry expression.

"Have you become a poet then, William?"

William smiled. "I have indeed. I am proof, gentlemen, that love will find a way. Though there be obstacles in your paths, I truly believe that love will conquer all."

"I believed that as well, I truly did, but it has not come to pass," Reggie said morosely. "I cannot change who I am, or not as much as apparently Miss Warner would wish me to. Perhaps she would be better off with someone of her own time."

"Nonsense," William said.

"I cannot help but feel that I have come between you and Miss

Warner, Reggie," Samuel said in an equally morose voice.

Reggie shook his head. "It was my words that Miss Warner objected to, Samuel, not you. I am the cause of the demise of our engagement. But I could not lie to her. Father would indeed never countenance a match between you and Miss Tollerton, and you must have his blessing."

"Because I have no income of my own," Samuel muttered.

"Yes, that is correct," Reggie said.

"But I could learn a trade myself. I wish to become a solicitor. Then I could support a wife."

"A solicitor!" William exclaimed. "What a capital idea!"

"A solicitor!" Reggie echoed. "When did you decide that?"

"Some time ago," Samuel said, "after I knew I wished to make Miss Tollerton my wife. I knew I should need a profession, and the law holds interest for me."

"Did you discuss this with Father?"

"Yes, I attempted to...on the same night that you stormed out and disappeared, a most inopportune time. He refused to hear of it and forbade me to speak of it again. I cannot study for the law without his financial assistance."

"Well, there is one thing that you can aid your brother with, Reggie," William said. "You can lend or give Samuel the money for his education, ensuring that he is able to support himself and a family independent of your father. For if you do not assist him, then what future has he as the second son of an earl? That of a poor *country parson*?"

At his last words, Reggie swung his head toward William who watched him with a raised brow.

"Egads!" Reggie exclaimed. "I had not thought of that. What was your future meant to be, Samuel? Did you and Father ever discuss such a thing? Surely, he didn't insist upon you taking orders, did he?"

Samuel shook his head. "No, nothing of the sort. I have only recently imagined that my life must have some meaning, a function other than that of second son to an earl. It was when I met Miss Tollerton that I realized I served no purpose. I neither added nor took from society...from the world around me. I simply existed to read books."

"An aimless existence," William said quietly.

Reggie studied his brother. "What do other families do?" he mused.

"I believe second sons take orders, take a commission in the Army or Navy, or become physicians," William offered.

"None of those interest me as much as studying the law," Samuel said.

Reggie stared at the brown liquid of his brandy. Images of Phoebe's distraught face haunted him, bringing an ache to his chest, but he tried to push them from his mind. His dimmed wits would only allow him to attend to one matter at a time.

"No, I cannot imagine you in any of those professions," Reggie said with a wry smile. "I will pay for you to attend school, Samuel. William is correct. That is one thing I can do for you, and I am pleased to do so. Whether or not you choose to marry Miss Tollerton must be your decision and your decision alone." He swallowed hard, trying to imagine what Phoebe might wish for him to say. "I will support you in your choice of wife, and she will be welcome in my home. I think she may wish to set up her own establishment though, and I imagine you would need to wait to marry until you have completed your schooling and are able to afford your own lodgings. I may be of assistance in that matter as well if you wish."

William rose and clapped him on the back with a broad grin. "Well done, Reggie! That is more than any brother could hope for, do you not agree, Samuel?"

Samuel jumped up hastily and began to pace, albeit with a drunken tilt. "I cannot accept your generous offer, Reggie. How could I ever repay you?"

"Do not be a pudding head, Samuel," Reggie said. "It is simply a matter of birth that I inherited my own money and you did not. I have enough for both of us." He rose. "The matter is settled. Though how you broach the subject with Father is not. If you wish, I can accompany you when you speak to him."

"About becoming a solicitor or my impending betrothal? For I do intend to ask Miss Tollerton to become my wife, Reggie."

"Yes, I am firmly convinced of that, Samuel. Both. I will stand by both your decisions. You may rely upon me."

"Thank you, Reggie. I could not wish for a better brother." Samuel bowed.

"Well, gentleman, a good day's work I would say. I must see to the rest of the house. My daughter must be wondering where her parents are. I imagine it is almost time for dinner."

"I am for the village. Do not wait dinner for me," Samuel said with a hesitant look in Reggie's direction. "Is there anything I can say to Miss Warner to ease the situation?"

Reggie shook his head. "No, there is nothing. Thank you. I have disappointed her. When I first proposed marriage, she said she did not know me well enough, but she acquiesced and accepted my proposal. It seems she has reverted to her original concerns that we do not know each other well enough, and I must honor that."

"I am sorry for it," Samuel said quietly as he followed William from the library, leaving Reggie still seated.

"Yes, I am too," Reggie said quietly. "Take a groom with you, Samuel. You have imbibed overly much to be alone in the saddle."

"I will," Samuel said.

****

An hour later, Reggie stepped onto the terrace of his new house and surveyed the soft purple hues of the river and the plains beyond as night settled onto the landscape. He should not have come but felt he could not stay at Ashton House for the moment. He did not think he could bear to see Phoebe at dinner, to feel the disappointment in her eyes as she regarded him over the dinner table. He had left a note for Mattie explaining that he would be absent from dinner, citing some vague errand.

He spied a stone bench against the wall that flanked the bay windows, and he sat down heavily. It seemed unlikely but it had only been a matter of hours since Phoebe had stood on the same terrace and admired the view, her hand entwined in his. The future had seemed bright and full of promise. Now, it seemed bleak and lonely. He had no intention of abandoning the purchase of the house for he would never return to his father's house—not while his father still lived. He would be master in his own home, and the "castle," as Phoebe had called it, would be his.

Soft moonlight glowed on the stone balustrade of the terrace, and he glanced up. The moon, seemingly still impossibly full, presided in the sky. Moonlight wishes, he sighed. They seemed so long ago.

He closed his eyes and tried to free his mind of all thought—memories both joyous and sad, smiles, embraces, the disillusionment in Phoebe's eyes when she turned away. Exhausted, he leaned his head back into a crevice of the wall and he relaxed into sleep.

The sound of a horse's snort and wheels awakened him, and he bolted upright, confused as to his location. The terrace of the new house. He turned to stride toward the front of the house but arrested when he saw Phoebe come around the corner. Moonlight lit her way.

"Phoebe? How did you come?"

She jumped as if startled by his voice.

"A groom brought me in the carriage. He's waiting for me," she said almost hesitantly. "I wasn't sure you'd be here, but I thought you might."

His heart pounded, and he knew not what to say. He held his breath and waited.

"I want to go home, Reggie, and you're the only one who can help me do that."

Only a superior strength from some inner aspect of his being kept him on his feet, for the searing in his heart seemed to weaken his legs. Could one man bear so much pain in a single day?

"As you wish," he said hoarsely. "What can I do?"

She looked at him, startled. "That's it? Okay? You're not going to argue?"

He had not thought Phoebe to be a cruel sort of person, but he wondered at her now. Did she not understand how much agony he suffered?

"A gentleman does not argue with a lady, Miss Warner," Reggie said in a leaden voice. "I would never seek to inhibit your desire to return to your own time."

"How nice of you," she muttered.

Reggie thought he saw the shine of moisture on her face but that seemed unlikely given her desire to return home. He had not understood the depth to which he had disappointed her. Her voice held a note of derision as if she despised him.

"Your moral codes and values will change over time, Reggie. It's just too bad some of them can't change sooner."

"Do you refer to Miss Tollerton?" Reggie said on a ragged note. He did not wish to discuss the wretched dressmaker.

"Partly, but mostly because you're willing to let me go without a fight."

Reggie shook his head. "A fight? Do you mean a tousle? Should I restrain you, hold you against your will? Ah! I know! Lock you away in an attic until you find a way to love me—all of me."

"I *do* love all of you," Phoebe shouted with a stomp of her foot. "More than you'll ever know. I'm sorry I hurt you. I'm sorry it's taking me so long to get used to some of the things around here—things that wouldn't be a problem in my time—but for crying out loud, I've only been here a few days!"

"Yes, that is true, Miss Warner!" Reggie said in a harsh voice. "And a few days is all it will be if you choose to leave tonight!"

"Well, I wasn't planning on leaving you, if that's what you're thinking," she sputtered. "I just need to get back and leave a note for Annie. I can't let her think you killed me and disappeared into England."

"Kill you! What are you talking about, woman?" Reggie thought he must be losing his mind.

"I just can't stop worrying about it, about her, about how much pain she'll be in."

"What about my pain?" Reggie barked.

"I'm not going to apologize for the way I feel, Reggie, but I did apologize for hurting you," Phoebe said.

"And I cannot apologize for the way that I feel. Whether it is fair or not, my 'moral code' is derived from the society in which I live."

"But it's wrong," Phoebe said, "and I know you know that."

"If you know that, then why did you storm out of the drawing room? Why did you abandon our betrothal so out of hand?"

"Because I was frightened and confused," Mattie said. "Because I love you, and I know that you're a fine man. I just hated to hear you say the words 'unsuitable.' Because I worry that you think I'm 'unsuitable.'"

"You *are* unsuitable, you minx," Reggie said. "And I love you terribly."

"I know what you did for Samuel. There's not much you can say to William that doesn't get to Mattie. She told me. William is so proud of you."

Reggie shifted uncomfortably. "The only admiration I seek is yours, Phoebe. I should stand by my brother. That is not a trait worthy of pride, but of filial loyalty."

"But it shows that you're willing to try to change...those one or two teeny, tiny things that aren't perfect about you." Phoebe's bright mischievous smile warmed his heart.

"I am forgiven then?" he asked.

"If you forgive me," Phoebe said.

"How could I not? Then you will stay?"

Phoebe shook her head. "No, I have to get back and leave her a note or call her or say something."

Reggie staggered back, landing heavily on the bench. He bowed his head in his hands.

"I am going mad," he moaned.

Phoebe bent down and took his hands in hers. "No, you're not. You're coming with me. And if we don't make it together, then you wish every day on the full moon that I come back, and I'll wish for the same thing. I just need an hour or so." She scrunched her face. "Well, maybe I need to look up the instructions for homemade antibiotics and central heating and grab one of Mattie's books, but after that, I'll be ready to head back."

Reggie shook his head. "It is too dangerous." He pressed her hands to his lips. "I cannot be parted from you, I cannot."

"We'll be together, Reggie. Always."

"I fervently hope this does not work," Reggie said.

"Don't say that. We have to wish on the same thing at the same time...and hope the moon is full enough."

"You are determined to do this?" Reggie asked.

"I am, Reggie. Maybe in two or three years, I won't feel bad about disappearing on the only family I have, but right now, it feels awful, and I know she must be crying her eyes out."

He sighed and rose, pulling Phoebe to her feet. "I will release the groom to return to the house. We cannot have him waiting about for days or a month, nor could I bear to have him witness my grief if we are separated." He crossed to the front of the house and sent the groom back to Ashton House with Sebastian in tow, and with a cryptic message for Mattie stating that he and Miss Warner would travel by moonlight but would return as soon as possible and would they please inform his family if they did not return.

"Repeat those words," Reggie instructed the groom, who repeated them accurately.

He returned to Phoebe who gazed at twinkling of the moon on the river.

"I love you, Phoebe Warner," he said as he took her hand.

"I love you too, Reggie Hamilton." She clung to his hand. "Don't let go."

"What is your wish, my love?"

"I wish Reggie and I were together at my apartment in New York City."

"I wish Phoebe and I were together at her apartment in New York City."

They clung together and looked up at the moon.

Nothing happened. They repeated the words again. Still nothing happened.

"Reggie?" Phoebe asked in a suspicious voice. "Are you really wishing for the same thing? You're not secretly wishing this doesn't work, are you?"

"I am conflicted, but I believe that I am wishing as you are. I know in my heart that I wish to be with you always. Is that not the same as wishing to be where you are?"

Phoebe sighed. "It should be. Maybe it's the moon. It can't really be a full moon, right? I thought the moon was only full one day a month, but look at it. It *looks* full."

"Yes, I agree."

"What if we don't hold hands?" Phoebe asked. "Maybe that's it."

"I am not releasing your hand, Phoebe! That will not occur." He tightened his grasp. Phoebe wasn't really serious about it anyway, because no matter what, she needed to stay with him.

"Okay, let's try one more time. If it doesn't work, we won't try again."

"I wish Reggie and I were together at my apartment in New York City."

"I wish Phoebe and I were together at her apartment in New York City."

Phoebe felt herself falling, and she screamed for Reggie.

"Don't let go, Reggie!"

CHAPTER EIGHTEEN

What seemed like only moments later, Phoebe opened her eyes and drew in a sharp breath. Reggie's hand still clasped hers, his grasp warm.

"Reggie?" she called. He lay next to her on the floor of the living room in the apartment in New York. They had managed to get back. Several lamps glowed, and Phoebe scrambled to her knees to look at Reggie. He opened his eyes and blinked.

"We are together," he said.

"Yes, we are," Phoebe said as she bent to plant a kiss on his lips. Reggie, still lying on the floor, grasped her by the shoulders.

"Do not ever leave me, Phoebe Warner," he said in a thick voice.

"Never," she whispered. "Even when I tell you I'm going to, I won't." She looked up. "We're here. I wonder if Annie ended up going to Hawaii. I hate that my disappearance probably ruined her trip."

She rose and tugged at Reggie's arm, unable to pull him up by herself. Reggie rose and straightened his coat and cravat.

"You and your clothes," she chuckled.

Reggie reached for her bonnet to straighten it.

"You and your clothes," he repeated. "A lady must always wear her bonnet correctly."

"I love you," Phoebe sighed as she melted into his arms. "Clothes and all."

"As I love you, my dear girl, in this century or any other."

A sound came from the bedroom, and they swung around. All was silent. They exchanged glances.

"Annie?" Phoebe called.

The door burst open, and Annie stood there holding a baseball bat.

"Phoebe?" she screeched. "Phoebe? Oh, Phoebe, where have you been? What on earth are you wearing?" Annie cried as she dropped the bat and crossed the room to hug her cousin.

"Oh, Annie, I'm so sorry we just disappeared like that. How long have we been gone?"

"A couple of days. I called the police, but they wouldn't take a missing person report until just this morning. Where have you been?" She turned to Reggie. "I thought for sure you had killed her and then run off to England. I tried calling Scotland Yard, but they thought I should contact the local police and provide your name. Not that I could remember your last name."

Phoebe listened to her cousin rant, and she let her vent while murmuring soothing words. Unconsciously, she kept hold of Reggie's hand, or he kept hold of hers. Just in case, someone wished something accidentally.

"You'd better sit down, Annie. It's kind of a long story. How about some tea?"

"Tea?" Annie said. "Gosh, you're really in character, aren't you? Don't think I don't recognize that outfit. You're doing a Jane Austen thing or something."

Phoebe shook her head and took off her bonnet, setting it on a table. "Okay, coffee then. Just relax. I can't tell you how sorry I am to have worried you. If I'd had a choice, I would have done it differently." She moved into the kitchen, pulling Reggie with her and making the coffee with one hand, not a difficult task with the modern coffeemaker. Reggie assisted her with cups and spoons.

"So, you didn't get to go to Hawaii, did you?"

"Not yet, but don't worry, I'll get there. Johan is waiting for me."

"I'm so sorry," Phoebe said in a mournful tone.

"Stop apologizing and tell me where you went," Annie snapped. "The best I can figure right now is that you were abducted by aliens, fans of Jane Austen, I would say."

Phoebe giggled nervously. She picked up one cup, and Reggie picked up another. He declined coffee for himself. They returned to the living room, and Phoebe handed Annie a cup.

"What? Are you two joined at the hip? Let go of one another. No one is going to disappear into thin air. I didn't hear the door open by the way. You were quiet...at least until I heard a thud on the floor in the living room. I'm not sure what you were doing."

Phoebe shook her head. "No, we can't let go of each other. At least, we don't want to. Drink your coffee and listen. Don't interrupt for questions."

She told Annie about Reggie's arrival, their own time travel back to

1827, their theory that wishing on the full moon was the catalyst, and that they were going to be married.

Annie choked on her coffee several times, and then leaned back onto the sofa and stared at them with narrowed eyes.

"Am I supposed to believe all that, Phoebe? Are you drunk?"

Phoebe shook her head. "No, it's true. I know it's hard to believe. I didn't believe it either, but look at him." She nodded toward Reggie who had remained silent. "Does he seriously look like he belongs here?"

Annie eyed him. "Yes, he looks like he belongs here. I thought you told me he was a model. He really does look like a cover model. I was nosing around in your stuff, looking for clues, and found all your paperbacks. He looks just like some of the guys on the books."

"Well, he might well be for all we know," Phoebe said with a smile at Reggie, "but that's another story. I came back, as scary as the trip was again, to tell you that I'd never just disappear like that because I knew you'd think I was dead somewhere." She looked to Reggie. "That reminds me, I should say something at work...about not coming back."

"Sinclair Publishing?" he asked with a private smile.

Phoebe chuckled. "Just so."

"Phoebe, you can't be serious. Time travel?" Annie asked.

"I am serious, Annie. How can I prove it to you?"

"I have no idea," Annie said.

"Wait! I know. I'll get my laptop. Maybe I can find Reggie's portrait on a search of his family's name. I just hope we don't see anything we don't want to see...like dates of death." Phoebe frowned. "No, I don't want to do that. Something else."

"I'll check it out," Annie said. "I won't tell you anything you don't want to know. Like I really believe all of this anyway."

Annie stepped into the bedroom and returned with her laptop, throwing skeptical glances toward them over the edge of the screen as she waited for her pages to load.

"Okay, what do I look for?"

"Lord Reginald Hamilton, Earl of Hamilton."

"Eighth Earl of Hamilton," Reggie amended.

"Earl?" Annie repeated. "I'm impressed." She keyed in the information, while Phoebe and Reggie waited. She cast occasional glances at them while she read.

Phoebe, her heart pounding, regretted the idea. It was less important to prove to Annie that they had traveled in time than to protect themselves from knowing the future.

"Annie, no matter what you find, please keep it to yourself," Phoebe said. She clung to Reggie's hand, and he patted her hand with his free one.

"I'm just reading stuff," Annie said. She paused at one point and peered closely at the screen.

Phoebe could have jumped up to look over the screen, but she held her position. "What are you staring at?"

"Nothing," Annie said as she glanced up. "Don't worry about it." She studied Reggie's face, and Phoebe suspected she had indeed found a portrait or some likeness to Reggie. She wondered what it looked like.

"Can I ask you anything?" Annie asked.

"No," Phoebe said firmly. She looked at Reggie who shrugged. "Maybe. I don't know."

"How about a name? Kind of like a test? Something I doubt you would really know."

Phoebe grew curious. "A name I wouldn't know? That doesn't make sense."

"Well, it's not really about you two. What about the name Tollerton? Is that anyone you know?"

"Tollerton," Reggie repeated faintly. "The dressmaker?"

Phoebe began to laugh. "Sarah Tollerton? You found a reference to her in a search of Reggie?"

"Well, not Reggie. His brother, apparently. You know, the solicitor?"

"Oh, see, Reggie?" Phoebe turned to Reggie. "It does work out. Hah!" She continued laughing.

"Leave off your guffawing, woman," Reggie remonstrated. "It is unseemly."

"I think I'll have her make my wedding dress," Phoebe chuckled. "In fact, I know I will."

"As you wish, my dear," Reggie said with a faint smile.

"Good news about Samuel though, right?" Phoebe said brightly.

"Yes, indeed. I am pleased though to hear that my brother succeeded in entering the profession of his choosing."

Annie snapped the computer shut. "Okay, I believe you."

"You believe us?" Phoebe stopped laughing abruptly and stared at her cousin. "Just like that? Time travel? That's okay with you?"

"Well, there's a portrait that looks a whole lot like Reggie on there, and it was painted in the nineteenth century."

"Don't say when!" Phoebe clamped her hand over her ears.

"I wasn't going to," Annie said. "It's all good though—long happy lives, both of you."

"Both of us?" Phoebe whispered.

"Both," Annie nodded. "But I know you didn't want to hear that."

"Very funny!"

"So, now what? You go back? And that's it? I never see you again?" Phoebe winced and gave her a faint nod. "That's about it, Annie."

Two tears spilled down Annie's cheeks, and she wiped at them with the back of her hand.

"It'll be like you died, Mouse," she said in a husky voice.

Phoebe jumped up and crossed over to the couch to kneel in front of her cousin. She took Annie's hands in hers.

"Oh, Annie, I'm so sorry. I don't know what to do." Phoebe glanced over her shoulder to Reggie whose face registered sympathy...and just a little bit of apprehension.

"I can't believe we're having this conversation. It's so surreal," Annie said. "But I believe you. You're in the history books," she muttered.

"*Am* I?" Phoebe whispered. She looked at Reggie again with a tender smile.

"Yes. Can't you come back at all? Even to visit?" Annie asked.

Reggie rose and came to sit on the sofa near Annie and Phoebe.

"We do not know if it is possible, Annie. We do not even know if it is possible to return to my time, but if it is not, I am fully prepared to live out my life here...with Phoebe."

"But you're there, both of you," she said. "I saw it on the Internet."

Phoebe shook her head, terrified Annie might accidentally reveal any more of her future...or past...than she wanted to hear.

"I'm not sure that's a guarantee," Phoebe said. "Who knows how this time travel thing works? We talked about this when we were in England. Can we inadvertently change the past by what we do now? If Reggie and I decided not to go back, then would you still see us there in 1827 or whenever you saw us listed?" Phoebe held up a hand. "Don't say what year!"

"But what if you do get back without a problem, isn't there any chance you can come back to visit...ever?" Annie asked.

Phoebe reached for Reggie's hand. She would let him decide. He seemed to understand her intent and he spoke.

"As long as Phoebe and I can travel through time together, there is a possibility we could try to return." He paused. "But once we have children, it will not be possible. I trust you understand why that must be so, Annie."

She nodded. "You can't risk the children or being separated from them."

"Just so," Reggie said. He smiled sympathetically.

Phoebe's mind had been brainstorming for the past few minutes.

"Come with us, Annie!" she exclaimed.

Both Reggie and Annie turned startled eyes on her.

"What? Are you nuts? I can't do that," Annie said. "I've got my life here, my money, Johan."

"Phoebe, my love, I do not think it is necessarily possible for Annie to travel as we do. Remember, as with Mattie and William and you and I, it is the power of our need for each other, our shared wish for love, that compels the travel through time...or at least so we believe."

Phoebe bit her lip. "He's right. If everybody could travel just by wishing on the moon, it would happen a lot more than it seems to. So far, we only know of one other woman who has traveled back in time. I don't know if it would work for you, not if you don't have a fervent wish to love someone in the nineteenth century."

"Well, I don't," Annie said with a skeptical look on her face. "And at any rate, are you guys sure that's how you travel?"

"The means are unclear, but it is true that I wished for my destiny, and Phoebe wished for...?" Reggie raised his eyebrows in question.

Phoebe blushed. "A Georgian man of my own. I remember the words."

"Ah! That would be me," he said with a smile. "As with the other lady who traveled, she tells us that she and her now husband also wished on a full moon for love, and their wishes were granted in the finding of each other."

"Gosh, you guys are way too romantic for me," Annie said with a grimace as another tear slipped down her face. "Stop!"

"I love you, Cousin," Phoebe said.

"I love you too, Minnie Mouse," Annie said. She extricated her hand from Phoebe's and rose as if to stretch her legs. She crossed over to the window to look out, and Phoebe and Reggie joined her there.

"How do you know if it's a full moon?" Annie asked.

"We don't," Phoebe said. "It seems to have been full for the last few nights."

Annie turned to Phoebe and Reggie. "You'd better go back tonight. If the moon doesn't stay full, you might not get back for a month...not that it would be a bad thing."

Phoebe nodded. "I agree...on both counts."

Reggie smiled. "Phoebe returned to say ease your worries about her disappearance."

"I know," Annie said. "Thank you."

"Well, I need to print out some stuff on the computer and grab a few things before we try to leave again," Phoebe said. "I can't stand leaving you here like this. It feels like forever."

Annie shook her head. "Johan is waiting for me. And maybe it's not forever."

Phoebe hugged her. "Maybe not." She turned and headed into the bedroom to grab a small cloth bag. Annie followed her into the room and sat down on the bed to watch. Phoebe threw a couple of I.C. Moon's books into her bag, especially those with cover models who resembled Reggie.

Annie picked one up. "Man, he really does look like the cover on this book."

Phoebe grinned. "I imagine he probably is. The author is a new friend of mine."

Annie chuckled. "Leave me what you don't take. Maybe I'll take a few to Hawaii with me and see what you think is so all-fired great about these romance novels."

"Maybe you'll fall in love like I did," Phoebe said with a chuckle.

"Oh, Johan would like that," Annie murmured in a sarcastic tone. "Are any of them set in Switzerland?"

"Nope, all England."

"Early 1800s England, huh?"

"Oh, that reminds me." Phoebe ran to her computer on the desk in the room and turned it on. "I'm going to need a few bits of information," she said. "Did I tell you that Reggie bought a little castle for me? It's a house, but it looks a little bit like a castle."

"Awwww," Annie said. "Really? So, he's got money to go with his title?"

"Yes," Phoebe said. She searched for a few items on the computer and then printed them to the printer next to the computer. She folded the papers and stuffed them into her bag before returning to the computer again.

"An e-mail to work, telling them I have to resign unexpectedly. I really hate doing this!"

"You loved that job," Annie said.

"I know, but it's not really all lost to me. I'll still be editing, just by hand though." Phoebe caught Annie's confused look and shook her head. "Long story."

She knelt down by the bed and retrieved a container of photographs from under the bed, rummaging through them hurriedly.

"Let's see, a couple pics of Mom and Dad, Gramma and Grandpa, and here's one of you! I'll take that," Phoebe said brandishing the picture.

Annie peered over her shoulder. "Oh, not that one! My high school prom?"

"You were beautiful," Phoebe said. "That red dress...stunning. You looked like a princess."

"Pshaw," Annie muttered. "I'll keep the rest of your stuff. It'll be here if you manage to get back."

Phoebe lowered herself to the bed next to Annie and took her hand. "I think I have everything I can carry...if I can carry anything. I don't know what else I'd take. I mean, I'd take everything I could to make life more comfortable there, but I'm kind of worried about getting back. Reggie's brother is in a bind. We didn't tell anyone we were leaving, exactly. Reggie just bought a new house, and I'm supposed to be getting married in a few weeks."

"Already?" Annie said. "I'm sorry I'll miss it. Send pictures," she said with a short laugh.

Phoebe chewed her lip. "Tell you what! I'm sure Reggie and I will travel to the States...sometime in our lives. I'll open up a safety deposit box at a bank, and authorize you to access it. I'll put stuff in it. I'm not sure what. That way, you'll know I'm okay, and you'll know I've been thinking about you."

"Let's see what bank was open then and is still open today." She peered at the computer screen again.

"No need," Annie said. "My bank, Bonner and Little, International, has been in existence since forever. In fact, they have a London office. Just get a box there, and I'll check it out next time I'm in London."

"Good! That makes me feel connected to you in some way," Phoebe said. "Too bad you can't send me a care package." She attempted to smile, but her face crumpled. "Oh, Annie, I'm going to miss you so much!" She caught her cousin up in a fierce embrace.

"I know, Mouse, I know," Annie whispered. "I'm going to miss you, too. We may not see each other all that often, but we've always at least been in the same century."

Phoebe gave her a watery smile. "It's getting late. We'd better go."

"I'll come watch," Annie said. "Hopefully, that won't hex you."

Phoebe rose and shouldered the bag.

"Please tell me you have at least one pair of decent jeans with you," Annie said as she wrapped her arm around Phoebe's waist.

Phoebe nodded. "I do, the ones I traveled in to get there."

"Thank goodness!"

They returned to the living room where Reggie stood near the window with his back to it. Phoebe looked at him questioningly.

"I did not wish to look at the moon lest I inadvertently make a wish," he said with a wry smile.

"Good plan," Phoebe said. She picked up her bonnet, set it on her head and tied the ribbons.

"Is it time?" he asked.

Phoebe nodded. "Before we lose the moon."

Reggie executed a deep bow in Annie's direction. "Farewell, Annie. Until we meet again."

Annie nodded, her lips pressed together. Phoebe could see she was trying to hold back tears.

With what felt like superhuman effort, Phoebe turned her back on her cousin and took Reggie's hand. She looked up at him and nodded, and they turned in unison to stare at the moon—shining brightly above them in the cloudless sky.

"I wish I was back in 1827 England with my own Georgian man, Reggie."

"I wish I was back in 1827 England with my destiny, my own dear love, Phoebe," Reggie said.

They smiled at each other.

CHAPTER NINETEEN

Phoebe awoke to the sound of Reggie's voice.

"Phoebe? Phoebe, dearest, awaken." He cradled her in his lap, stroking her cheek.

She opened her eyes to darkness, lightened only by the bright moon overhead. The same moonlight reflected against the bay windows of the house.

"Are we back?" She felt her bonnet on her lap. Reggie must have removed it. Her bag lay by her side.

"Yes, dear, it would appear we are. Exactly where we left."

A sharp pain seared through her chest at the thought of Annie, and yet she couldn't deny the joy she felt at their successful to return. A tear spilled down her face, and she wiped at it.

"I know, my love," Reggie murmured. "I know."

She swallowed her pain and reached up to kiss him. "I'm so glad we're still together."

He cupped her face in his hands. "As am I," he said softly.

"Look at how the moon glows on the windows of the house," Phoebe said. "Isn't it gorgeous? Let's call it Moonglow Castle. What do you think?"

Reggie leaned his head back against the stone balustrade and studied the house.

"I shall enjoy calling it Moonglow Castle."

"Very new agey yet medieval," Phoebe said with a sigh.

"New agey?"

"I'll explain another time, dear." She rose to her feet and grabbed her bag. "As happy as I would be to sit here in your lap all night, it's kind of chilly. We could see if the door is unlocked and spend the night inside."

She grinned mischievously. "Since we're going to be married and all."

Reggie stood up beside her. "No, madam, that will not do. We must still observe the conventions of 1827." He kissed the top of her head. "That is to say, as many as we can still salvage. We have ignored so many of them to this point that it seems foolish to insist on the few remaining rules for behavior that we have not violated, but indulge me in this one last attempt to salvage your reputation." Reggie laughed, but Phoebe knew he was serious.

"My reputation," she sighed. "Do you think that's salvageable?"

"When you are the Countess of Hamilton, no one will dare question you." He drew himself up with that haughty posture that she loved.

"Oh, Reggie! You're so cute when you get all aristocratic. Really!" She grabbed his lapels and pulled his face to hers.

"Minx!" he said with a laugh when she let him up for air. "Come! We must find a way back to Ashton House." Despite his words, he tried the handle on the door leading into the house, but it was locked.

"Too bad," Phoebe teased.

"A pity," he said with a broad grin. "I might almost have been coaxed into staying."

Phoebe laughed, and Reggie took her hand. Together, they set off down the long lane to head to the village. The moon still shone brightly, lighting the way.

"Don't make any wishes," Phoebe warned.

"I have everything I wish for at my side, Phoebe. There is nothing else I need."

"Me, too," Phoebe said. "I don't think I could be happier."

****

Two weeks later, Phoebe knew she was mistaken. She could be happier, and she was—on her wedding day. As she and Reggie drove away from the church in a carriage festooned with ribbons and flowers, she held his hand and relished in that happiness.

The past few weeks had flown by. They had made it to the village on the night of their return, and Reggie awakened the innkeeper who rustled up a carriage and driver at the inn willing to transport them to the Sinclairs' house. They had arrived almost at midnight, awakening Mattie and William, and telling them of their successful trip between the two times. Samuel had thankfully slept through the commotion of their arrival, and so they didn't have to tell him about the time traveling...yet. Phoebe suspected he would find out someday. After all, even Lady Hamilton knew. Samuel and his father were the last to know.

The following morning, Reggie had the banns posted when he and William had gone out to arrange the ceremony at the church. Phoebe had driven into town with Mattie to visit Sarah Tollerton and collect the two dresses that were ready. She had commissioned a wedding dress, and Sarah had been grateful and awed by the commission, much to Phoebe's discomfort.

"Oh, gosh, Sarah! It's just a dress. Something simple, but elegant. Satin though. I do like shiny!" Phoebe had said. Both she and Mattie regarded Sarah with bright smiles in the secret knowledge that she was going to be their sister-in-law one day. Phoebe had shared what few details she knew of the future with Mattie.

Lady Hamilton had come by that afternoon ostensibly to visit Mia, but she asked to speak to Phoebe and Mattie in private before seeing her granddaughter.

"Uh oh," Phoebe said. "I think it's time for *the talk.* You know, the 'are you a time traveler talk.'"

"Oh, boy," Mattie said. "I really never get used to being alone with her...without William around. I wish he and Reggie would get back. I was hoping she wouldn't be back so soon, but I should have known she couldn't wait to find out about you."

Phoebe straightened her hair in the mirror of her room and turned to grab Mattie's hand before they went downstairs.

"We'll be fine. She's just one woman."

"Hmmm..." Mattie muttered. They hurried down the stairs and entered the drawing room where Lady Hamilton awaited them.

"Hello, Lady Hamilton. Would you like some tea?" Mattie asked.

"Yes, that would be nice, thank you."

Mattie turned and nodded to John to bring tea.

She sat down on the sofa opposite Lady Hamilton, and Phoebe sat next to her, waiting expectantly. Lady Hamilton smiled pleasantly and appeared to be waiting as well. A brief uncomfortable silence ensued.

"So, Lady Hamilton, how is Lord Hamilton? Is he better?" Mattie asked.

"He is, thank you," she said. "He insists on eating foods that disagree with him, and when he is upset, his stomach pains him."

Phoebe's instinct was to say she was sorry to have been part of his upset, but she bit her tongue...and waited. She didn't have long to wait though.

"Miss Warner. We have not had a chance to become acquainted," Lady Hamilton said. "And yet you are already betrothed to my stepson. Such haste," she murmured.

"Yes," Phoebe said succinctly and without explanation. Lady

Hamilton had said the same thing the day before. Phoebe suspected she should try to establish some kind of relationship with the woman, but she was irritated by the implied criticism.

Lady Hamilton quirked an eyebrow and waited, but Phoebe masked her face and stared back. Two faint pink spots appeared on Lady Hamilton's cheeks, and she turned to Mattie.

"Mattie, may I ask if your cousin is from the America that you know?"

Just then John returned with the tea, and they were silenced for the moment until he left. Mattie poured tea.

"Phoebe?" she said. "Do you want to tell her or should I? We might as well."

"Yes, Lady Hamilton. I am from the America that Mattie knows, though I lived in New York City, and I believe she lived in Seattle. But if you're asking if I traveled in time from the twenty-first century, then yes."

Lady Hamilton tightened her lips and nodded. She studied Phoebe curiously.

"How many of there are you?" she asked, looking at both of them.

Phoebe shrugged. "I think we're the only two I know about. Are you worried that hordes of Americans will come over here from the twenty-first century and snatch up all your young men?"

"Phoebe!" Mattie gasped with a nervous chuckle.

To Phoebe's surprise, Lady Hamilton didn't get angry. "I have been thinking just that, Miss Warner," she said with a wry smile.

"Well, just so you know, it will become fashionable—and necessary—for some of the men of the English aristocracy to marry American heiresses later on in the century. You know, money for the coffers. But not me. I'm not wealthy."

"Miss Warner," Lady Hamilton began. "You *do* know that it is vulgar to discuss money, do you not?" Her hand shook a little as she sipped her tea, but she appeared to be holding back a laugh.

"I do," Phoebe smiled. "And yet still I do it. I don't know what's wrong with me."

Mattie broke out into laughter. "Oh, Phoebe, I'm so glad you're here," she said as she reached to pat Phoebe's hand.

Lady Hamilton sobered. "I think perhaps I am glad you are here as well, Miss Warner. My daughter-in-law has not had a proper female companion since my own daughter left for America, and she has been lonely for a friend." She looked to Mattie whose face reddened. "Long ago, I expressed my fears to Mattie that she would take my son away from England and from his inheritance—to the future, but that has not come to pass, and it appears my fears were groundless. I have been hard on Mattie, and she does not know how pleased I am to have her as a daughter-in-law. She has become a fine wife to William and a good mother to her daughter. I dare say that I am quite proud of her." She lowered her eyes to sip her tea again as if she'd said nothing.

Phoebe turned to Mattie who stared at Lady Hamilton with rounded eyes.

"Thank you," Mattie choked out.

"Yes, well, perhaps Miss Warner could tell me a bit about herself," Lady Hamilton cleared her throat and changed the subject. "Are you truly cousins?"

Phoebe, delighting in the way Mattie seemed to relax in her mother-in-law's company, spent the next hour discussing her own background and arrival. She deliberately omitted any comments regarding Mattie's novels or the fact that Reggie and Phoebe had traveled back to the future only the night before. She suspected Lady Hamilton would argue Mattie's scandalous vocation, and that she would worry about Reggie disappearing and leaving his inheritance behind. She also skipped over the part where Reggie spent the night in her bedroom, albeit passed out on the ottoman at the foot of her bed.

"So, that's about it!" Phoebe said. "And just to reassure you, Reggie and I intend to stay here in England."

"Lord Hamilton does not know about the time travel, and I think it best he does not. But I feel I could speak for him were he to know, and say that he would be utterly happy to hear the news. I did make it clear to him that, in purchasing a house in England, Reggie has clearly abandoned his desire to relocate to America for an extended period."

"I wouldn't mind visiting the United States, but I'm happy here," she said. "And I have a new friend." She reached for Mattie's hand.

"And family," Lady Hamilton added. "I may have lost a daughter to America, but I have since gained two daughters-in-law, albeit one by marriage."

"Oh, good! Can we call you Mom?" Phoebe chuckled.

"Mom?" Lady Hamilton repeated faintly. "Certainly not!" Mattie burst out laughing, and even Lady Sinclair laughed.

It was to this laughter that Reggie and William walked in. The men stopped short and stared at the odd sight.

"Come in, gentleman," Mattie said with a broad smile. "How did it go?"

"Very well," Reggie said. "The wedding is set for Tuesday fortnight." He came around the sofa to stand behind Phoebe and lay a hand on her shoulder. Phoebe realized he did it as if to protect her from his stepmother.

"Lady Hamilton has just been inviting us to call her mom," Phoebe said with a mischievous grin.

"Miss Warner jests, gentlemen." Lady Hamilton rose. "I think my daughter-in-law and future daughter-in-law might address me as Lucy if they were of a mind to, but not *mom!*" She inclined her head and nodded. "I am so pleased to hear that preparations for the wedding progress. Please let me know if there is any way in which I may assist. Now, may I see my granddaughter?"

Mattie sent for Mia who ran to her grandmother when Jane brought her in.

"Grandma!" she cried out happily as Lady Hamilton picked her up.

"A walk in the garden, my pet?" Lady Hamilton asked. "We will return directly." She carried Mia out and Jane followed, leaving the men staring at her back in some disbelief.

"What has possessed my mother?" William said.

"I don't know," Mattie said, "but I like it. Did you hear Mia call her grandma? Your mother didn't blink an eye."

"Lady Hamilton seems to have softened," Reggie said in a voice of wonder.

"I think she's realized that we're not all going to disappear on them. You know, take off for the Colonies," Mattie said. "She seems pretty tickled to hear that Reggie isn't leaving either, or maybe his father is."

"Yes, she did mention that your father assumes you'll stay in England since you're buying a house here."

"I believe that is our wish, is it not, Phoebe?" Reggie looked down at her.

"Your wish is my command," Phoebe couldn't resist saying with a grin.

"Never a command, my dear one," he said, bending and speaking near her ear. A delicious shiver ran up her spine.

"I'd say get a room, but don't," Mattie chuckled. She rose. "Come on, William. I think we'd better leave these two alone and go see if your mother really does chase after Mia." William smiled broadly, and they left the drawing room.

Phoebe pulled Reggie down and kissed his lips. "It's an old saying, Reggie. You know I don't mean that."

"A lord can only hope that his commands will be obeyed," Reggie whispered against her lips.

"Oh, puhleeezz," she breathed. "Try wishing for that on the moon."

EPILOGUE

Annie thanked the bank clerk and stared at the safety deposit box. So, Phoebe really had gotten a safety deposit box. Would anything be in there? Phoebe had only been gone for a couple of months. It wasn't like Annie missed hearing Phoebe's voice every day since she and her cousin had often gone for months without talking on the phone or seeing each other. But knowing that she might never see Phoebe again felt like death, and Annie had come to London to see if Phoebe had bought a safety deposit box as she'd promised.

Annie found it hard to think in terms of the time travel. If Phoebe had only been gone for a few months, had she had time to find anything to put in the box? With a wedding to plan? And a house to move into?

Yet in reality, Phoebe had actually been gone almost two hundred years, plenty of time to make memories and include them in the box. Annie felt nauseous, as she always did, at the thought that Phoebe had already lived her life and died. She had seen the date of Phoebe's death when she looked at the computer that night in her apartment months ago. Phoebe had lived a long life, but it didn't change the fact that she was now dead.

And Annie was now without family—and without Johan, the flake. She had no idea what she had been doing with him anyway. He was nothing like her. He shared none of her interests really, not even a common culture, and she hated skiing. The high mountains scared the dickens out of her. He had been the proverbial fish out of water in Hawaii. She had said goodbye to him in Hawaii after only two days.

Annie hadn't wanted to admit it to Mouse at the time, but the thought of going to Hawaii, knowing she was saying goodbye to her cousin forever, had been too much to handle. She had gone but could not forget

Phoebe, and she felt she had left something behind, something unresolved.

When she returned to New York, the apartment seemed empty but filled with Phoebe's things. She had packed them up and stored them, unwilling to get rid of anything—just in case Phoebe was able to come back or had to come back. It was possible that things had gone wrong, that Phoebe couldn't abide life in 1827—no matter what the Internet showed. Since Annie hadn't looked at Phoebe's information during the past two months, she didn't know if it had changed. Maybe the past did change by the actions of those in the future.

She sat down on the stool in the vault and stared at the box. Well, clearly, Phoebe had made it back to England because here was a safety deposit box in Annie's name and in Lady Phoebe Hamilton's name. The bank clerk had informed her that other relatives of Lady Hamilton's had also been authorized to access the box, and Annie worried they had taken things out of it meant for her—letters, photographs.

With a shaking hand, she inserted the key into the old-fashioned steel box and opened the lid.

The box was filled almost to the brim in an untidy mess of papers and photographs. Photographs!

Annie pulled out the pictures on top and examined them, surprised to see them in color. Various groups of people posed on a lawn in the first picture—almost as if it were a picture of several generations of a family. A summer photo—some wore jeans or shorts, a few wore dresses and suits, especially the older ones. Small children sat cross-legged in the front. She turned the picture over.

The Hamiltons, Summer 2010, Bedfordshire

Summer 2010? Had Phoebe come back to the present but stayed in England? She scanned the picture for Phoebe's face but didn't recognize anyone who looked like Phoebe.

The next picture, also in color, looked much like the first but was dated 2000. Other pictures in earlier decades with the same composition showed the family group changing—new people showed up, some disappeared.

She dug further into the box, pulling out black and white photographs. The clothing changed in the 1960s and 1950s, as it did in the 1940s and 1930s. The quality of the photography changed as well as did the background. Occasionally, a large imposing house could be seen in the background. In others, family members posed on a terrace of some sort with a river visible in the background.

Annie smiled as she pulled out pictures from the turn of the century— the twentieth century. Such beautiful dresses, and the men were so handsome. None of the women wore slacks by then as they had in the photographs beginning in the 1920s or so.

At last, she pulled out a photograph where she recognized Phoebe. 1890. Phoebe with white hair, in a dark Victorian dress with a brooch visible at the high neck, sat in a rocking chair with a wide smile. Reggie, looking much like his male cover model self, albeit with white hair, rested a hand on her shoulder. Young men and women lounged around them in lighter shades of clothing as if they had been playing tennis. Small children hardly seemed to sit still in the photograph.

The Hamiltons, Summer 1890, Bedfordshire

The earliest image was 1850, a daguerreotype, showing Phoebe and Reggie, younger now, with several young adult children and two who looked like teenagers, all in Victorian dress.

Underneath those were several small painted portrait miniatures of Phoebe, Reggie, and their children. Annie snatched one up. The wedding portrait! She smiled.

The portrait, probably painted before the marriage, showed Phoebe in a white empire-waisted dress of some shiny material, sitting next to Reggie. White flowers were interspersed throughout the curls on top of her hair, and she looked like a woodland fairy. Reggie looked resplendent in a cutaway coat of royal blue and beige pantaloons, a top hat perched dashingly on his head.

She found a thick folded note beneath the pictures, sealed with wax, and she stared at it for a moment. Her name was written on the front: *Miss Annie Warner.* She hesitated to break the seal and wondered if she should take it to an expert in historical documents. It looked old.

But she knew it was from Phoebe. Who else? And written in the last two months, or almost two hundred years ago.

Annie pried the wax off the letter and opened it carefully. She unfolded the thick paper and read, the writing clearly done by ink with a few splotches.

Dear Annie,

It's me! If you're reading this, then you found the safety deposit box. I'm so glad you did. I've run up to London several times to put things in it, and had Reggie drop some things into it as well. I instructed my children to toss in a family portrait every decade, and I left a note in my will, stating I hope their children continue the tradition. I wanted you to see that we're doing well. I'm happy and well and so is Reggie. We're still chugging along. No terrible plague or anything yet!

Annie ran her finger over the smiley face Phoebe had drawn.

If I had it to do all over again, I'd probably bring a few more things with me, but the recipe for holistic antibiotics has been a blessing. It has gotten me out of a jam or two! And Mattie was so happy to have central heating installed. William and Reggie worked together to install it in both of our houses. I think it saved us during last year's wet English winter.

We have a baby now, a little girl! You'd love her. I never thought about children before I got married, but now that I have one of my own, I think about you, and I wonder if you married and had your own children. I'm sure you did. I wish I could meet them.

I don't know when you'll check the box, or if you ever will, so I don't know how many years have passed since I left...in your time. I've wracked my brain but can't think of a single way you can "drop me a line" to let me know how you're doing. There's still no way to send me a care package, or at least a photo of you and your family.

I hope you and Johan are well. Maybe marriage? Little Swiss children yodeling? I can see it now.

Another smiley face was drawn.

I'll let you go for now. I miss you, Cousin, and I wish I could see you, but you'll remember that we don't dare try to travel back while we have a child. The risk is too great. I love you, Annie.

Minnie Mouse

Annie smiled tenderly and folded the letter to return it to the box. Everything had gone well. Phoebe had lived a full life and her descendents lived on through her, even carrying out her wishes. She picked up the photograph at the bottom of the stack—the one dated 2010.

The Hamiltons, Summer 2010, Bedfordshire.

Bedfordshire.

Her next destination.

ABOUT THE AUTHOR

I began my first fiction-writing attempt when I was fourteen. I shut myself up in my bedroom one summer and obsessively worked on a time-travel/pirate novel set in the beloved Caribbean of my youth. Unfortunately, I wasn't able to hammer it out on a manual typewriter (oh yeah, I'm that old) before it was time to go back to school. The draft of that novel has long since disappeared, but the story still simmers within, and I will finish it one day soon.

I was born in Aruba to American parents and lived in Venezuela until my family returned to the United States when I was twelve. I couldn't fight the global travel bug, and I joined the US Air Force at eighteen to "see the world." After twenty-one wonderful and fulfilling years traveling the world and the birth of one beautiful daughter, I pursued my dream of finally getting a college education. With a license in mental health therapy, I worked with veterans and continue to work on behalf of veterans. I continue to travel, my first love, and almost all of my books involve travel.

I write time-travel romances, light paranormal/fantasy romances (lovelorn ghosty stuff), contemporary romances, and romantic suspense. Visit my website at www.BessMcBride.com

Made in the USA
San Bernardino, CA
20 February 2015